This book is a work of fiction. Any references to historical events, real people, or real places are used fictitiously. Other names, characters, places, and events are products of the author's imagination, and any resemblance to actual events or places or persons living or dead is entirely coincidental.

Editing by Studio ENP

Cover Design by TRC Designs

For my dad
Thank you doesn't seem quite adequate enough for all you do for me.

Playlist

Chlorine - Twenty One Pilots

Euphoria - bülow

Ribcage - Plested

MonyOnMyMind - UPSAHL

Bloody valentine - Machine Gun Kelly

Way With Words - The Wrecks

Lies - Ivy Adara

Save Yourself - KALEO

Introduction & Warning

Hello dear reader!

This is a dark mafia romance with themes consistent with my style, included but not limited to dubious consent and violence. Our hero and heroine both behave questionably at times.

I recommend reading Ruthless Saint prior to Savage Prince.

xoxo,
Sara

CHAPTER 1

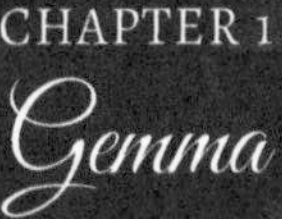

He comes to me in the dead of night.

I haven't slept in two days, and my hands tremble slightly when I hold them out in front of me. There's a single lamp on the floor of this room. Otherwise, the place is deserted.

I've been hiding out in my Aunt Mary's house. She uses Rose Hill as a sort of safe escape from the city. We had parties here growing up, and I slept in this very room more times than I can count. After my mom died, my aunt stepped in as my designated female role model.

I never blamed her for that. She was pushed into it by my well-intentioned father.

She left with the rest of the women a week and a half ago.

My brother followed her route less than forty-eight hours ago... and thus began my sleepless patrol.

I left a cookie sheet leaning against all the doors, and the loud clanging alerts me to his presence. I stand and move to the bathroom. My phone has been plugged in, waiting. I shoot off a quick text, then seal it in its plastic bag and drop it into the back of the toilet. Carefully, I replace the ceramic lid and move away.

I imagine he'll do a sweep of the downstairs, then venture up—and I'll get another warning.

Snap-snap-snap.

Mouse traps. A layer of them on the first four steps of the staircase. I thought it might be overkill, but only three go off. Still, I've got to give him props: he isn't swearing. He's not making any noise at all. They may not have caused any damage. Like the cookie sheets, they were there to sound an alarm of sorts.

I close my eyes and try to remember what Dad told me before he left.

He pinched life into my cheeks, then kissed my forehead. A way of saying goodbye, I think. Even though this was mostly my idea, my nerves were shot.

"You're saving us, Gemma," he said.

The need to be important had puffed my chest, but now I wonder why I must be the one to save them.

Wilder DeSantis was murdered eight weeks ago. My family watched from the sidelines as they hunted for the truth... but the truth led them to us.

The Wests and the DeSantises have never seen eye to eye—not in business, territory, socially, and certainly not morally. The feud goes back generations. And the stories my father used to tell Colin and I before bed were enough to turn my stomach. I didn't want the violence to live under my skin. Colin, though... he ingested the loathing without question.

We didn't speak about what happened to Wilder, but if I had to guess? It was someone in my immediate family.

Aiden DeSantis, Wilder's brother, seemed to land on the same conclusion. Rumors spread through the boroughs that he was looking for my brother.

Dad forbade me from asking Colin about it. How do you

accuse your own brother of murder, anyway? The papers wrote a short article about Wilder's death, painting him as a good Samaritan and businessman, but there's been hardly any mention. No police visits, no investigative reporting. It's like the world forgot about him.

"Gemma."

My gaze snaps to the door.

Aiden is little more than a silhouette in the dark, a version of Peter Pan's trickster shadow. I would recognize him anywhere—and that's where the danger lies. In the way he says my name, and how he holds his shoulders. And my *recognition*.

I turn away from him, smoothing the front of my dress.

"You're the only one here," he says. "Why?"

I laugh. I can't help it.

Three years ago, he gave me the best day of my life. It seems so distant now, the way he smiled. The carefree feeling that lit me up like a sparkler. I was sixteen and miserable, and he knew how to make it better.

If I'd only asked his last name before I'd climbed in his car...

Part of me knows, deep down, *that* betrayal is one of the reasons why I'm here.

He's waiting for an answer, but I don't have one.

I lift the bag at my feet, slinging it over my shoulder. "What will you do with me?"

"They left you here." He crosses his arms, unfazed by my packed bag.

He didn't answer my question.

I have toiletries and a change of clothes. A card preloaded with money hides under the sole of my left boot, just in case this gets away from my control. It's laughable, really—I have no control. I lost it the moment Aiden stepped foot inside the house.

If I move too quickly, my ankle feels the wrath of the knife strapped there. It's in a sheath, and the whole thing is barely hidden under the top of my boot, but that means nothing.

To have a fighting chance, I've got to keep my shoes.

My mind threatens to run away from me with that sort of logic, so I head toward Aiden. It's a bit like approaching a lion.

"They didn't leave me here," I counter. "I stayed."

Now that I'm closer, I meet his burning eyes.

"Quite a distinction," he says lightly. "Where's Kai?"

I swallow. My Aunt Mary's son used to go by Kaiden, but it was apparently too close to Aiden's name for his liking. He started helping my father more and became *Kai*. Is that who Aiden expected to find tonight, sitting in the dark? Kai and Colin are close.

Where one goes, the other follows.

Ironically, Kai became more like Aiden as he got older. He had darkness inside him that scared me as a child. I outgrew it —came to appreciate it, actually. He taught Colin how to protect himself from everyone, including himself.

But I'm not scared now. Determination fills me.

Aiden shakes his head. "Come now, princess. If you're going to be the bait, at least make it worth my while."

I grip the strap of my bag and keep my expression bland. On the inside, though, my heart has grown hummingbird wings. It takes everything I have not to give in to the frantic feeling.

"Do you want me to dance?"

"Maybe." His eyes darken.

I lift my chin.

The truth is, Father and I hadn't planned for more than this moment. I knew I would get caught, whether it be by Aiden or his brother, Luca. But now that we're here, I don't know what to expect next. I didn't think I would have to convince him to take me.

Deep down, I've been preparing for him to beat me, drag me out of here by my hair. The violence of it soothed me for the past two nights.

Whatever befalls me won't reach Colin.

"Okay," he says, quietly coming to some sort of decision in his head. "Let's go."

"Go?"

He smiles how a wolf might smile at its prey. "You're packed. It implies you know what I mean when I say *go*."

I flash back to sixteen years old. Aiden sitting beside me on the curb. He nudged my arm and offered me a tissue, then gave me his hands and helped me to my feet. And away we went. I didn't question it. I was so ready to leave school behind, and so we left.

"Where?"

"You're in no position to ask questions." He strides across the room and stops just within reach.

The lamp at his back casts his face in shadow. I don't think I'd be able to read his mind even if I could see his eyes, though.

He offers his hand.

This is wrong.

But he's right: I'm not in a position to ask questions.

I slip past him, out of the room and down the hall. I avoid the last trap he didn't spring: a metal bucket of water precariously perched on a side table, and the string about an inch off the floor that would've brought it down.

His chuckle follows me. "This is like *Home Alone*."

How many times did I pace this hallway in the dark, wondering if he was going to slip past my defenses? It's part of the reason I haven't slept in so long. Exhaustion tugged at me constantly, but the ebb and flow of adrenaline wouldn't let me do more than doze.

I'm wide awake right now. I'll crash eventually. When I'm safe, or when my body gives out.

"You're not as talkative as you once were, Gemma West."

I flinch. "I was taught to not talk to our enemies."

He's right behind me on the stairs, and he stops me with a hand on my shoulder. He pushes me against the wall. "Is that what I am?"

"You and your mind games," I huff. "Yes, you are. You're a DeSantis. You're hunting my family down like a wild dog. Did you expect a warm reception, Aiden? Or did you think a fight might be more suitable for our environment?"

He grins. "You really do put on a strong act."

I meet his gaze. "You could've told me your name when you kidnapped me."

"Ah." Aiden's smile widens. "I did, don't you remember? I told you my name."

First names only. For an afternoon, I was just Gemma. I contemplate what that must've been like for him—to be just Aiden with me. A moment in time where our families didn't exist.

But the whole time, he was talking to his dad. There was a photo later, proof that he had me in his car. It was just of my profile as I stared out the window, but when Mom showed it to me, I wondered how I'd missed it.

How did I miss that an afternoon of walking the pier and eating ice cream could've been threatening? Did he have a knife in his hand when he guided me along? Or was I that easy to manipulate?

"Did they keep you in the dark, dear Gemma?"

I stiffen.

He touches one of my loose curls. "When did you start to believe in monsters?"

I knock his hand away. "Don't touch me."

It happens too quickly: he grips my chin and yanks me forward. My chest hits his arm, and I inhale sharply. He smells good—but that's not what I need to be focusing on, brain.

"You're not in charge," he says in my ear. "You gave that up the moment you decided to remain behind."

I jerk my head to the side and stare back up the stairs. "You'll never understand why I stayed back."

His gaze sears into the side of my face, but I don't face him. Uncomfortable heat winds under my skin as he examines me.

"Maybe not," he allows. "But now it's time to go. I expect whoever you warned of my arrival will be waiting for us downstairs."

I narrow my eyes.

He takes my arm. He lets me lead the way, but he doesn't release me. I focus on the intake of breath, on my exhales. The house is silent and still.

No one is coming for me.

What's the point of a sacrifice if we get blown to bits before it comes to fruition? I see myself as the roadblock. I stop—or at least distract—Aiden from continuing his hunt.

By now, Colin should be well out of town.

Dad is probably back home in Brooklyn.

Neither of them will spare me a second thought.

"No one is out there," I say suddenly.

We navigate past the mouse traps and into the foyer. This house is old, Victorian style. Many hallways and hideaway spots. He seems to realize the pitfalls because we creep through it slower.

"Quiet," he orders.

I bite back my retort. We head for the front door, and I spot the fallen cookie sheet a few feet away. It was bold of him to come in the front—but nothing I wouldn't expect from a DeSantis. This neighborhood wouldn't be awake at this hour. It's inching toward three o'clock. There are faint, faint pink streaks in the sky, visible through the window.

"Smart," he says in my ear. His breath creates goosebumps down my neck. "I wasn't expecting you to be crafty."

"Did you think I'd just hide in the closet?"

He pauses.

I hate that I want to know what he thinks I'd do. How accurate of a picture he has of me.

But he doesn't end up answering me at all. He swings open the door and guides me through ahead of him.

I'm his shield, but the street is utterly silent. Just his car parked in front of the house, only yards away.

"You really think I lured you here as a trap." I grimace. "I'm not stupid."

Aiden DeSantis is cunning. It's part of his allure—and what makes him lethal. People have tried to trap him and failed.

Take, for example, the Eldridge family.

Here one day, obliterated the next.

Aiden wears *that* on his conscience... if he even has one.

There's a rumor he's lacking in that department.

"You're not," he agrees. "Which is why, when I put you in the car, you're not going to move."

I almost ask for clarification, but I don't want him to have that satisfaction.

We make it to the car, and he opens the passenger door for me. Everything is a test, it seems. Am I going to get in and be a willing participant in... whatever scheme he's about to fulfill? Or will this be by force?

I contemplate him for a moment, then get in the car. He slams my door closed and goes to the trunk. He jogs back to the house with two jugs. I'm still trying to figure it out when an orange glow appears in one of the windows.

No.

I scramble to open the door, falling on my face in my rush to get out. He's setting Aunt Mary's house on fire—he *can't*.

That's years of West history stored in those walls. Memories with my parents. My *mother*.

Without thought, I run inside.

Stupid Gemma.

I only take a moment to curse myself before I remember the fire extinguisher on the wall going down to the basement. The shelf was lined with dust-covered things: old paint, folded canvases, tools, and *that*, the red canister.

I don't see Aiden on my way to the basement door. Flames crackle up the curtains in the living room. This house is made of old, dry wood. Dark smoke billows up to the ceiling, drifting inches above my head. I cover my mouth with my shirt sleeve and lunge for the extinguisher.

Working it is another issue—and where to start?

I hate the panic clawing at my throat. It's suffocating.

Focus. I run into the kitchen.

A roar echoes through the house.

Perhaps he's realized I came back in—that I *am* the idiot who's prepared to burn with her family's heirlooms. Aunt Mary was the gentle history-keeper. There's an opal ring in my bag, luckily still in Aiden's car, that belonged to my mother. I found it yesterday in Aunt Mary's bathroom, and I knew immediately who it used to belong to. My heart ached when I thought that of all the possessions Aunt Mary *could* take, she didn't take the reminder of my mother.

A blast throws me forward, into the sliding glass door. Searing heat burns my back. I drop the extinguisher and slide the door open, falling onto the patio.

I think I'm on fire.

I hazard a glance back. The hem of my dress is, indeed, on fire. I don't think—I just scramble forward and launch into the pool.

Cool water envelopes me. The sky suddenly bursts orange, and I hover under the water. Little bubbles stream out of my nose, rushing up. Was it an explosion? Did the fire hit the gas —*ah*, that's it. Aiden probably turned on the stove and blew out the flame. It explains the sudden blast that put me against the door—although I'm lucky it wasn't worse.

It certainly seems *worse* now. My back stings, and my dress tangles around my legs.

I kick back to the surface and pop up near the far edge, glancing back at the house. The fire rages now, lighting up the whole backyard. Black smoke belches from the windows on the second story. There's a sharp ringing in my ears.

Someone hauls me out of the water, hands under my armpits. I'm set on my feet and spun around, and I take too long to register Aiden's furious expression. He pats me down roughly, all over. If the knife is still strapped to my ankle—*it must be*—he doesn't feel it. And then I realize his lips are moving.

"I can't hear you," I say.

I think I say it.

He scowls, turning my head to the side. He touches my earlobe and shows me the streaked blood on his finger.

Shit. That explains the ringing.

He resumes scanning me, and my skin prickles. My dress was loose, but now it's like a second skin.

"I'm fine," I tell him.

"Good," I think he says. And then he puts his hot hands on my hips, lifting me...

Up and over his shoulder. I'm no better than a bag of sand.

The ringing in my ears is rather violent, but it's lessening. I can start to pick up other sounds—mainly, the sirens.

His car beeps, but he doesn't set me down. I only catch a glimpse of the trunk opening.

Oh, that motherfu—

CHAPTER 2
Gemma

He drops me into the trunk.

"No!" I squeal, pushing up on my elbows. "Aiden—"

"I'm *this* close to strangling you," he shouts in my face.

I rear back, blinking in surprise. I'm not sure why that stings as much as it does.

He slams the trunk closed, and I'm left in darkness. The sharpness of his words retreats. Anger takes over. I pound on my low ceiling, yelling at the top of my lungs. It smells like gasoline in here.

The car engine turns over, and I slide as he shoots away from the curb.

My stomach rolls. I have a turbulent relationship with cars —and motion sickness. Now would be an awful time to lose it.

I pitch onto my side and gasp. I feel around me. My fingers land on thick rope, then a roll of something smooth—tape, I'd guess. And a box. Since I have nothing better to do, I work the edges until the top pops open. The box is just bigger than my palm. I run my finger over the contents, trying to visualize it in the dark.

We hit something—a bump or a pothole—and I'm weightless for a split second. Whatever's in the box clinks together.

I pull one out and run my finger over it. It's smooth and cylindrical. Maybe a cartridge for a gun? Makes sense, seeing as how he's a freaking hitman.

Settling back, I close my eyes. There's no point keeping them open, and now that I'm caught… my sense of self-preservation is draining.

Well, we can agree that it was already nearly gone. I ran into a burning building. My long-sleeved dress is ice-cold, and before long I'm hunched in a fetal position. I can't stop shivering. My muscles ache from the exertion, but I'm not warming up. If anything, my temperature is dropping.

What feels like hours later, the car slows to a halt. A door opens and closes, and then the trunk clicks open an inch.

He doesn't open it farther, though, and the barest amount of light seeps in through the crack.

Huh.

A trap for me, then? Payback is a bitch.

I shove it open and peek out. My nerves are shot, and my tremble is too rough to go unnoticed. The car is parked in a garage—no big surprise if we're in downtown Manhattan—and the only light is a fluorescent bulb that flickers overhead.

Slowly, I climb—eh, more like barrel-roll—out of the trunk.

My heels hit the floor, and pain spikes up my legs.

I hate him.

For burning down my aunt's house, for putting me in the trunk, for coming after us in the first place. For ruining my life one step at a time.

Decimation is a process.

I stare around the garage. We're on the slant between levels. I could go up to an elevator, the *exit* sign glowing, or down to what I would guess is a side street. Freedom is in that direction, and at this rate, I can't breathe with how angry I am.

Down, then.

Someone steps out of the shadows at the base of the ramp. A man—but not Aiden. He's too bulky to be him. He folds his arms over his chest, and the way he tilts his head is a challenge to keep coming at him.

No thanks.

I pivot and go back the way I came. A quick check of the interior of Aiden's car reveals my bag is gone. I bite the inside of my cheek to keep from screaming, then move on. No point in getting pissed when he's not around to witness it.

The elevator door is open and waiting. I step inside and hit a button at random.

Nothing.

I try another, keeping one eye on the man. He's meandering toward me, his hands in his pockets now. He gives off a carefree vibe, but it's a lie. He probably knows who I am, and both those things translate to danger.

None of the buttons light up, but the doors close without warning. If there was ever a way to make sure a girl didn't run...

I cross my arms over my chest. The dress now seems like a bad move, because I'm being whisked into the center of my enemy's lair. Armor would've been more appropriate.

Even after the long ride, water drips from the fabric. I wring it out as best I can, leaving a puddle in my wake.

The elevator chimes and slides open on the seventeenth floor, revealing a hallway with only a few doors. It's more like a lobby than a hallway.

I try the door all the way to my left, but it's locked. Same with the second. The third opens easily, swinging inward. At first, I don't understand. It's... a kitchen?

Commercial, from the look of it. There are many stations, and everything is deserted. Only one row of lights is lit, illuminating the way. I've got to believe I'm on the right path, whatever that means.

My footsteps echo on the tile.

I try to home in on my anger, but finding my way through a maze has blunted it. I walk into the dining room and try to get my bearings. Two walls are just glass, giving an unobstructed view of the surrounding skyscrapers. It's growing lighter by the minute outside, but it's still too early for the lights across the street to come on. I guess the fact that we can look across the street into the next building is the definition of an obstructed view, but whatever.

There's a light on at one of the tables.

Aiden sits leaned back in his chair, gaze on the view.

Not on me.

I come to a stop beside him.

"Hungry?" he asks.

I shake my head. My stomach is in knots—I'm sure I'll be hungry soon, but I can't fathom eating now. Not with him.

He sighs and pushes away the water glass. "Okay."

"Why are we here?"

He nods to the view. "That doesn't seem familiar?"

I frown and spare it a glance. "No."

He rises and leaves me standing there. I squint across the street, wondering what I'm missing, but I don't want to be abandoned. I hurry after him.

"Where'd my bag go?" I call.

He doesn't respond. I follow him up two flights of stairs, puffing by the time he stops and unlocks a door.

We go down a hallway, and he unlocks another door.

"This is where we wait," he tells me. He turns on a light and waves me ahead of him.

I step into the room, spinning in a slow circle. Bed, desk, chair, television. It does a good impression of a hotel room. At least it's warm in here. "Wait for what?"

"For *whom*," he corrects.

I cross my arms. "Wait for who?"

He smirks. "My father."

Ah. All this has been subterfuge. Delaying the inevitable. He's going to let his father decide what to do with me because that'll be easier.

"That's cowardly," I point out. "You can't make up your own mind?"

He frowns and takes a seat. "Why did you run back into the house?"

Why, indeed?

"*That house* held a lot of happy memories, and you just destroyed it. Why would you do that?" A question for a question seems fair.

He stands right back up again. "You're not in charge here, Gemma. If you want to stay alive, you're going to remember that."

I push my shoulders back. I shouldn't provoke him, but it's so easy. "And you're saying you're not, either."

He frowns, but then it's gone.

"It's been two months, Aiden. You're the new heir, aren't you? And instead, you're wasting your time hunting down my family instead of doing whatever it is heirs do. What's your plan? Or your dad's?"

I never had a chance to be an heir. First born, but a girl. If that weighed on my parents' minds at all, they never said. They just let me be a regular girl... until Aiden took me the first time. Then it seemed that the lightbulbs went on for them that I could be more than ordinary.

But Colin... he was raised knowing he was going to take over.

Aiden regards me. "I haven't decided."

I wonder how I come across now. Sopping wet clothes, hair. Waterlogged boots. I'm still trembling from the cold, my muscles twitching involuntarily. I'm outgunned and, at this rate, probably outsmarted. *His territory*, after all. He's at an advantage.

I've never been one for helplessness. In fact, I've gone out of my way to avoid it.

Aiden brought me here, but he doesn't have a plan to get me out.

Think. My sudden predicament has me chewing at the bars of my cage—and I've only just arrived.

"Well, let me know when you do." I turn away from him and go for the door. "I'll go."

"You won't," he says quietly.

I pause with my hand on the knob. "And why not?"

"Because I'm afraid you won't like what's on the other side, especially once they start waking up. A mad lot, especially in the morning." He brushes his hands over his thighs and cocks his head. "But do go ahead and try."

I tilt my head. "Is that it, then? Your way or—"

The door swings open, knocking me back a few steps.

Jameson DeSantis, Aiden's father, fills the doorway. His gaze flits from me to Aiden, then back again. He looks me up and down, lingering on my chest. "Well, well. You caught a West."

Don't back up, don't back up. Showing fear is deadly, especially in this viper's nest.

He doesn't ask my name. There's no need, really. The only Wests worth capturing are ones in direct relation to Lawrence, the head of the family. Cousins, nieces and nephews, distant relatives... they're expendable. To an extent, anyway. Kill one and there will be retribution. Kidnap one for leverage?

Not likely.

"The daughter, then?"

Aiden sighs. "Obviously."

"We'll keep her with the others," Jameson says. He takes my arm, pinching just above my elbow. "To lure Lawrence out."

"No." Aiden stands. It seems he's decided, after all.

Jameson stops. He's imposing, almost as tall as his son and just as broad. His goatee is neatly trimmed, and he seems too put together for dawn. Like he's already been working for hours.

"No?" he drawls.

"I've already claimed her." Aiden comes forward and stares pointedly at his father's hand, until the latter releases my arm.

Lead balls drop into my stomach. This is a worst-case scenario—he's *claimed* me? What the hell does that mean?

I try not to let my confusion show.

"Claimed," Jameson repeats drily. "You've fucked girls before, Aiden. There's no need to get attached to this one."

My face flames.

"She agreed to marry me," Aiden says. "So, no, she won't join the prostitutes."

Married? I stare at Aiden.

I couldn't have guessed *this* would be his chosen path. Why he'd want to be stuck with me for the rest of his life is beyond me... unless he plans on killing me later. After my family's businesses are under his control. Yeah, that seems more likely. He's feeling a bit possessive and doesn't want me sold for sex, but the marriage thing is just a line of crap to buy us time.

There's always an endgame with a DeSantis.

Jameson grunts. "She doesn't appear to be on board with that plan, son."

The muscle in Aiden's jaw tics.

"I'm totally on board," I blurt out. "I, um, Aiden and I—"

Jameson narrows his eyes.

I get the impression I'm doing more harm than good by speaking. I close my mouth and shrink back against the wall.

They have a nonverbal exchange. I can't make sense of these miniscule actions that belie a silent conversation, but then I don't have to.

"Prove it," Jameson says to Aiden. "That you've already taken her—and will again, of course. If she's your wife, prove that she's willing."

Aiden rolls his eyes, but the bastard doesn't object.

"Come here," he says to me.

I almost shake my head but think better of it. What's my other option? Joining the whores the DeSantis family keeps? Let Jameson do God knows what to me? I don't doubt it would be more insidious than anything Aiden has planned.

The sinking feeling in my belly gives way to anticipation. I'm nothing if not a glutton for punishment.

I go to Aiden.

I'm not quick enough for his liking, though, because he grabs my neck and hauls me to him.

His lips slam against mine.

It's shocking.

Horrific.

...Pleasant?

My thoughts screech to a halt, and I fight him. I push at his chest, but it just incentivizes him. He spins us, shoving me against the wall. His tongue invades my mouth as he lifts me. I automatically wrap my legs around his hips.

This is an act.

Say it, Gemma.

This is an act. To trick his father. To save me from his wrath and so much more.

His hand has navigated under my dress, to my core, and I inhale sharply.

He strokes my center. I grip his shoulders, turning my head away abruptly. This cannot be happening.

Aiden thrusts his finger inside me, and his lips move to my throat. I gasp and let my head fall back to the wall. It's sensation overload mixed with extreme embarrassment. My whole body is crawling with fire—good and bad. I waver on which way to lean... into the pleasure or *other.*

My gaze goes to Aiden's father. He stands there, expressionless, and I tense. I can't help it.

Aiden stills. He has two fingers inside of me, and, well, *those* don't stop moving. "Do you mind?"

His father nods once, even though I'm the only one who catches it. The door closes, and then it's just us. Now that we're alone, the ruse can drop. He'll set me back on my feet and sit back in his chair and contemplate what he just did.

But if anything, the door closing pushes him on. He tugs my panties farther to the side, rubbing my clit in small circles. Electricity builds under his touch, and I dig my fingers into his jacket. I can't take the pressure.

"What are you doing?" I ask on a whimper.

He puts his mouth to my ear. "I'm going to make you come, princess. And when I do, it better be my damn name that comes out of your pretty mouth."

"Stop," I whisper. I can't do this. Not when we're alone.

He bites my neck. "No."

"Aiden."

"That's a good girl," he murmurs. His free hand wanders up my side. "Say it again."

I press my lips together and let my head fall back on the door. If he wants me to say his name, I'll go to hell in silence.

He slows until my whole body trembles, left dangling on an unknown edge. He pulls away from me piece by piece, but we're so tangled together. His fingers first, then his grip on my thigh. I put my feet back on the floor.

The wild part of me would say anything to feel his touch again. To push me off the cliff.

But sensible Gemma takes charge, and I put a hand on his chest. To get him away from me, to be able to breathe, I don't know. I just need *space*.

He gives it to me. His own breathing is ragged, and he sharply turns away from me.

I let loose a sigh of relief.

"Your bag is in the bathroom. Shower if you want. Put on dry clothes." His gaze sweeps up and down me, heating slightly. But he tears himself away and leaves me in the middle of the room. The door closes behind him. It's impossible to miss the *snick* of a deadbolt sliding home from the outside.

I rush to the door and try the handle anyway, but the wood rattles in the frame. Stuck and definitely not opening.

Great.

But my bag—that's the first piece of good news I've had today.

I lock myself in the bathroom and strip off my boots. I turn them upside down in the sink. A fair amount of water splashes out.

Oops.

My body aches, but I register that I'm safe here. At least for the moment.

My life has narrowed to *moments*.

I peel off my soaked socks, then the dress that did a shitty job keeping me warm. The hem in the back is burned black, and parts of it flake off under my touch. It's an inch or two shorter than the front. I add my underwear to the pile and turn on the shower. I crank it as hot as it'll go and wait for steam to fill the room.

At some point, I stopped shivering. But my hair is a wet disaster plastered to my scalp, and my skin has pruned.

I carefully undo the Velcro straps around my ankle and remove the knife. I set it on the counter, then eye my bag. It's zipped up tight, but I wouldn't put snooping past Aiden or one of his goons.

I sift through it and find the tiny travel bottles of shampoo and conditioner. It seemed natural to pack light—like I'd be held hostage and then released, beaten and defeated.

I had been mentally preparing for a fight. Or punishment. Instead, my core tingles and pulses like I've never been touched before.

Well... I haven't.

I touch my lips. He *kissed* me, and more... with a witness.

Ugh.

I step into the shower. The water is scalding, but I need the cleansing fire after what I just went through.

Priorities, Gemma.

I need to figure out what Aiden wants from me.

This was never...

Don't be daft. This was always going to be a permanent thing. My father's sorrow before he and Colin left echoes inside me.

They abandoned me.

I shake my head at the intrusive thought. *No*. Dad instilled in us that family comes first, always. That doesn't mean leaving someone behind. I'm meant to save Colin—but not at the expense of my own life.

I'll make my own plan of escape.

They can't keep me in this building forever.

Or... can they?

Knowing Aiden, he might try.

We're two stories above the restaurant. The view out the window—in both the bathroom and the bedroom—allows me to catch a glimpse of the buildings around us and the tiny street below.

If I want to get out, I need to get down more than nineteen flights without being seen.

Or sounding an alarm.

I finish washing my hair and scrub my body. My back stings when the soapy water rushes over it, but I can't twist around far enough to see the damage. There's a bit of blood in my ears, although the ringing has faded.

I'm glad my hearing returned.

Once I'm clean, I step out and get dressed as quickly as possible. The knife first, then the jeans and thick socks, a t-shirt, and the sweater over it. Last are my boots, still soggy, but I don't have another choice.

I like layers. Colin always made fun of me for being eternally cold.

I had a disposable phone hidden in the bottom of my bag, but I don't immediately spot it. My search becomes a bit more frantic.

How am I going to contact my father?

My own phone is probably a crispy shell now, unless the toilet miraculously saved it. I couldn't risk taking it with me after I sent the last message.

This burner cell was my one lifeline to the Wests.

Someone bangs on the bathroom door, and I almost jump out of my skin.

"Open up," Aiden says.

I shove everything back into my bag and stand, hesitating for a moment. Then I open it.

He leans against the frame, glowering at me. "What were you doing?"

"Showering. You told me to."

He rolls his eyes. "Come on. You've had your solitary hour. It's time to go."

I sling my bag over my shoulder. Pain bursts across my skin, and I cringe.

"Are you hurt?"

"No," I lie. I can barely take a deep breath.

He watches me. He could be trying to figure out if I'm telling the truth or not.

He snatches my bag and tosses it on the bed, maneuvering me around. I stiffen with him at my back. His fingers are gentle, though, as he pushes my t-shirt and sweater up.

"Fuck, Gemma," he groans. "You should've mentioned this."

"I don't even know what *this* is," I snap. And then, quieter, "How bad is it?"

He ghosts over a spot on my lower back, near my spine. "A burn. It's... not great. You'll live, though." He tugs my shirt back down and takes my hand. He grabs my bag with his other.

"Where are we going?" I ask.

He leads me down the hall, back to the elevator. "Up. I don't trust you here."

We glance around at the same time. This floor seems quiet.

"You don't trust *me* here," I repeat, putting the emphasis on a different word. It isn't that he doesn't trust me *here*, on this floor. I'm the issue.

Once we're in the elevator, he releases me and fishes something out of his pocket.

I suck my lower lip between my teeth. My phone—the burner, not the cell phone. Which means he went through my bag. I knew it, but the confirmation is... unpleasant.

"Give that—" I reach for it.

He tuts, sticking it back in his pocket.

"Are you going to tell me anything?"

Aiden grins. He's thoroughly enjoying this. "No."

I narrow my eyes, fighting a wave of exhaustion. I just want today to be over. "Why did you tell your dad you claimed me?"

He glances at me, then back to the closed doors. "Truth?"

"Please."

"I knew you would belong to me when I found you crying on the curb three years ago."

We jolt as the elevator zooms upward.

I'm dumbfounded. *Then?*

No.

"Come on, Gemma. You either come with me or I'll let my cousins do what they've always dreamed about doing to a West princess."

The door dings and opens to reveal a small lobby-like entrance. There's only one door ahead of us, and he unlocks it with a keycard. He steps aside to reveal a huge apartment, then leaves me standing in the elevator with his threat hanging above me.

My legs carry me out. Seems like I have a sense of self-preservation after all... Well, my brain does.

I'm not so sure about my heart.

CHAPTER 3
Aiden

I close my eyes, and Wilder's death plays out in front of me again.

The crack of a gunshot, the spray of blood. They got him in the chest, slightly off-center. The guests screamed and ducked, hiding in the pews. It's the natural response to fear: to flinch away from it.

Luca and I didn't. Violence moves in our veins the same way blood does.

He went after the bride, Amelie, and I located the shooter. They were in the choir section on the second floor, but by the time I got there, they were gone.

It had Lawrence West written all over it, but we had no proof. The place was in chaos. We shuffled everyone to my father's estate in Beacon Hill. We'd spent a lot of time there in the summers—everyone escapes Manhattan in the summer—and the wedding party had been preparing it for the reception for most of the week.

It ended up being a refuge for our shocked guests.

My father told us that Wilder hadn't made it. They were on their way to the hospital, but he died in the ambulance.

The rage I felt was like nothing I'd ever experienced before. It lived inside me, festering for weeks.

It didn't help that some boneheaded cousins sought immediate gratification and attacked the Wests. They, in turn, tried to intimidate us on our own property. No one close to Lawrence, the head of their family—no one under his direct orders would be so stupid. Jameson cracked down on our family, too.

Everything was tense.

I followed the trail from loose-lipped acquaintances and business partners to seedy bars. The Wests were practically untouchable, but I wasn't looking for the law to side with me. I was looking for enough evidence to exact my revenge.

The only way to pay for Wilder's death was through blood.

Then finally, *finally*, someone gave me a valuable piece of information.

Colin and Kai had been training at the shooting range for months. Both of them ran into Wilder a week before his death and threatened to end the DeSantis line. Cocky teenagers running their mouths is what it was brushed off as.

Wilder was the heir, after all. He was going to take over for my father. He was poised to take control of everything—and he wasn't meek. He would've gone after the entire city, pushing the Wests to the suburbs. Greedy or optimistic... I couldn't say which he was.

Smart, though. Devious.

He wanted to rule in an official capacity.

We played two different games, and Wilder was too confident in his safety. In his power. He might've let his plan slip a little, and in doing so painted a large target on his back.

No one could tell me where Colin and Kai were on my brother's wedding day.

More proof, but too flimsy.

There's a scuffing noise behind me, and I'm on my feet with my gun out before I've fully registered the movement. My apartment is nearly infallible—but that doesn't mean people haven't broken in before. Usually, assholes wanting something from me... or one of my brothers.

Just one brother.

I've learned that nothing is truly infallible.

But on the other end of my firearm is Gemma West, her eyes open impossibly wide. She opens her mouth and then closes it, and I can't tell if she wants to scream at me or pretend I'm still not pointing a gun at her.

I stow it back in its concealed holster and go to her.

She backs away from me.

"I do love a chase," I say.

She shakes her head but stops moving. *Good.*

"What time is it?" she asks.

"Almost nine."

She slept for fourteen hours and still seems exhausted. When I found her in that house, she was more ghost than girl. And her eyes held a haunted look, as much as she tried to hide it. I recognized it because it was a mirror of my frozen expression for a solid month after my first kill.

Gemma is soft where I'm hard. Quiet and meek. But she didn't go down without a fight, I'll give her that. And running back into the burning house took courage.

It scared me half to death. How someone could care that much about a structure that they'd risk their life for it. If this place caught on fire, I'd walk out with nothing but the clothes on my back.

"When's the last time you slept?" I ask, if only to curb my line of thought. "Before today."

She shrugs and glances away.

A better question occurs to me. "When's the last time you ate?"

Her stomach growls in response, and I smile. Food, at least, I can do. My parents were no help in the cooking department, but I learned to take matters into my own hands when I moved into my own space. What began as a terrible experiment transformed into something fun.

She follows me into the kitchen.

This apartment takes up half this floor and a quarter of the one above it. Once upon a time, Wilder lived above me. Dad liked to keep all of us close, and I think he bought into the idea that a skyscraper was easier to control than a neighborhood. That's not to say he doesn't have spies all over the city—and beyond. If he wanted to raise an army, he could easily do so.

But it certainly takes less energy to keep us all in a one-block radius.

I fill a pot with water, and try not to focus too hard on Gemma. She's an enigma. Something about her called out to me when I first met her, and she managed to tattoo herself in my brain. I've kept a tight lid on my fixation, but having her in my apartment is almost too much.

She slides up onto the counter and pulls one leg up, wrapping her arms around it.

Her blonde hair is wavy—something I don't think I knew about her. In public, it's always been ironed straight or pinned up.

I like this. It's not much of a difference; just another layer that's peeled away.

"What are you making?" Her voice is low and haunting.

I glance over my shoulder. "Spaghetti."

She frowns. "Why are we here, Aiden?"

I step away from the stove and lean against the counter opposite her. I can easily recall the way she squirmed beneath my fingers, and my heartbeat picks up.

"The doc checked your back while you slept." I raise the

cream he gave me, then return it to its spot on the counter. I had to carefully lift her so he could wrap gauze around her torso, but I keep that quiet. She was putty in my arms—both asleep and when I had her pressed to the wall. What I wouldn't give to do that again.

Now isn't the time.

The family doctor needed a good amount of persuasion to even look at her. He eventually did—there might've been a threat to kill everyone he loves if he didn't, but Gemma doesn't need to know that.

She doesn't need to know a lot of things.

Like why she's here.

"This will help with the pain," I say.

"And my phone?" She raises her eyebrows. "And my *life*? What'll help with that?"

I step closer, stoked by her dramatics. "Your life is mine."

She keeps her knees pinched together, and I notice she's still wearing her boots. Even when she passed out in my bed.

I grab her boot and yank it forward. "Why did you sleep in these?"

She cringes, and my curiosity piques. She doesn't stop me from unlacing it and dragging it off. Such a simple action, but I find myself savoring it. I drop the boot and try not to get fucking turned on that she has a knife strapped to her ankle.

It's half covered by her sock—and, I'll admit, an impressive hide. The leather of her boot made it nearly impossible to feel.

She snatches the hilt and yanks it free, pointing it at me.

My attention goes from the trembling tip, hovering inches in front of my nose, to her face. I have to take a moment to register the emotion whipping through me. It's *glee*. It's the ever-present violence—and the challenge she presents.

"I hope you're prepared to use that," I say.

Her fingers tighten. "I am. Let me go."

I nod and drop her ankle. The sudden shift of her weight sends her off-balance, and she slides forward, off the counter.

As much as I'd love this to play out, part of me is concerned she might actually stab me. I grab her wrist, twisting it until she cries out. The knife falls to the floor between us, and I spin her, putting my palm between her shoulder blades and lifting her wrist. The pressure folds her in half. Her face hits the counter. I'm careful not to touch the burn when I lean over her.

"Maybe one day I'll show you how to use a knife with intention."

Her foot stomps down on my toes, and I groan. I only removed *one* of her boots. She digs her heel down, putting all her weight behind it. Damn, it hurts. But the pain only serves to wake me up—and I have to wonder if she likes this, too.

"What's your goal, princess?" I move my foot out of range. It isn't like me to wander around without shoes—lesson learned around this girl. "To spy and send information back to daddy dearest? To bring home my head?"

Dark thoughts, indeed. I've been turning over the puzzle of why she's here all day, to no avail.

She just... gave herself up.

Who does that?

"Why didn't you go with the rest of the women in your family?"

I'd never seen such a large exodus of West women. It was impossible to miss, even if they thought they were being sly about it.

It's in my nature to keep an eye on things.

On *everything*.

Gemma presses her forehead to the counter, giving in to my hold. "I couldn't."

I grunt and haul her up. "I'm beginning to think your family doesn't deserve you, Ms. West."

She's eager to put distance between us. I can tell in the wideness of her eyes, the way her lips are parted. The predator in me wants her to run—because the chase is half the fun. But right now, she's not at full capacity.

I box her in and lean close. "I'll figure you out, Gemma. That's a promise."

She stiffens. "I just want to pay my penance and go home."

That brings me up short. *Penance for what?*

"Your water is boiling," she says suddenly.

I automatically glance behind me, and she slips under my arm.

Damn it.

CHAPTER 4
Gemma

What the fuck is wrong with me?

Last night, he guided me into a bedroom and disappeared, and it wasn't long before I fell asleep. I have a vague memory of him lifting me into his arms, but the crash I was anticipating happened sooner than I expected—and it left me no choice but to surrender to his mercy.

Luckily, I didn't wake up tied to a bed or surrounded by sex workers.

I stomp upstairs, and I breathe easier with some distance between us. But I can't stay here forever. Not when my hunger is so bad I can barely stand. My stomach cramps, and I press my palm to my abdomen.

I yank off my other boot and throw it into the room Aiden put me in. My meager possessions are still in the bag on top of the dresser, but the thought of unpacking nauseates me.

Spaghetti doesn't sound bad—and *that's* why I'm questioning what's wrong with me.

Eating with my enemy.

I wouldn't have thought we would end up here. I cross to

the window and look out. Rolling clouds block out the stars, casting a dark gloom over the city. Any higher and we'd be inside the clouds.

Sighing, I leave my boots behind—sans knife—and go back downstairs.

The apartment must've been designed with an industrial theme in mind. There are metal rafters visible through the drywall, and besides the monochromatic color scheme, everything is bare. No photos, no extra decorations.

It's like he lives here as a visitor.

I go downstairs and pause on the bottom step, focusing on Aiden in the kitchen. His presence is too much. Impossible to ignore. I let my gaze sweep over him. The way he moves quietly and efficiently. He is so distinctly different from any man I've ever met.

A touch feral, too.

I force myself away and flop on the couch. The television is already on, playing some action movie. I pull the blanket around me and zone out.

I'm not processing. I can't seem to wrap my brain around anything that's happening, so instead... nothing. It explains how I was able to sleep for so long, in any case. But self-diagnosis is frowned upon.

My father would be furious at the turn of events. Aiden *touched* me, and part of me enjoyed it. Truth be told, if I wasn't experiencing a major case of emotional whiplash, I'd be furious, too.

I gag—did I really just think about what Aiden did and what my father would think back-to-back?

Gross, Gemma.

I don't know how long I sit before Aiden sets a plate in front of me. When I don't touch it, he sits beside me, so close that his thigh presses against my knee.

"Are you going to eat?"

I glare at the pasta. It has a red sauce with chunks of meat. The whole thing is swirled like they would in a fancy restaurant, complete with green garnish on the side.

"It's not the plate's fault you hate me," he says. "But don't you think you'll need your energy for whatever it is you have planned?"

"I do hate you," I agree.

He nods and lifts the plate, forcing it into my hands. "Eat."

So fucking bossy.

It doesn't help that it smells amazing. I give in to my temptation and twist the noodles onto the fork, carefully bringing it to my mouth.

A riot of flavor assaults my tastebuds. It's so much better than it smells, even.

"Oh my god." It's ridiculously good. My hunger overtakes my senses, and I bring the plate to my face. I shovel the pasta in, barely chewing. I'm pretty sure I'm making asinine noises of appreciation.

Now who's the wild animal?

He watches me for a moment, then abruptly stands.

To get away from the crazy woman, I'd bet.

I get to the bottom of the plate and set it down gently, wiping my mouth with the back of my hand. All I need to do to completely horrify the memory of my mother is to belch.

Aiden returns with water for me, and a dark-amber liquid in his glass. He takes a seat next to me again and regards me. "When's the last time you ate?"

I shrug. "I don't know. Maybe yesterday morning." A granola bar...

"You need to take better care."

I scoff. "Seriously?"

"Yes, Gemma. You can't just starve yourself."

"Well, excuse me with being a bit preoccupied with my

impending abduction." I shuffle myself to the side, putting space between us.

"Right, that. What was your plan, anyway? Or were you just being a good daughter and following orders?" He's suspicious. Rightly so.

I shoot to my feet. "You think—"

"Sit down." He narrows his eyes, and the warning in his tone is clear.

I comply… slowly. "Dad didn't order me to do anything. It was my decision."

He sips his drink and watches me over the rim. "Why?"

"Isn't the answer obvious?" I fold my legs under me and gulp my water. It's one thing to know my own motivation, and another thing entirely to share it. Or have it spread. The *last* thing I want to be is predictable.

But in that regard, I feel more like the mouse than the cat. I'm being herded in whichever direction Aiden pleases—and that might be right off the balcony.

Splat.

"It's not obvious," he says. "But I suppose I can guess."

"Guess, then."

He smiles. "You think you're enough."

I go still.

"You think you're enough to save your cousin and brother. You think that by being here, I won't look for them. That maybe I'll take the pound of flesh we're due from *your* skin." He leans forward and puts his hand on my knee. "Or maybe you were just driven by the need to do something—anything—to clear your conscience."

I rear back. "No."

"I'm wrong, then." Aiden raises his chin.

"I…" I did think me being here would be enough to satiate the DeSantises' bloodlust. I thought my sacrifice would curb

Aiden's need for revenge. I thought *I* would... be enough. Just as he said.

But I was wrong.

The need to warn my father is almost unbearable. There must be some way to tell him that Aiden won't stop until he spills more West blood. A life for a life. That's always been the way of things, and he won't kill me.

Stupid.

I'm a dumb girl trying to change decades of Mafia warfare madness.

"I want to be alone," I say woodenly.

"No." He faces the television and reaches for the remote. "You want to sulk? Do it here."

I stand anyway and go toward the stairs. He can bite me for all I care. What I need to do is find the phone he stashed, or *any* phone. Even his personal one.

An arm bands around my waist, hauling me back.

I squeal and kick out, but he lifts me clear off my feet.

"You. Just. Don't. *Listen.*" He's got me in one arm, supporting most of my weight just by cinching me to his side.

Spikes of pain zip down my back from the pressure, but the fight is more important.

"I don't want to be around you," I say, clawing at his arm.

"Lucky for me, you don't make the decisions around here." He sits and drags me with him.

I land on his lap awkwardly. He doesn't release his arm from around my waist, so I'm forced to either tense, straining forward, or use him as a backrest.

He's smug, and it only seems to get more intense when I sag backward. He takes the brunt of my weight and adjusts slightly. I can't help but wish that he doesn't make it more comfortable for both of us.

I close my eyes and breathe deeply. "Your hand better not wander."

He chuckles.

"I'm serious, Aiden. Don't—"

"Maybe rethink your need to give me orders," he says in my ear. "We know how well that works out."

I press my lips together. His arm hasn't moved, but now his thumb edges under the hem of my shirt. He swipes it back and forth across my hip.

He's maddening.

My skin is hot.

I have a desire to ruin it.

"Why did you yell at me for going back into the house?" I ask.

His thumb stops.

"I mean, it would've been easy to let me die. Wouldn't that have been—"

"Payment?" he finishes. "You think if you died in a *fire*, it would be better?" He pulls me closer. "What did they raise you to believe, princess? That your life is worthless?"

I stiffen. "My parents taught me that my life isn't more important than anyone else—"

"Bullshit."

It's amazing how we can have a conversation without looking at each other. That the words are actually coming out, instead of clogging in our throats.

"You think you know who I am," he says quietly. "The stories your cousins must've told you about the bloodthirsty DeSantis brother. Middle child. Forced to carve out a place in the world—and I did it by being the best. The most savage. The most daring. And you think I would stop with you?"

I push against his arm. "You could change your mind."

He laughs. "I won't, princess. You gave yourself up willingly. But don't confuse this with warmth toward you or your family. They're going to fall."

They're going to die.

"Wilder—"

"Do not say his name."

I wet my lips. My heart pounds against my ribcage. I get the feeling I'm walking on thin ice, but who would I be if I didn't blunder forward?

"He was supposed to take over when your father stepped down." I blow out a breath. "And now it's you. It has to be you. That's why you can't go back, or let my family go."

Aiden is silent at my back.

"He died, and your world exploded, too." I lift my chin, staring at the window. "I think that's why you're doing this. It's less about revenge and more duty." In that, at least, we can relate.

His grip shifts. His fingers dig into my jaw, forcing me to meet his gaze. His grasp is bruising. "So many theories bouncing around in your pretty little head. Is that your best one?"

I narrow my eyes, ignoring the wings fluttering in my chest. I do like a challenge.

"Hmm," I say. "Maybe you arranged for Wilder's death because you wanted what he had."

Aiden smiles—not the reaction I was expecting. "Anything else?"

My mind races over what I know of him. But to know his motivation? He's right: I *don't* know him, even if I thought I did. "Not yet."

He hums and releases me. "Go."

My skin tingles where he held me. "Go…?"

"Away. Retreat, Gemma West." His smile is menacing. "Or you won't like where this goes."

The threat is clear. I shiver and stand on shaking legs. He doesn't stop me from stepping away from him, and I back up until I'm clear of the couch. Then I bolt.

CHAPTER 5
Gemma

"Gemma, wake up."

I groan and roll over, burying my face in a hard pillow. My body aches from the past few days, and all the sleep I got only seems to have made me stiff.

I was in the middle of a dream about my brother. We were arguing about the best way to get someone to give you twenty bucks. I had an idea, but every time I opened my mouth, I kept saying Aiden's name. In response, Colin dropped to the floor, blood pouring from his eyes.

Actually, I'm glad to be awake.

Bloody tears. That has to be a bad omen. A dream interpreter would have a field day with me.

"I know you're awake, little princess."

I groan and palm the pillow.

The hard pillow that is very unpillowlike.

I'm going to kill him.

I open my eyes, and no lie, I'm wrapped around Aiden like an octopus. How did I not notice this? How did my sleeping self allow this to happen? My arm is around his waist; I'm pretty sure I just burrowed my face into his chest. Our legs are intertwined.

"I'm not awake," I inform him, pulling back. "This is an awful nightmare."

He smirks. "You're cute when you're flustered."

I roll away from him and try to be subtle about wiping my mouth. "Why are you in my bed?"

"My bed, you mean?"

My face flames. "I don't know how to respond to that." Because I'm the idiot who should've done a better job scoping out the bedroom. I should've known it was his. He's already demonstrated a possessive streak, and putting me in his bed is just another step.

He reaches over me and grabs a remote from the nightstand. I flatten to the mattress, loathing the way my skin tingles where he touches me. I'm in the one t-shirt I own and my panties. The bag didn't allow for much extra, and I didn't plan for *this*.

If I had foresight, I would've brought a freaking chastity belt. But then I remember what Aiden told his father yesterday morning. His decision of what to do with me. And suddenly I realize I don't know enough about the DeSantis family to survive. I've only got the stories that were whispered in the dark, the pieces of conversation I snatched from my hiding places.

I've been kept away from the politics of my family for too long.

"Why did you tell your father we were getting married?"

He clicks a button and then relaxes back onto his side of the bed. There's a whirring noise, and the shades retract up the walls. Sunlight floods the room, and I drop my head into my hands.

"I told him that because I had to make a decision." He slides out of bed.

I peek at him, then immediately avert my gaze. He's only in a white t-shirt and black briefs. His thigh muscles bulge, and embarrassment sweeps through me.

My god. I've done my best to avoid anything sexual, and in the span of forty-eight hours, he's made me soar high—and then crash.

"And I already told you, princess. I knew you'd be mine three years ago."

He reappears from the closet, and my gaze automatically drops to his briefs. To his cock, which strains against the fabric.

He smirks. "I think you might come to like this."

I stand and take the sheet with me, keeping it wrapped around my body. I'm not naked, but I may as well be. "I was sixteen. It was one afternoon. You can't just... say someone's going to be yours from one day."

He shrugs, seeming indifferent. "I did."

I scowl. "Why?"

Aiden pauses, and his face closes off. "You should get dressed. My cousin will be here soon."

He knows why he chose me. Why I intrigued him three years ago.

And maybe why I appeal to him more now.

I could say no just for the hell of it. To be fickle. But the thought of someone else seeing me without any sort of armor makes my skin itch. So I nod and inch toward my bag.

We both get dressed in silence. His bathroom has two sinks, and it's weird that we both brush our teeth at the same time. My stomach growls, which elicits a throaty chuckle from Aiden.

"My fridge is stocked. You cook, right?"

I frown. "Of course I do."

Well, sort of. We had a maid at home, and a chef. People to clean our house and keep it sparkling. But if I think too much of home, my heart beats faster and my chest tightens. The key to surviving here is to ignore the before.

I know how to make cereal, and I could probably figure out the inner workings of something easy, like a sandwich. Or mac 'n' cheese. Who doesn't know how to make that staple food?

Someone bangs on the door downstairs. I follow Aiden to the first level but hang back on the stairs. He unlocks the door —interesting that he keeps it locked in his own family's skyscraper—and a man pushes past him. His dark hair is cut close to his scalp, and he wears a red-and-black-checkered flannel over a white t-shirt and tan pants. On the first impression, it seems he works with his hands.

And then he turns to face Aiden. The back of his flannel has caught on the handle of a gun, like he shoved it there and forgot to hide it. I sink onto the second step from the bottom, hoping that maybe I can just fade into the background.

"We have a problem," he says without preamble. "The shipment we had scheduled to come in today is gone."

Aiden goes rigid. "Gone how?"

"The ship arrived this morning, but our container was empty. This was supposed to be our supply for the rest of the busy season." He runs his hands through his hair. "Jameson told me to find you since Luca is—"

"I'll handle it." Aiden's attention snaps to me. "Gemma."

The man—his cousin, I have to assume—whirls in my direction. "Oh, fuck."

I frown and stand.

"You have a *West* in your apartment?" He glowers at Aiden.

I, for one, am more than a little surprised that he recognizes me. Or maybe it's my name—it's always been the unusual one in a crowd. How many Gemmas are out there—and worse, how many are entangled in Mafia schemes?

You don't know that's what this is, a little voice counters. But what else could it be? A container of what? Do drugs or guns have a busy season in New York?

"Hi," I say, forcing myself forward. "Yes, he does have a West in his apartment."

The man blinks.

"And you are...?"

"Sam." He moves past Aiden without touching him, slipping out the door.

The silence is deafening.

"I have to go," Aiden says. He scribbles something on a pad of paper on the kitchen counter. "If you need anything, text this number."

I cross my arms. "I don't have a phone. You took mine, remember?"

He frowns and seems to contemplate it. "Then I guess you'll have to do without."

My mouth drops open. "Wait—"

He comes closer, stopping just in front of me. "Listen to me. If you leave this apartment while I'm gone, I can't protect you."

"But—"

"Only a small handful of people saw you come in. Sam is one of them now, and I'll make sure he doesn't say anything. My father is another. But I doubt he would busy himself with the likes of you. Out of sight, out of mind." He narrows his eyes. "Stay in the apartment, Gemma."

I nod. Out of sight sounds just fine to me.

He searches my gaze, then seems to decide I'm telling the truth. He leaves me standing there without even a goodbye.

I sigh and kick out at the stair. Of all the things to happen, I didn't expect distance. The silence seems harsher now, testing me. Waiting for my realization... that I'm all alone once again.

* * *

THREE DAYS FEELS like an eternity when there's nothing to do. I've exhausted the list of movies that were saved on the television. I found an apartment-sized washer and dryer in a back closet—that kept me busy for all of ten minutes.

The highlight was going through every *inch* of Aiden's belongings.

Am I sorry?

Nope.

I found a safe behind a panel next to the bed but couldn't figure out the passcode. It flashed red at me after my second attempt, so I closed it. Knowing him, it would detonate after the third wrong code and kill me.

My sleep is off, too. I find myself staying up too late and sleeping in, only forcing myself out of bed when my stomach aches with hunger. I can barely reach my back to apply the cream for the burn. When I finally got up the nerve to inspect it in the mirror, that is. It isn't as bad as I expected. Just angry red over my shoulder blade, down to the bottom of my ribcage.

All in all, I'm *not* thriving.

I'm in a cage of glass and metal.

It reminds me of Amelie Page. She survived two weeks of this, and I'm pretty sure it was in a smaller room than this. Maybe one of the hotel-like rooms Aiden took me to when we first arrived.

I shudder.

The fourth morning, I find a notepad and pen and sit on the floor of Aiden's bedroom. I sketch the skyline, frowning at the view. It's nice enough, if you like skyscrapers. Or heights. Or a lack of fresh air.

I tilt my head when I realize a banging noise is drifting

toward me. It takes another few moments to put together that someone's at the door.

"Oh, shit," I murmur, scrambling to my feet.

I hurry downstairs and look through the peephole. A woman raps her knuckles against Aiden's door without pause.

I take a quick step back. My hair is wet—*thank you, shower number fifty-seven*—and I had pulled on a pair of Aiden's sweatpants and t-shirt. The shirt smells like him, but more like the laundry detergent. It made me a little less apprehensive about wearing his stuff.

The sweatpants are giant on me, so I've rolled the waistband and the cuffs at least three times.

One might say I look like a homeless person squatting in Aiden's apartment.

"I know you're in there," the woman calls. "Did he tell you not to open the door?"

I hesitate, then say, "Yes."

She scoffs. "He's an ass. I'm Cat, one of his cousins. And you're Gemma?"

I unlock the door and crack it open, keeping my foot against it in case she tries to force her way in. She's pretty, with long dark-brown hair and tanned skin. She's taller than me by a few inches.

She frowns. "What on earth...?"

I stay silent. Frankly, I'm not sure what the proper etiquette is here, anyway. Smile and pretend like our families don't hate each other? I'm all too aware of Aiden's threat—that if I leave this apartment, I'm vulnerable.

"Cat," she repeats, like I forgot. "Why did Aiden take in a West?"

Her tone doesn't *seem* aggressive. Not even upset. Just openly curious.

And it would be nice to talk to someone other than Aiden.

I pull the door open farther, stepping back to allow her inside. "Why does Aiden do anything?" I reply.

She snickers. "That's true."

"How did you find out I was here?"

Cat goes to the center of the room, dropping her purse on the kitchen counter. "Sam is my brother," she says. "He mentioned Aiden had lost his mind over a pretty enemy."

I narrow my eyes.

"Then again," she continues, sitting on the edge of an armchair, "it took him a few days to mention that you were *here*, stuck in Aiden's apartment. Did you bewitch him?"

"No." I cross my arms. "Did you come just to question me?"

She lifts one shoulder. "Maybe. So, Gemma West, tell me about you."

I shake my head and pour myself a cup of coffee. "I don't think so." Some details should be private, and I'm still trying to figure out her motive. I'm not some spectacle to be stared at. I return to the couch and smile as sweetly as I can. "Why don't you tell me your life story?"

She pauses a beat, then raises her hands. "Okay, I see your point."

"Thank you."

"So you and Aiden met and just... hit it off?"

"He says we're getting married," I inform her. I've always been a fan of the shock factor—it tends to get genuine reactions out of people. Well, the only people I've tested that theory on was family... Still. "It was very sudden."

I suppose if I tell people, he can't decide to kill me before the ceremony. I wouldn't put it past him. He's used to dealing with the scourge of the city. I'm nothing compared to those people. Maybe even too easy in contrast.

It takes me a moment to realize Cat is silently choking on her laughter.

"Let me in on the joke," I say drily.

"Sorry," she gasps, wiping under her eyes. "God. I've known Aiden since I was a baby. He's always sort of terrified me. The idea of him settling down with... well, with *you*? You look sweet and innocent, and he's anything but that."

"Yeah, well." I glance away. "I'm not."

I totally am.

She sighs. "And he left you up here because he was worried how our family would react, I'd bet. He's breaking practically all the rules. Did you meet his father?"

I settle back and push away the one time I met Jameson. It was one time too many, if you ask me. "Unfortunately, yes."

She shudders. "Sam and I are lucky. Our mom is Jameson's youngest sister, and she managed to stay mostly out of the life. She moved back to Italy when we were six, left us with our dad. Dad... well, he's a diehard DeSantis fan, if you know what I mean. She just couldn't deal with the fact that he'd pick the family over her, and he wouldn't let her take us to Italy. So she left us with him."

"Does he help Jameson?"

Her gaze flickers away, then back. "Well, he's one of the captains. Leads a crew when stuff gets brutal, enforces policies, et cetera. We'd been in peaceful times up until Wilder was killed. He was happy just collecting debt on the street and earning his pension."

I grunt.

"Who was it?" she asks suddenly. "A cousin looking to prove himself? Some overeager hotshot? Or maybe your brother?"

I tense, and a slimy feeling crawls up my throat.

I wish I knew. Except, I really don't. Sometimes being left in the dark is safer than harboring the truth.

"I think it's time for you to go," I say. I'm done with this pseudo-interrogation.

Her eyes widen.

"Now." I stand and point to the door.

She leaves without saying anything, and I exhale in the sudden silence. My mother, rest her soul, would berate me for treating a guest like that.

She wasn't a guest—she's just another snake.

I just need more reminders that I'm far from home. Kicking Cat out is *not* how I'm going to make friends—or survive. I can't just slam the door shut when someone asks me about my family. Deep down, I know they're going to ask. They have to. It's their duty just as figuring them out is turning into mine. Some sort of sick curiosity and fascination... and maybe a bit of revulsion.

Everyone talks about peace, but there's still been bloodshed.

Dad kept me ignorant of the business. He wanted me to be a carefree child, to live happily. And I *was* happy... until Mom died eighteen months ago.

Thinking of her hurts. Old wounds rip open. She was the best person I knew. She was dangerously smart, but with good intentions. Dad relied on her input, cherished her. He loved her.

We all did.

I lock the door and press my back to it, sliding down. I bring my knees in and hug my legs. Mom would know what to do, or how to get out of this. She'd probably tell me to look at this as a good thing. To learn something new, to expand my world view.

No thanks.

I long for our Brooklyn house, for the coziness our home managed to provide. It was old. It creaked whenever anyone went up or down the stairs, and the attic had one of those pull-down ladders. It was impossibly drafty in the winter. But

I had seventeen years of holidays and birthdays with both parents, parties in our backyard.

And after I turned sixteen, I didn't spend much time there, anyway. I was tucked away in Manhattan, where Dad believed I was safer.

Too many houses, and none of them fit me anymore.

Still, I didn't think leaving would be this difficult.

"This was your choice," I remind myself, if only to break the silence.

Sometimes it cloys on my tongue until my stomach spins, and a scream builds up behind my teeth. No one would care if I screamed here. They wouldn't come running.

I open and close my mouth, and ultimately decide against it.

To scream would be to give in, and I am stronger than that.

Resolve fills me. I'll figure out Aiden DeSantis's game—maybe I'll even sabotage it. But what I won't do is surrender. He can marry me. He can try to control me. And I'll just wait for the perfect moment to take everything I know back to my father.

CHAPTER 6

Aiden

Sam appears beside me. He's a quiet fucker when he wants to be, and right now is all about silence. He's joined me in the control room of the shipping yard, but he isn't looking at the monitors like I am. His gaze bores into my back.

"What?" I snap.

I'm in a foul mood. Our container was empty—left untouched once discovered, per my instructions—but no evidence of a break-in. The two padlocks were intact, with no signs of scraping that picks usually leave behind.

It's supposed to be inspected upon arrival, go through customs, and collect paperwork for it to enter the United States, then be cleared for pick-up. The harbormaster has been in our debt for years. Father allowed him to live, even when he owed us nearly five hundred thousand dollars. Any other man, in any other position, would've had their hand cut off. A broken kneecap, maybe. Or death—strung up in his shipyard, left for dead on the streets for the crows... The possibilities were endless.

Instead, he received a warning.

We've been collecting what's due to our family slowly, funneling our legal and less-than-legal shipments through this port. Our harbormaster has always greased the wheels and cut through the red tape for us.

It never failed before, and I'm not certain it failed now.

"What are you going to do with him?" Sam finally asks.

I glance at the harbormaster. Even if he's not guilty, he deserves a little terror in his life. He's hogtied and gagged, face down on the ground. Not injured, but I think he pissed himself when I shoved him to his belly and placed my knee on his back. Other than the quiet trembling, he hasn't tried to plead for his life. Nothing.

Whether that means he knows he's a dead man or just knows how we operate is what I'm currently speculating.

"I haven't decided."

The harbormaster groans, trying to inch away from us.

I crouch next to him and pull my blade from its sheath. I drag the point down his temple, and he stills. The whites of his eyes are bloodshot, lips pale. His skin is a sickly shade of green, and he can't decide whether he wants to watch it or me.

I press the knife into his cheek and rip the gag down. "Tell me again, Martin."

He heaves. "I don't know, I don't know."

The knife cuts into his skin, and a trickle of blood runs down his face. It gives the appearance of red tears, but I shove that weird thought away.

"Who could get into our container?" Same question, new hour. "Who had a key besides you?"

"Just Jimmy, our customs officer, but he knows not to touch yours. He's good people. I swear. Worked here for years and years. We went to school together." He rolls onto his side, trying to get away from me. His back hits the wall. "I don't know more than that, man. My wife—"

Everyone plays the wife card. The family card.

I have a wife, kids, please don't hurt me.

I don't give a shit. If their husband or dad has gone so far off the path of good and ordinary to be dealing with me, then chances are strong that they don't deserve the wife or kids. What kind of man goes half a mil into debt with the Mafia and lives to tell about it?

What kind of man puts his family through that?

"Jimmy and you," I repeat. "That's it? Think."

"I swear to God, Aiden—"

I stuff the rag roped around his head back into his mouth.

"Maybe an eye would be decent payment, since you should've been *watching*." I pause.

He lets out a muffled wail, his feet smacking the floor.

"Do you think he takes me seriously, Sam?" I've about lost my patience with this whole mission. And *them*. This shit-storm could've been avoided if people did their goddamn jobs, and if Luca was around to help me enforce it.

The harbormaster had the audacity to ask me what we were bringing in the other week.

Well, it wasn't drugs like he suspected. He stepped right over the line and accused us of it, actually.

Not drugs, but there were enough firearms hidden in the container to bring down Brooklyn. And we're taking a hit on this either way.

Our buyers won't give us the money back. Whoever stole them might be selling at cost when we don't come through.

Fucking Wests.

This has their name written all over it.

A vile smell fills the small room, and I grimace. His piss is worse the second time around.

"I think he takes you seriously, boss," Sam replies.

I shove at Martin and rise. "Get him the fuck away from me."

I'll deal with him later.

Sam cuts the harbormaster's feet free and hauls him up. The man can barely stand, but my friend isn't known for being gentle. He guides him down the steep stairs and away.

Finally, silence.

I take shallow breaths and rewind the tapes farther. I've gone back in increments from Sam cracking open the shipping container at 2 o'clock in the afternoon, two days ago. There was a buzz of people around, ready to unload. When cargo ships arrive, the whole yard seems to come alive. A giant crane unloads them, sometimes in stacks, other times directly onto the backs of waiting trucks.

That sort of energy is good. Productive.

This, however, is a whole bunch of stale air.

My phone rings, and I don't speak after I hit the green *accept* button.

"Report," my father commands.

I glare at the ceiling. "I have jack shit. The harbormaster swears he didn't see anything. Surveillance is flimsy at best. My leads are dwindling." It's been three days of trying to figure this out.

"Failure is unacceptable."

"Right. I haven't—"

"And your glowing bride-to-be?" His voice is insufferable. "Where did you leave her?"

"She's out of the way." I rub my eyes. The smell of piss is overwhelming in here.

I move to go outside, but something on the screen catches my attention.

Nothing more than a silhouette of a person slipping down the aisle between containers in the middle of the night—but it's something. More than I had before. They're headed for the DeSantis container.

"I've got to go." I hang up before he can respond. I'll catch flak for it later. He'll probably come up with some inane punishment for disobedience, but that will stall when I show him something. Proof, if I can obtain it.

Well, I just won't return until I have evidence.

I click around, bringing up the other camera views. The person remains a shadow, vanishing around a corner. And I lose them.

"Fuck," I mutter. I take a quick picture of the time stamp, then shut down the screens and step outside.

I have a harbormaster who was supposed to be under our thumb asking too many questions, a missing shipment of expensive marble, handcrafted tiles, and the firearms that would've greased our bank accounts for months. And now a mysterious person on *one* camera of dozens.

Ridiculous.

"You okay?" Dr. Matthews asks from below me.

I squint. "Why are you here?"

"I came to talk to you about Gemma."

I trot down the steps and blow past the doctor. "No offense, Doc, but I don't have time for this."

"Your brother kept a girl hostage, don't you recall?"

My rage has been stewing for days, and I don't want it to boil over in front of the doctor. He'd probably just bring it back around to my father. So I ball my fists and pivot slowly. He must see what I'm trying to hold back, because he takes a step away.

"I'm worried you're going to get home and find her dead," he says. "You know your family."

I laugh. "I do, and I'm the worst of the lot."

"Do they know she has your protection?" He lifts one shoulder. "Her burn concerns me, and you're out here—"

I growl, and he clamps his mouth shut.

"I'm out here doing my job. Trying to find my brother's killer, which has proven next to impossible, and now there are more fires to put out. So the West princess can stay in her tower until I return. If you're so worried about her, check on her." I raise my eyebrow. "Or maybe you're worried the family will turn on you?"

He bows his head. "I'll check in on her."

When he doesn't say anything else, I nod curtly and continue on my way. The doctor is a good man—one of the better ones I know, anyway. Loyal to a fault, practices smart medicine. He cares about his patients and doesn't usually let something like ethics get in the way.

Or, perhaps he's aware that there would be a lot more damage caused if he wasn't there to patch us back up.

I can't imagine my father in a hospital. I almost didn't have to imagine it, if Wilder had made it that far.

Died in the ambulance. Sudden and shocking. The bullet didn't kill him as quickly as it should've. It shredded his heart just enough to cause pain, but it still beat. Ten minutes, maybe longer. Then, flatline.

Sam waits for me at my truck, a rag in his hand.

"Well?" I demand.

He shrugs. "Started begging for his life as soon as you were out of earshot. I think he just wants to go home."

I sigh. "Fine. Have someone watch him. One step out of place, and we pull him back in."

He nods.

I hand him a radio. "He can sit for a while. Right now, I need you to do something for me."

He perks up, until I lay out my plan. Then he becomes slightly less thrilled.

But I don't really give a fuck. This is part of the job.

Sam climbs back up to the control booth, and I wind my way between shipping containers.

"There," he says over the radio, along with a burst of static.

Not sure what the hell *there* is, so I crane my head and glare at the camera.

"I see you," he says.

I lift the radio to my mouth. "No shit. Which way?"

Sam guides me down the stacks, following the path our mystery figure took. I don't know if that person is involved—I'm just going on intuition. And part of intuition is follow through.

"Stop," Sam says. "He takes a left, and our cameras don't pick him up again."

I round the corner.

"Okay, you're gone." Sam waits, and when I don't respond, "Aiden? If you're standing still, you're in a blind spot."

"Get the fuck down here." I sigh and step forward, around the pool of blood.

A man is slumped against one of the containers. His eye is gone—the exact threat I issued to the harbormaster only minutes ago. Blood is soaked into his light-blue collared shirt. It says *Shipping Customs* on the sleeve.

Jimmy, then.

There's a God-awful amount of flies buzzing around the body, and the smell turns my stomach. He doesn't look great —bloody foam collected in his nostrils and lips, and his body has begun to bloat.

I crouch beside him, tilting his head to the side with one finger. His eye was obliterated by a gunshot, the back of his head cracked open where the bullet exited. The blood on his skin has dried. They probably killed him four days ago, the night we were stolen from. Enough time for rigor mortis to pass and decomposition to begin.

Sam skids to a stop. "Shit."

"Yep. The customs officer."

"He was alone on camera. Who killed him?"

I sigh. "Someone waiting? I don't know."

I sound like the harbormaster, repeating *I don't know* until the opposite becomes true. I search his pockets. Something clanks, and I draw a key ring out of his slacks pocket. "They took his wallet but not his keys?"

My friend grunts.

A mystery. I take a picture of the body and stash my phone, then rise.

I try to shake off the nagging feeling. "Call in Detective Sanders on this one. I need to have a chat with Martin."

Sam nods.

I fist the keys and head back to my truck and Sam's van. I've got a harbormaster to interrogate and a lead to follow.

CHAPTER 7
Gemma

I experiment with the blinds in the bedroom. I refuse to think of it as Aiden's bedroom, especially since I've been living in it on my own for the past five days. It's neutral for now. But anyway, this is peak boredom because I've been counting the seconds. Another restless night, another morning of no Aiden—absolutely nothing but me and my thoughts.

The blinds retract slower than they drop. Gravity plays a role, of course, so the logic works in my head. I'm surrounded by drawings of the city, and I can't help but retrace my steps up here. Into the elevator, through the kitchen on the seventeenth floor.

My mind stumbles on what Aiden said to me, and I instinctively reach for the sketch pad. From my position on the floor, I scribble out what I remember.

He asked me if I recognized the view.

Manhattan. A different side of the building, facing another direction. I never spent much time in this end of the city. I preferred the quiet of Central Park. The Empire State

Building is a few blocks north of us, then even farther up the park begins. Far from where I think we are.

But, because I was in a trunk, I really have no idea.

My windows face east and north. I pretend I can see the tall spire through the gaps of other buildings, and beyond that the trees that guard the entrance to the park.

Wishful thinking.

We're too high up, so I can't see the street names. None of the surrounding structures have defining marks. In other words, I'm out of luck.

Someone knocks on the door. Not to the apartment, but to the bedroom.

I bolt up and sway as the blood rushes away from my head. I have to stand still for a moment, the room swinging around me, until I can move.

"Who is it?" I demand.

"Dr. Matthews," a man responds.

I jerk back. His voice is familiar, but I can't place it.

"I've brought you a friend," he adds.

I glance down at myself. My t-shirt and Aiden's rolled sweatpants. No use changing if I'm not leaving, right?

Still, I only crack the door open and peer through with one eye. Dr. Matthews has a nice enough face. A bit older, closer to my dad's age than mine, with flecks of gray in his dark hair and goatee. Cat stands slightly behind him on the landing.

"I didn't scare you off?" I blurt out.

She laughs. "Hardly."

I open the door wider. "You should've knocked."

Dr. Matthews shrugs. "I did, but you didn't answer."

Oh.

"I just wanted to check on your back. I'm not sure if you remember me from the other day, but I looked at your burns and prescribed the cream." He waits.

All I remember is Aiden rocking me in his arms—and at

that memory, my face flames. The doctor ignores it, though, and motions for me to turn around. Cat goes with me, so I'm not just staring at the wall.

I flinch at the snap of his gloves, and then his cold touch on my lower back. He lifts my shirt up and touches around the burn. It hurts, but I grit my teeth and concentrate on something else.

"We're going out," Cat tells me. "And you clearly need a new wardrobe, right?"

I perk up. "Out?"

"As in, out of the apartment." *But not out of the tower.*

My face falls. "Oh."

She sighs. "I share an apartment with my brother. It's a few floors down, and I need to get rid of some clothes."

There's at least three inches height difference between us, but I don't say that. Maybe she likes capri pants and crop tops, and they'll look like normal clothes on me...

"I'm sorry for being so nosy yesterday." She offers her hand. "I wasn't thinking about you or your feelings. Just that we had an outsider in our tower. Sam made you sound like bad news."

I laugh and take her hand, pulling her closer. "I *am* bad news."

Dr. Matthews tugs my shirt back into place. He clears his throat, and for the first time I must ask myself if he—or Cat—won't take every part of this interaction back to Aiden.

"It's healing," he says. "It might scar."

I nod. "I'm okay with a few scars."

Wouldn't be the first, probably won't be the last.

He leaves, and Cat waits for me to hunt down my shoes. She leans against the wall, seeming to contemplate something.

"Spit it out," I finally say.

"Were you at Wilder's funeral?"

I freeze, and the rush comes back.

Two months ago, give or take, I ran into Amelie Page on the streets in Brooklyn. A random encounter with the girl who married into the DeSantis family. The whole city had been talking about Wilder's death on the altar. Some online tabloids distributed photos of her in a bloodstained wedding dress, although I doubt she ever saw them. They vanished shortly after they were posted.

We knew her parents were desperate. My father wanted to take down their company and demolish the building they owned, turn it into high-rise apartments. The Pages couldn't keep up with the hits on their delivery trucks, the steep rising cost of supplies.

The rumor was that they married her off to one of Wilder's brothers. I didn't realize how desperate I was for it to not be Aiden until she confirmed it herself, standing in front of me.

Relief, gratitude, annoyance. A flicker of pity.

I brushed it off and moved on. It wasn't like Aiden would swoop in and steal me away, even if, in the darkest recesses of my mind, I *wanted* that. Dreamed about it.

But then, a month later, she texted me. Luca kept her locked away under the guise of protection, but it was a jail cell.

I mentioned to my father that maybe he should pay his respects at the funeral. Cause a stir, anyway. He agreed. I roll back the memory of that day: watching the entrances of the church for Amelie to step out, quickly mimicking her makeup and hair, pulling on a dress similar to hers. The veil was a nice touch—reminiscent of her wedding veil, except in black.

The mausoleum where Wilder was going to be put to rest was tall and bleak, the weather mirroring the DeSantis family's moods. Depressing.

And, yes, Amelie and I switched. She got in a car with my cousin, Kai, and I went and talked to her parents. They didn't notice I wore the same clothes as their daughter—something that irked me later. They really didn't give a shit about her.

But Cat waits for an answer, even though I know she knows I was there.

I kept my back to Luca and Aiden the whole time I talked to people, accepting condolences for a man I hated.

And I wondered if Amelie felt the same way about him.

"The girl was skin and bones," I reply. "She needed to get away from them."

She surprises me by nodding. "Luca talked me into being her keeper. Bringing her meals, checking on her..."

I appraise her in a new light. Seeing the difference in Amelie from the day on the street to the funeral was shocking. It reaffirmed in my mind that the DeSantises were bad people... but maybe it was just one person who was bad.

Or two.

"You brought her the phone?" I ask.

She doesn't look away. "I did. I couldn't outright let her go, but... I did what I could."

I nod. "It worked. She's free."

And she owes me a favor. It doesn't matter, though. Amelie is a world away, and I'm stuck in a tower.

Our roles have officially reversed.

Cat's smile trembles. "That's so good to hear. Now, come on, let's get *you* out of this apartment for an afternoon."

That's what we do. She shows me around the lower floors, opting for the stairs instead of the elevator. Her apartment is only a flight below Aiden's, but the difference is startling. The living area is warm, creams and browns with pops of orange. A dark leather couch faces a television, a wooden dining table by the windows. It has two short hallways on either side, leading to bathrooms and bedrooms.

"This way," she says, leading me toward hers. The three walls are eggshell blue. White floor-to-ceiling curtains are swept open to reveal the huge windows. We've rotated again, I notice. Different view. The morning sun hits the opposite building, so we must be facing west now.

"Does the restaurant look this way?" I ask.

She pauses. "Um, no. South, I think."

I grunt.

"Sit on the bed."

I perch on the white and turquoise blanket. Cat pulls open her closet doors and stares into it for a second, her hands on her hips.

"Okay, do you want comfortable or...?"

I shift. "Um..."

She snaps her fingers. "Both."

"You didn't list another option," I mutter.

Cat glances back and winks. "Trust me."

Trust her—what a concept. I don't trust Aiden. I barely trust myself. The only ones who are worth putting my faith in are Wests. My blood. I'm here to save them, and I need to hold on to that.

"Anyway," she continues. She tosses items onto the bed beside me. A few soft shirts, a sweater or two, a mini skirt.

I press my lips together.

The pile grows. Jean shorts and a few dresses, hell, she even gives me socks.

"Okay," I interrupt, standing. "That's a lot."

She frowns. "Oh. Well, you should try some on just to make sure it fits."

Right. I grab the jean shorts and a t-shirt and lock myself in her bathroom, shedding my clothes. The shorts fit well, only gaping a little bit at the waist, and the t-shirt's bottom hem coasts just above the denim. Not quite a crop top... until I raise my arms, anyway.

I stare at my reflection in the mirror and shudder. I don't look great. Dark circles under my eyes, not a speck of makeup. I find a hair tie and twist my blonde locks into a new braid.

But this is fine, because Aiden isn't here. I used to be a social butterfly before my parents forbade me from going to school. And... well, most places where they couldn't hover.

Cat knocks. "Gemma?"

I unlock and open the door.

Aiden stands behind her, glaring at me.

Shit.

He stalks forward and grabs my upper arm. He drags me out of the bathroom, straight past his cousin. She shoots me a wide-eyed expression that I'm not sure how to interpret. I'm pretty sure we both broke Aiden's rule of me not leaving the apartment, and I don't know what that means for her. I don't know what it means for me, either.

My heart kicks up speed when he practically throws me into the elevator at the end of the hall. I spin around, pressing my back to the wall. Sam, Cat's brother, watches passively from outside their door. That's the last thing I see before Aiden steps inside and the doors slide closed behind him.

He hits the button for the twenty-fourth floor. I make a mental note of what I know of the building, trying to distract myself from Aiden's scowl. He seems content to stand there and glower, though, instead of saying what must be on the tip of his tongue.

Cat said anything above the twentieth floor is DeSantis only. Restaurant on seventeen. The rather bland room we waited for his father in was on the nineteenth. Cat's apartment, twenty-third. Aiden, twenty-four.

Still too much mystery for my liking between here and the ground.

"She was being nice," I finally say. I can't help it. The need to defend her is overwhelming. "She came with Dr. Matthews when he—"

"Be quiet."

I raise my eyebrows. "Seriously, Aiden? You shouldn't—"

The elevator chimes as it arrives on his floor.

"Go on. What should I not do?" He's immobile in front of the doors.

Is he just oddly curious? Or waiting to see if I'll dig myself into an even deeper hole?

Definitely the latter, but I keep pushing.

"You can't control every aspect of my life." I straighten my shoulders.

He smirks and steps forward, wrapping his arm around my waist. It seems like he might kiss me... or maybe now he's going to kill me. The elevator is all metal sheeting. Probably easier to clean than the floor of his apartment.

Blood spatter is a nasty thing.

How would he do it? There's no saying he even has to draw blood. He could pinch his hand over my nose and mouth and suffocate me. Wrap his hands around my neck—

"Gemma."

His hand at the small of my back applies pressure, guiding me off the elevator to his door. Inside. The lock *snicks*, and that unlocks my muscles.

I don't want to be alone with him.

I bolt toward the stairs and make it into the bedroom, my fingers grasping at the knob of the bathroom door. He catches me there, his weight hitting my side. I lose my hold, and we hit the floor hard. He flips me onto my stomach and pins me to the carpet, capturing my wrists in his hands. He straddles my thighs, keeping them pressed together, and his ankles hook over my calves.

I'm trapped.

My struggle is worthless.

"Am I controlling you now?" he whispers in my ear.

"Physically." I try to shift, but it's impossible.

His lips touch the back of my neck, and I freeze. He peppers my skin with kisses, and heat rushes through me.

I hate him.

I hate the way his palms cover the backs of my hands, his fingers threading between mine. Loathing crawls through me, chased by something darker. The knowledge that there's a part of me that wants to be touched.

Wants *his* touch.

His mouth travels up my neck, to my ear again. "Physically. Mentally. Emotionally. I know what thoughts run through your head, princess. I know what you're trying to hide." He slides his hand down my arm, my side, and wedges it between my hips and the floor.

I bite my lip to try to stop my gasp, but there's no denying my breathing is too fast. He cups me through the jean shorts and stops. All I can hear is the sound of my heart pounding, and shame fills me.

All over again, I can see my mother's worried face as I stepped off the elevator at sixteen. Her firm grip on my shoulders, the wobble of her chin.

Because of him.

She was always afraid of Aiden DeSantis lurking around the corner, ready to steal her baby girl.

He pulls away and climbs off me. But something still presses me into the floor, heavier than shame.

Disgust.

My hands tremble.

He leaves me there. His footsteps pound on the stairs, then the slam of the outer door hits me. I still can't move for a long moment, waiting for those emotions to subside. He brought them out in a vicious way, but it's me who holds on to them. They linger on my skin.

I hoist myself to my feet and look around the room. My drawings are still scattered across the floor by the window. I sloppily made the bed this morning, and the crinkled blankets seem to scream at me.

It can't be a mistake that he didn't throw me on the bed.

My cheek stings, carpet marks indented in my skin. The burn at my back aches, too. Everything hurts more than it should, like Aiden came in and flayed open all my nerves just to watch me burn.

Do something, Gemma.

If that's my voice in my head or a ghost from my past, I can't tell. But I listen. I creep downstairs and into the kitchen. I have to haul myself up on the counter to reach the top shelf, moving aside some spices to reach the liquor.

Yep, Aiden has a secret stash.

I don't know why he hides it, though. As far as I can tell, it's only ever been him living here. I rise higher, straining to see farther into the cabinet, and my heart damn near stops. The bottle of tequila hides a tiny gun in a holster... and a burner phone.

I'd bet money it's mine.

I grab it and flip it open, staring down at the screen. Do I send a message? Call for help? Update my father or brother?

The sensor on the outside of the door beeps, and it scrapes as it unlocks. I shove the phone back into the cabinet and move the tequila and spices back in place. I hop down just as the door opens, and Aiden and Sam enter.

The former glances at me and grimaces.

"Go upstairs, Gemma."

I cross my arms. "Seriously?"

He narrows his eyes. "You're being allowed a lot of freedom right now."

"You're being a dick." The words are out before I can stop them, and... well, judging from the look on his face, I probably should've gone for something softer. Like... *jerk* or *control freak.*

Eh, either of those would garner the same reaction.

He glances at Sam. "Excuse me for a moment."

Fuck.

His cousin's expression is amused, and he watches from a distance. Aiden stalks toward me. I backpedal, inadvertently boxing myself in the kitchen. He stops inches away from me and leans forward. Nose to nose.

I can't breathe. I shouldn't be afraid, and maybe it isn't fear, exactly. But my brain isn't cooperating, and I can't seem to function.

I've short-circuited.

"Problem, princess?"

"I..."

He nods and squats suddenly, grabbing my hips. He wraps his arm around my legs, just under my ass, and rises. I could be flipped over his shoulder, I suppose, but I remain straight, Still, when he turns, I waver and grip his hair.

"Put me down."

He scoffs.

"It's bad enough you kidnapped me." I kick my feet, trying to hit him where it counts. The best I get is his shin, and he grunts but keeps moving. "Now you're fucking manhandling me—"

"Stop."

I yank at his hair, pulling his head back to look at me. "Don't tell me to stop, Aiden, because you brought this on yourself."

He meets my gaze. The lack of emotion behind his eyes is amazing. A flicker of jealousy stirs inside me. Feigning being impassive is a trick I wish someone had taught me. Any sort of survival kit would've been nice to have in my arsenal, actually. As it is, I just have the books I lived on and whatever I picked up from my brother, cousins, and father.

Which isn't much.

"What do you want, Gemma? You want to sit at the big girl table?"

"I want to know what you were doing for the past five days," I mutter, breathless.

We get upstairs and into the room. He loosens his grip, and I slide down his front. I release his hair, too. Regrettably. It's actually a lot softer than I would've imagined.

"Hunting," he says. He steps back, turning to go.

Why would he stay, after all? His cousin waits for him to discuss... I don't know, the demise of my family? All I've done is delay the inevitable: that he's going to isolate me again.

But you found the phone.

Still.

It isn't enough.

I grab his arm before he leaves, wanting to make sure I understood him correctly. "Hunting who?"

He gives me a measured look. "Not your brother. Not yet."

I stumble backward, and he leaves. The door closes behind him, and I close my eyes at the definitive turn of the lock.

Not yet, he says, as if my sacrifice means nothing. And it's true—I gave myself up thinking it would be enough, but it isn't. It won't be for him, for his father.

They want the sort of justice that comes with blood.

CHAPTER 8

Gemma

The sun is low by the time Aiden unlocks my door. He leans on the jamb, arms folded across his chest. I'm up against the windows. I have been since he left me here six hours ago, trying to pretend I'm a bird.

"I'll be back later," he says.

I don't acknowledge him, and he leaves.

Still thinking *trap*, I wait an hour before I venture downstairs. It's empty, so I push my luck further and stride out into the hallway.

I find my way to Cat's apartment and bang on the door, surprised when she actually answers.

"Gemma?"

"I'm not going to let that asshole dictate my life," I seethe. "And yeah, I know he's family to you, but he keeps manhandling me. That's not okay."

She beckons me inside. "Agreed."

"So that, coupled with the fact that I'm pretty sure I locked myself out..."

Cat laughs. "Great, well, you picked a good night for a rebellious stage."

I follow her farther into the apartment, grinning that the clothes she was going to give me are still on her bed. Plus a few extras.

"Here," she says, tossing me a white t-shirt and black shorts. "There's a big card game starting soon. It's open to friends of the family, so no one will blink twice if you're with me."

I raise my eyebrow. "Right."

"We'll just omit who you are..." She shrugs. "It'll be fun."

"Sounds fun... And maybe dangerous." I grin. "It'll drive Aiden nuts when he finds out."

She cackles and shoos me to her bathroom. "You're devious, Gemma West."

A half hour later, we're dressed and in full faces of makeup. She tried to get me into a bright-pink lipstick, but I opted for dark red.

"You're right," she says. "That's a good color on you. I've never even worn that one."

My smile—and confidence—grows.

We head out, and I expect to go downstairs. Instead, we step into the elevator, and Cat presses her thumb into a scanner, then hits the button for the twenty-eighth floor. There are only twenty-nine accessible by this elevator.

I don't know if this is the same as the first elevator I took when I arrived, but it would make sense if there were more. The different security measures catch my attention, too, and I file it away for later. Keycards, thumbprint scanners. I eye the ceiling and locate the camera in the corner.

"Is there a roof?"

She glances at me. "Yep. Not sure if you should go up there, though..."

I shrug. "I don't have plans of going anywhere alone."

"Just to my apartment."

"Well, that was easy to find," I reply.

The elevator chimes, and the doors slide open on the twenty-eighth floor. It seems like a huge... recreational area. Like a millennial co-op break room. You know, the sort you'd expect to see at tech companies in Silicon Valley. Floating chairs and an open kitchen, comfortable couches in circles. It's got a darker, warmer feel to it. Like we're not in a skyscraper, but a downtown bar.

"Wow."

There are more DeSantis men and women here than I've seen since... well, since Wilder's funeral. Then, I was in disguise. And I guess I'm in disguise here, too, unless they *all* know me. Who I am and why Aiden brought me here.

"Here," Cat says. "This is one of Sam and Aiden's friends."

She leads me to a man standing next to a beer tap. He finishes pouring himself an ale and turns around, grinning first at Cat, then me.

"Jack, this is Gemma. Gemma, Jack Morrin."

"Not DeSantis?" I raise my brow.

He winks. "I wasn't born into the family. Just raised by it." He offers his hand. "Pleasure to meet you."

I take it, and we both pause. He pumps up and down, then releases my fingers with a soft smile.

He tilts his head. "Sorry, I feel like I know you."

"She's just my guest," Cat says evenly. "Maybe you saw her from a bar or something."

Jack grins. It's possible he doesn't suspect I'm a West—or he doesn't give a shit.

"Are you staying long?"

I shrug. "As long as they'll have me."

I'll grudgingly admit that Jack has his own immediate charm. He gives off *normal* vibes, if such a thing even exists in this building.

"We have a game starting in a minute." He gestures to the room behind us. "I assume that's why you came."

"Exactly." She takes my hand, lacing her fingers with mine. "This is the fun part. Just relax and no one will think twice."

This new room's ambiance is that of a den: intimate, compounded by the haze of cigar smoke. Bookshelves frame in the room. There aren't windows in here, just warm lights that give it the intimate vibe. There's a bar in the corner, this one manned by a bartender. Two waitresses in sequined dresses stand off to the side.

They've set up three tables for the games.

"Poker at the middle table, blackjack at the other two," Cat informs me. "I don't have the confidence to play Texas Hold 'Em. Some of those guys are ruthless."

A few of the ones at that table appear to be grandfather age—but I don't let that comfort me. Just because they're old as shit doesn't mean they wouldn't hesitate to put a bullet between their enemy's eyes. Part of me wonders if they'd take one look at me—the only blonde in the room—and shoot on sight.

But none of them even look up. Their backs remain to the door in a display of power. It's not often we see old Mafia men. It's considered a miracle to get past forty-five.

Cat grins at me and drags me over to the far left table, farthest from the door. Jack is already seated there, and she pushes me down into one of the empty chairs.

Our dealer smiles at Cat. "You got out of it this week?"

Cat shrugs. "Pawned it off on Bea—I've been showing Gemma around."

The dealer turns her gaze to me. Her skin is the color of honey, and every part of her outfit seems to accentuate that feature. She flips her dark-brown hair over her shoulder. "Gemma. Visiting someone in the tower?"

I swallow and force an affirmative.

"Welcome."

Cat pulls out a stack of hundred dollar bills, dividing it and setting part of it in front of me.

My eyes go wide. "Cat—"

"Don't," she says. "This is nothing."

Jack snorts and leans toward me. "She's a shark. She's saying it's nothing because she'll win it all back by the end."

I clear my throat, feeling a bit out of place. Not just a bit—a *lot*. Half of the men in the room are in various states of business casual: collared shirts, some jackets flung over the backs of their chairs, loosened ties. Like they came here after a hard week's work and will be *decompressing* for the rest of the evening. My outfit isn't out of place between Jack and Cat, in their jeans.

I lift one shoulder. The dealer snags the cash from in front of me, replacing it with a stack of chips. Cat hasn't said much of anything, except that this was an event I couldn't miss.

It's been five days since Aiden left, but only two since Cat first knocked on the apartment door and coaxed me into opening it.

It's been over a month since I had any fun.

Cat nudges me. "You only need to beat the dealer."

"Cat won so much, they made *her* a dealer," Jack says under his breath.

I angle toward him, raising my eyebrows. "Why?"

"To win money for the family," another man says. He cranes around Jack. "You're Cat's friend?"

I nod.

He's a bit older. Gray peppers his otherwise dark goatee, but the hair on top of his head is thick and brown. His skin is weathered, and he's got a scar that runs over his jaw and down his neck. It disappears into his black shirt.

"Gemma, this is Mac," Jack introduces. "Mac is Jameson's brother."

He grunts. "That's one way of putting it. I knew a Gemma once."

Our dealer shuffles the cards with quick hands and offers the deck to Mac, who puts a white plastic card in the middle. She cuts it and slips it into a machine, making sure everything is just right.

"Have you played before?" Cat asks.

I stare at one of the waitresses moving between the tables, taking drink orders. It seems too normal—like this is a usual occurrence for them. It shouldn't surprise me, but it does. Just another layer of the DeSantis family pulled back.

"Gemma?" Cat pokes me.

"No," I lie, shaking my head. "I haven't played. Are you any good, Mac?"

"Sometimes," he allows.

Memories of sitting on my mother's lap as the adults played filters through me. When I was old enough to sit in my own chair, they let me play. Mom's voice whispers game theory to me, how to keep count. A hushed tone. Illegal, of course, as all things were that happened in the dark.

I can't remember all the faces now. My father sometimes hooked people that way. Lose enough money, owe enough, and a man will do anything you ask. Anything to avoid broken fingers or kneecap. Anything to avoid the shame of admitting they've lost everything.

My parents only let me play when it was safe. When it was family and friends gathered around their dining room table or their den, the curtains drawn and a fire crackling in the hearth.

Nothing like this. Here, I'm surrounded by snakes.

"And that's all there is to it," Jack says.

I belatedly realize he just explained all the rules. Maybe not all... I have a feeling he left out quite a bit.

"Thanks."

"Jess," Cat says, "we should make this more interesting."

The dealer grins. She hasn't begun to lay out the cards. Judging from the murmuring conversation at the other tables and the clink of chips, she's the only one.

"Winner of the table takes all." Cat announces. "And by *all,* I mean winner's choice, since we're playing until only one of us remains—obviously they walk away with the money."

I raise my eyebrows.

"What?" she says. "It isn't your cash."

I laugh. I can't help it. Jack had just finished warning me she was a card shark, and here it is in action. She's right: it isn't my money. But what she may choose, if she wins, could be worse than money. A favor, perhaps.

"Count me out, Catrina," Mac says. "This old man has lost too much to you. I'm wise to your tactics."

Even with the high stakes, I love a challenge. "I'm in."

"Sure," Jack says evenly.

We start the game, and I let Cat and Jack try to teach me. I can't ask any of the questions I want, though. The important questions that have nothing to do with blackjack and everything to do with Aiden.

Every so often, Mac's gaze beats into me. Each time, I catch it and offer him a brilliant smile. I should be scared—I should bend my head and remain weak. But that's bullshit, isn't it? I can't hide who I am forever. And being confident doesn't translate into me being a West.

Mac seems familiar, like he might've come to my parents' home once upon a time.

The Wests and DeSantises run in the same circles—it would be nearly impossible for us to have never seen him. I mentally shuffle through public events: charity dinners and luncheons, a ball once hosted by a politician trying to win favor—a waste of time, in my opinion. Grand openings.

Nothing rings a bell.

Jack is a bad player, and he laughs amicably at his mistakes.

I nudge him when he wins, and he returns the favor. He doesn't get upset when his stack of chips quickly depletes itself. For someone I've just met, there isn't any tension between us.

Cat, on the other hand, is an aggressive player. I can see why they made her a dealer. She's smirking before she even knows the outcome, cocky in a way that I'm coming to learn is a trait of the family.

"I'm Gemma," I say to the final man and woman at the table. We've been playing for almost a half hour at this rate, and they're the only ones who haven't tried to make conversation. They seem to be a couple, leaning into each other, and it's the woman who reaches out and shakes my hand.

"Darcie," she says. "And Tim."

He keeps quiet but offers me a slow nod.

I force myself to lose repeatedly, winning only enough to keep myself in the game. Sweat prickles the back of my neck. No one paid attention to us when we entered, but I have a feeling Cat is going to draw their attention. Her laugh grows louder, and she orders both of us drinks when a waitress passes.

Darcie goes out, and Mac is soon to follow. I glance around the other tables between hands. It seems once you've run out of money, you're done. The crowd isn't thinning—those who aren't playing linger around the edges of the room, watching—but the number of players dwindles.

Someone touches my shoulder, and I look up. It's just me, Jack, Cat, and Tim. But Mac is behind me, and he leans down. "It's about time someone showed them up," he says. "That goes for Aiden, too."

I frown.

I'm in no position to show anyone up.

But the tide shifts when Jess stops to shuffle the deck

again, and she slides the stack to a stop in front of me. I meet her cool gaze and push the white plastic into the center.

"Having fun?" Jack asks me.

"Not until I start winning." I smile. "I could use a favor or two."

Cat grins.

The fresh deck doesn't help, but I quickly get the count in my head. They don't notice when my bets increase, but within the hour I've doubled my chips.

Jack plays his last few and loses. He sags back in his chair and eyes me. "Beginner's luck?"

"Maybe."

We've captured the attention of the room now. The back of my neck burns. There are too many eyes on me, when all I've really wanted was invisibility. They react to everything I do: a hit, splitting my cards, passing.

I glance over my shoulder and wink at Mac.

Cat groans and hangs her head. "I don't think this is beginner's luck."

There's only a few chips left in front of her, thanks to some clever maneuvering on my part. My parents taught me how to play the game, but I taught myself how to manipulate it.

The quiet man goes out, his chair screeching backward.

The room is silent on the next deal. I take the low card Cat needs, and she busts. So does the dealer. And that's it. Jess swipes the last of Cat's chips and pays me out. I stare at the mountain of chips in front of me.

Some of the crowd whoops and cheers. A few reach out and pat my shoulders, my back. It's nice, like they're happy I won.

Last woman standing.

"You're a hustler," Cat squeals, hitting my arm. She only

hesitates a second before wrapping her arms around me. "That was *amazing*."

I tip my head back and laugh. "That was fun."

"*WHERE IS SHE?*"

Everyone goes still. I recognize the voice—*how could I not?*—and my heart jackhammers.

The door crashes open, and Aiden storms through. His gaze swings around, and it lands on me. His face is etched in fury.

Cat's arms slip off me, and I glance at her pale face.

Uh-oh.

The people surrounding us quickly back off. Aiden projects his anger, silencing the room. He stalks over to me and grabs my arm. He lifts me out of the chair and hauls me over his shoulder.

I squeal, grabbing his shirt. My ass is in the air. Humiliation burns through me, but I don't resist him. That darn self-preservation has kicked in again, hoping to lessen the damage. I raise my head and catch Jack's eyes. He seems confused and slowly shakes his head at me. Cat bites her lip, but no one stops Aiden from sweeping me away.

He carries me to the elevator and doesn't set me down when it jolts into motion. We ride in silence, my face pressed against the small of his back. There's a faint metallic smell clinging to him.

We enter his apartment, and he locks the door.

It's only when we're upstairs that he leans forward, throwing me on the bed.

"Are you deaf?" He's too calm.

He loosens his tie, and the motion draws my attention to the front of his shirt. He's covered in blood. Dried, judging from the rusty color, but *blood*.

His jaw tics.

"I'm not deaf," I say.

"Stupid, then."

I narrow my eyes. "No."

He yanks off the tie and sheds his leather jacket. His fingers work at the buttons of his shirt, until he stands before me in just his black pants. "There must be *some* reason you disobeyed me, little girl."

I stand and plant my arms on my hips. "I'm not a dog. You can't just say *stay* and—"

"You're not a dog," he says. "You're a fucking doll to sit on the shelf and look pretty. You don't speak. You don't leave. And you certainly don't make fucking decisions to play poker with my whole fucking family."

I flinch. My anger is waking up, fanned by his passive face. There are too many emotions under both our surfaces—we're going to explode one of these days. I went to bed every night while he was gone, trying to picture where he went. What, exactly, carried him away.

Hunting, he said. I get even angrier, with both of us. For allowing myself to think that he might care about me. Why would I even delude myself into thinking that?

It's bullshit, just like this engagement.

"Blackjack." I grit my teeth. "You're an asshole. This isn't how you treat someone—"

"This is how you deserve to be treated until I say otherwise." He comes forward and traces my jaw with his finger. "And I think we need to make sure that sinks in."

"Fuck you," I spit.

His eyes light up.

Psychopath, my mind whispers.

"Give me your hands, Gemma."

A thrill goes through me. I understand the warning in his voice and narrow my eyes, but I do as he asks. For once.

Maybe for the last time.

Call it curiosity, or the stupidity he accuses me of having, but I want to see how this plays out.

He retrieves his tie and turns me around, pulling my arms behind me. He wraps the tie around my wrists and binds them together, then rotates me back to face him. He takes a seat on the edge of the bed and stares at me like he doesn't recognize me.

My body trembles. I can't stop it. Fear blooms on my tongue. I lace my fingers together.

"Who did you talk to while I was gone?" He tugs me forward a step by the waistband of my shorts, then fingers the button. It pops open, and he pushes the fabric down my legs. He catches my panties with his thumbs. They make small circles on my hips, and the sensation sends shivers up my spine.

I step back, but he grips my hips and drags me closer.

I'm naked from the waist down. I'm sure he can see the way I quake, but he doesn't comment on it. Anticipation underlines my fear.

Slowly, he unbuckles his belt and slides it from his pants. "Gemma."

I jerk. "What?"

"Names."

I can't rat out Cat. He'd probably kill her just to spite me —family or not. I press my lips together. Jack, Mac, Darcie, Tim. They were innocent parties.

Too quick to process, he guides me forward and down. I exhale sharply, lying flat on his thighs. One of his hands presses down on my spine between my shoulder blades. His fingers catch in my hair.

No.

"Names, Gemma," he prods.

He barely waits a moment for an answer. The leather belt hits my ass, and pain explodes across my flesh.

My scream lodges in my throat. Call it pride or vanity, but he *wants* me to suffer. Loudly, I'd bet.

"No one can hear you," he tells me. "So scream."

"Fuck you," I repeat.

He hits me again, and I buck against him. He's got me thoroughly captured. My shoulders protest the angle of my arms, but it's a reflex to try to make myself smaller. I can't stop fighting. The fight or flight urge rises like a tidal wave, and nausea spins my stomach.

Smack.

Smack.

Smack.

It goes on and on until I do break.

My scream rips out of me. My ass is on fire, and when he switches to the other cheek, it's somehow worse. At some point, I register an awful heat spreading through me. It grows with every strike.

But it isn't awful. It's the same way I felt when he shoved me against the wall and thrust his fingers into me. Like the helplessness is just another fire to burn under my skin.

I cannot be turned on by this. By *him*. I bite my cheek, wrangling my emotions. They're out of control—I'm as out of control as Aiden.

Tears run down my cheeks when he finally stops. The belt is on the floor, but I can't think. I don't know how long it's been there, how long he hit me with his hand instead of the leather.

His fingers dig into my ass cheek, harsh and then gentle.

I groan. This new sensation is good.

The only noise that fills the room is our twin breaths—both labored.

His finger slides into me without warning. A whimper slips out past my clenched teeth, and he growls.

"Fuck, Gemma." He continues a lazy rhythm, dipping in and out of me.

I tense around his finger and rotate my hips, trying to get more friction. This is agony and foreign pleasure winding together, and it might be sweeter torture than the *spanking*. No one's hit me like that... well, ever.

My cheeks flush hot when I realize I didn't mind it. This precarious position only serves to make his finger push deeper inside me.

And all at once, he stops. The loss of him shocks me. I bite my lip hard enough to draw blood.

He puts me on my feet and unties me, then disappears into the bathroom. I sag to the bed and rub my wrists. The sudden quiet... my stomach is in knots. There's no relief in this ending, just an ache between my legs.

Tentatively, my fingers creep toward my core. I lie back and close my eyes. I've avoided exploring my sexuality, but now it's easy to find my clit—it pulses with its own homing beacon, alive from Aiden's touch.

Just a touch, just a moment.

I can't help but whimper again, and I rub in tiny circles. The climb is familiar, but I don't stop. I grind my hips into my own hand. My legs tremble, and I press my toes into the floor. The rational side of my brain wants to stop. To stand and pretend this didn't happen.

But I just keep driving myself to the edge.

I make the mistake of opening my eyes.

Aiden stands in the doorway to the bathroom. His cock is in his fist, and he strokes himself in quick, jerking movements. His gaze is fastened to the apex of my legs.

"You're afraid," he says.

My face is on *fire*, my ass throbs. My abdomen clenches when I take in his erection. I have some sick fascination in the way he's sliding his hand up and down his length.

No, I almost say, but I don't have it in me to lie.

I sit up and close my legs, flushing. "I haven't—"

He tilts his head.

"Done any of this," I finish lamely.

He pushes off the wall and stalks closer. "Kiss?"

I purse my lips.

"Besides me." He tsks, like that caveat is obvious.

"No."

He kneels on the floor and pulls me forward, until my knees bracket him. "Sucked someone off?"

"No."

"Touched yourself?"

I hesitate. "Until now, no."

He meets my gaze. "Orgasm."

My cheeks heat.

"Sex?"

My gaze flicks to the ceiling. "You know I haven't."

He slowly lowers himself and touches his lips to the inside of my knee. "You're so fucking pure."

I try to draw away, but he holds my calves firm.

"Poor princess," he breathes on my sensitive skin. "I left you hanging, didn't I?"

He's inching his way higher. Up my thigh, his breath hot on my skin. He licks me without warning, and I jump. His tongue dances over my clit, alternating sucking and teasing me. I squirm and slide my fingers into his hair.

He groans.

The vibration is a new type of sensation, and I let my head fall back. And then his mouth moves a bit lower, and his tongue plunges in me.

"Aiden," I moan, squeezing my eyes shut. "Oh God."

He fucks me with his tongue relentlessly, but it's the sudden switch back to my clit that sends me flying. It doesn't take much—I was already sensitive from his belt and hand on my ass. My grip tightens in his hair, and I try to tug him away. It's too much. He ignores me and slides two fingers inside me. I clench around his finger and ride out my orgasm.

I soar for too long, and my body is slick with sweat by the time I've returned to my body.

Embarrassment is quick to follow.

He just...

He stands and takes my hands, drawing me back into a sitting position. But he doesn't stop there. I must be his puppet, because I'm letting him guide me wherever he wants.

To my knees. He tilts my head back and stares down into my eyes.

"Open your mouth like a good little doll," he orders.

Loathing cuts through the bliss, but I do as he says.

"If you bite me, I'll knock your teeth in." He runs the tip of his cock over my lower lip. "Nod if you understand."

I nod quickly, my lips still parted.

He keeps his hand on the back of my head and pushes his dick into my mouth. It's obtrusive—too big. Saliva fills my mouth, and I try to fight it. I plant my hands on his thighs.

"Relax," he says. "Suck."

I allow my tongue to curl around his length, retreating slightly.

He hisses.

Naïve as I feel in this moment, it doesn't feel like rocket science. My hands creep up from his thighs and grip the base of his cock, helping guide it in and out of my mouth. I mimic his movements, fast and then slow.

"Gemma," he grunts. "God, why are you good at this?"

I refuse to grin. He tastes unique, and I'm shocked that I like the flavor of him.

He rocks his hips forward, and he hits the back of my throat. I gag around him. Tears spring into my eyes. Something savage takes over—not only in him, but me, too. I let my hands fall away, and he pounds into my mouth. I do my best to keep up, but he doesn't care. My eyes flick up and meet his.

He comes with a guttural yell, spilling down my throat.

I swallow around him.

He pulls out carefully and sinks to his knees in front of me, so we're eye to eye. He brushes the tears from my cheeks, and I wipe my mouth.

I sniffle.

"You okay?" he asks in a low voice.

I nod once and stand. My skin crawls with what we just did. The horror of giving in to Aiden DeSantis is overwhelming. I grab my underwear and tug it on, followed by sweatpants I snatch off the floor.

He eyes me without comment.

I leave the room. I can't... I can't be in the same bed as him. He just fucked my mouth, and some dark part of me enjoyed it. So, yeah. That's a big *no*. I need distance and mouthwash and maybe a lobotomy.

I settle on the couch and toss the blanket over me. I'll wait for that mouthwash once he's asleep. Yep, I'm hiding from my future fucking husband.

Maybe he'll let me out of it.

I dismiss the thought immediately. He doesn't seem like the type to go back on his word—ever.

I squint in the dark, sensing movement. I tense a moment before Aiden grabs me, throwing me effortlessly over his shoulder. It's his go-to mode of transportation for me, I'm learning.

"Put me down." I struggle against him, raining my fists down on his back.

He doesn't say anything until he drops me on the bed. I move to get up, but he blocks me.

"No," he says—he's the epitome of calm. "You can't run from me. Or hide. Sulk, if you want. Be fucking embarrassed that we gave each other orgasms. But you can do it in front of me or not at all."

I cross my arms. "I happen to value privacy."

He laughs. "You had days of it, and you threw it in my face the first chance you got. You're mine, Gemma. Now, in a week, on our wedding day. It doesn't fucking matter. And one day, maybe you'll feel the same. Either way, you're here and I'm not letting you go."

I groan. "I need to brush my teeth."

He doesn't stop me from rushing into the bathroom. I slam the door shut, feeling for all the world like a dumb kid. I press my forehead to the frosted glass and say, "You don't like me, Aiden. You want to own me. That's completely different."

He doesn't respond.

But then again, I didn't expect him to.

CHAPTER 9

Gemma

The whir of the remote-controlled shades wakes me up. I face the windows, so the sun hits my face before I even open my eyes. I groan, flipping onto my back. I'm not ready to be awake. There's no agenda, no plan for me. Nothing to *do* but waste away hundreds of feet off the ground while Aiden searches for my brother.

Someone steps in front of the sun, blocking it, and I squint back in the direction of the windows.

Aiden crouches in the center of my drawings, the ones I managed to forget about. The ones I *should* have packed up and kept in the nightstand, or ripped up and flushed down the toilet. He stares down at them all, not moving to touch them. They're just cityscapes, anyway. Some other drawings from memory, or imagination.

He glances at me.

"You're talented," he says quietly.

I say nothing.

One catches his eye. He scoops it up, then folds it in half and sticks it in his pocket.

"You—"

He silences me with a look and comes over, kneeling beside the bed. He raises his hand and smooths back my hair, and the gesture is so unexpected, I almost flinch.

Almost.

"Get dressed," he says.

I raise my eyebrow.

"Cat is taking you shopping for clothes that actually fit." He frowns, maybe already regretting his words. "You'll be accompanied by guards."

That means there's a catch—or this is a test. Or a reward for a stunning blow job last night.

Ha, I crack myself up.

Once I worked up the nerve to come out of the bathroom, I laid on the edge of the bed. Aiden dragged me to the center and rolled me to face him. I couldn't help but notice how careful he was of the healing burn on my back.

But he wedged his thigh between mine, snaked his arms around me, and told me to sleep. And even with claustrophobia pressing in, and a sense that I should be trying to get as far away from him as possible, I relaxed.

I slept.

Now he's giving me an inch of freedom?

"Are they there to keep me safe, or just keep me?"

His brow lowers. "Let's just say both, for the sake of argument."

"You do realize I came here willingly, right?"

"That doesn't mean you might not regret your decision."

I glower. "I'll only regret it if you keep searching for my brother. He's not involved."

It's the first time I've denied it. I don't actually know if he had anything to do with the shooting because I refused to ask him. I thought it would make me safer, but now... now I wish I knew one way or another.

"Lies," Aiden dismisses. "You'd say anything to save him."

That's… true.

"You don't have proof, do you?"

I can't concentrate with his hand stroking my hair. The gentleness of his actions versus our harsh conversation.

"Why are you letting me leave the tower?" I ask instead. "I thought you'd keep me locked up here until you forced me to marry you."

I sit up and wince. My ass stings with the remnants of his punishment. His hand slides off my head, and he smirks like he knows exactly the issue. He remains crouched beside the bed, though, so I'm looking down at him. I don't like this new side of him. Him being cordial, at the very least. *Nice*, even. It sets me on edge, and I'm not fully awake yet.

"Cat convinced me that you being locked up would do no good in the long run." He rises. "Get dressed."

In the long run? I shudder. "How long will you keep me?"

He pauses in the doorway and glances back, his gaze inscrutable. "Until Wilder walks back into the DeSantis tower alive, princess. Which we both know isn't going to happen."

I close my eyes.

He leaves me. I slowly glance around, like the walls will spill his secrets for me. I don't think I moved at all while I slept —a surprising change from previous nights. But then my attention snags on the other side of the bed, the dented pillow. The comforter and sheets are folded back into position, like when he woke up, he took a moment to make it seem like he wasn't ever there.

My stomach twists.

My weakness smacks me in the face. Aiden's demonstration last night just proves how helpless I am in this situation. How much control he holds. He's right: he can control me.

I climb out of bed and straight into the shower, dousing myself in cold water. I slide on the same shorts Cat gave me yesterday, then pick up the tube of cream for the burn.

This is the worst part.

I struggle to reach it all that I don't give it a second thought when Aiden appears in the doorway. He leans against the frame, watching me for a moment, then steps forward. He plucks the tube from my grasp and motions for me to spin.

I just stare at him.

"Turn around," he says.

I hesitate, then I follow his direction. His cool fingers press into my shoulder blade, and I shiver. One finger skates down my spine.

Goosebumps rise on my arms.

He swipes on the cream impossibly gently. It barely hurts. Then turns me back around, and his gaze drops to my bare chest.

I reach for my shirt, but he stops me. There's a look in his eyes that I don't understand, but it draws me in. It isn't his usual anger or stoicism.

His hand slides under my hair, around the back of my neck. He tugs me closer, flush against him, and I automatically tilt back to meet his gaze. I don't know what's happening. I've lost sight of the fact that we're fighting—even if it's just in my head.

My tongue pokes out, sweeping my lower lip, and he releases a frustrated growl.

"Even when you infuriate me, I can't resist you," he murmurs.

Our lips connect, and I rise on my toes to meet him. It shocks my brain into blissful silence, but then my body kicks back into gear. I concentrate on the quick beat of my heart, his lips sliding against mine. This is better than the show we put on for his father.

Better than last night. He didn't kiss me then. It was more of a punishment than anything else. But this... there's a difference.

I hold on to his wrists. This kiss feels like one out of a romance novel. All-consuming.

And I do let it fully consume me for a handful of seconds. My ears ring. My skin is electric. The outside world is blocked out as Aiden touches me. I reach down and loop my fingers in his belt loops, yanking him even closer. His erection pushes into my belly, and I gasp into his mouth.

His lips move to my ear. "Surprised?"

No time to answer. I don't have a brain, anyway, because he lowers himself and kisses my breast. Then nips my flesh.

All my rational thought is gone.

"What are you doing?" I manage. My voice is strangled—maybe I don't even want to ask.

He pinches my nipple, rolling it. I clench my thighs together and fight back a groan. His dark eyes meet mine, and I have a moment of déjà vu.

It hangs around me, a weight of *this has happened before*, before he focuses back on my chest. He sucks my nipple into his mouth. Little sparks flicker in front of my vision. I tip my head back, bracing my weight on the counter. He can't keep doing this, or I'm going to explode.

"Aiden."

He breaks away suddenly, taking a few big steps backward.

"What—"

He stares at me like I'm a ghost. Or maybe a figment of his imagination. The déjà vu feeling is back, this time like ice water dripping down my spine. The way he's looking at me... I hate it. He grabs my shirt and presses it to my chest, then walks out of the bathroom.

It takes me a while to put myself back together. The pulsing between my legs, the flush of my cheeks. I splash water on my face and will away the memories, but my lips are swollen. There's a red spot on my breast, teeth marks. It didn't feel hard enough to leave a mark, but the evidence is on my skin.

I turn away harshly, yanking my shirt over my head. I haven't been able to wear a bra because of the burn, but it isn't like I need it. And at the end of the day, I don't really give a damn if people care.

I brush my hair out, then continue reapplying my makeup. All the while, I'm terrified that Aiden might come back up here and finish the job—rather, finish *me*. My innocence sits heavy on my shoulders.

But who do I blame for that?

Myself, for not being more outgoing?

My parents for keeping me homeschooled the last few years of high school?

I don't know. Maybe all of the above.

His questions from last night come back to me, and I touch my lips. Is the only thing left to do... sex? I shudder and shift my weight, ignoring my butterflies. I know, with certainty, that he's going to cross that off the checklist, too.

After another minute of stalling, I zip on my boots and go downstairs. Aiden is gone, but Cat and Sam wait for me. The latter scowls, while Cat beams.

"I convinced him this morning after I gave him a piece of my mind. Carrying you off like a caveman." She comes over and hugs me. "Well, Sam convinced him, I think. My dumbass brother can be good for some things."

I can't seem to unlock my muscles until she withdraws. It isn't that I'm not used to hugs—I'm a hugger when the mood strikes me—but it's this family. She's not being nice because we're friends. She's a DeSantis, for God's sake. And yesterday was fun, but not life-changing.

Her ulterior motive will reveal itself with time... just like Aiden's.

Either way, I don't know now and I won't show my suspicions by asking. Who would ever tell me the truth about that, anyway?

I follow Cat out of the apartment and into the hallway. Sam trails after us, shooting her a questioning glance.

It occurs to me that I didn't get my earnings from last night, and my pride won't let me ask. I file away the fact that Jack and Cat owe me favors, though. Until I have a plan to use them, I've got to stay under the radar.

And that includes in this mall. I can just follow Cat around and see what she picks out. But I'm not going to turn this down—it's an excuse to get outside. To breathe fresh air.

We exit the elevator into the parking garage, and Sam now leads the way to a dark SUV parked halfway down the ramp. His sister opens the back door, gesturing for me to climb in. Once I'm seated, she slams the door and circles the vehicle. She sits beside me, bouncing up and down.

"I haven't had an outing in ages," she says. "Not a fun one, anyway."

"Why?"

She looks away. "Well, we were on lockdown."

Oh, right. A flash of guilt hits me, but I shove it away. *I* didn't force them into lockdown. I didn't kill Wilder.

We lapse into silence after that. Maybe it's just my imagination that it's tense, but I can't open my mouth to break it. The sun slants across me as we exit the parking garage, and I tilt my head to face it. Too late, I realize I should be paying attention to where we are in the city.

We navigate out of Manhattan, crossing the bridge and finally pulling into a giant mall parking lot.

"Here?"

I came here as a kid. Paced the stores behind my mother, or got smoothies in the cafeteria with friends. Mom liked it because it had a lot of options, and not many people recognized us.

Sometimes being a West was dangerous—and dragging a guard around behind us always drew attention. How safe we were just depended on if the people knew what to do with that attention.

"Ready?" Sam asks. He climbs out of the car without waiting for us.

After a beat, Cat and I scramble after him.

I keep my promise to myself and tag along behind her through the store, pausing a few feet behind her when she does. My anxiety creeps higher and higher the longer we're in the store—and it's only the first one. Sam seems on edge, his gaze never stopping for too long.

Finally, Cat scowls at me. "What are you doing?"

I raise my eyebrows. I'm about to climb out of my skin, but I don't say that. This is her excursion, after all. I'm just the excuse she needed to have a day out of the tower.

"You're following me around. This is supposed to be for *you*, Gemma." She steps forward, trying to get me to look at her.

My cheeks heat, and I fidget with my nails. I may as well just come out and say it—especially since she thinks I'll be racking up a huge credit card charge. I do have one in the sole of my boot, but it's for emergencies only. As in, emergency escape.

So I blurt out, "I don't have any money, okay?"

Sam chuckles.

"Stop that," I snap at him. "It's not like I wanted to admit it, all right?"

Cat grabs my hands, squeezing them gently. "I have Aiden's credit card. This is a DeSantis-approved field trip. So just... find stuff you want to wear. He's paying." She tows me toward a rack of athletic gear. "You strike me as a runner."

I scoff. "Not sure where you got that idea."

Yoga is my go-to. If I'm under duress. I definitely try not

to run... well, ever. Although, I suppose I might have better chances of surviving if I'm more in shape. Still, I shudder.

Horrible thing, running.

"Okay, so...?"

"I like dresses," I give. "And comfortable clothes. I'm sick of wearing Aiden's sweatpants."

My face is on fire, but she doesn't comment on that. She just grins, and the tension between us breaks.

"Was that so hard?" she teases. "Besides, I saved your winnings. I'll grab it from the apartment when we get back. Right now, though? We're in the wrong store. Come on."

CHAPTER 10

Gemma

"Try those on." Cat points to my armful of clothes. "I'm going to look at the swimsuits."

We've been to at least six different stores. I can't decide if Sam's here as security or to carry our bags—he's doing more of the latter currently. He stops outside the entrance to the fitting rooms and turns around, tracking his sister across the room.

"Go on." He glances at me. "I'm starving."

I grunt. I am, too. We had soft pretzels about an hour ago, but it wasn't enough. My stomach growls at the thought of food. One of the attendants hands me a colored tag to hang on my door, and I step into an empty fitting room.

It's decently sized, teal walls and a large mirror on one. There's a row of hooks opposite, and a wooden chair in the corner.

Almost immediately, the door knob turns and the door is forced inward.

"This one is occupied—" I rear back when I register *who* is slipping into my space.

My brother grins at me. "Hey, Gem."

He locks the door and looks me up and down. I do the same, trying to take in everything before it's ripped away. He's taller than I am—overtook me a few years ago, despite being younger—and his lean body is packed with muscle. His hair is light, like mine. Green eyes, freckles. Objectively speaking, he's handsome. As a sister, I hate the attention he gets from girls. I understand it, but I still want to punch anyone who flirts with him.

Still, the relief that crashes through me is swift. He's safe.

For now.

I lunge forward and throw my arms around his neck. "What are you doing here?"

He returns my hug tightly, lifting me off my feet for a moment. "Dad told me what you did. Taking the fall—or, I don't know, did you actually admit to doing it?"

I step back. "I didn't admit anything. They're hunting *you*. I just... You're supposed to be upstate. Why would you risk it to come back here?"

It sounds silly. *And* there's a DeSantis right outside. One who would probably happily take Colin back to see Aiden. What would my husband-to-be do? Torture a confession out of him?

"Colin." I grab his hand. "Did you do it? Kill Wilder?"

"I don't have long, Gem. That's what you want to ask me?" He pauses, attention drawn down to my neck. "Are you okay with them? Are they hurting you? Say the word and we'll get you out of here."

I think of Aiden's idea of marriage, his fingers on my skin. His lips on mine, or his face buried between my legs. The fire at Aunt Mary's house. Standing in the window waiting for him to arrive. Every moment with him rewinds, until it's just my father and me standing in the dark house. Deciding. Choosing what path to go down.

I thought I knew what I was getting into, but the truth is...

I still don't know what I've done. What he's capable of doing to me.

"I'm okay," I say.

"Gemma?" Sam calls.

I motion for the chair, and Colin gingerly hops up onto it.

"You okay?"

I roll my eyes at my brother. "Perfectly fine," I say. I inject attitude into my voice. "Why? Am I taking too long?"

"Suck-up," Colin mouths.

"No, no," Sam backtracks. "Just... stay there."

I grab one of the dresses off the hook and put Colin at my back. I ditch my shirt and slide the silky fabric over my head. It fits well and looks fine, so I barely spare myself a glance in the mirror before I move on to the rest of the stuff. Well, some of it. A few pieces Cat threw at me because she thought I'd like them, but...

Well, we're not on that good of terms yet. She doesn't know my style.

"Gem," Colin whispers hoarsely. "What happened to your back?"

I glance over my shoulder at him. He's paler than he was a few minutes ago.

"He set Aunt Mary's house on fire, and I stupidly tried to rescue it." I shake my head. "Blast from the kitchen threw me into a wall. I had to jump in the pool."

His eyes widen. "You could've been seriously injured."

"I know." I take his hand and squeeze. "I wasn't running on common sense. Believe me, I realize how dumb it was."

"Where are they keeping you?"

"Twenty-fourth floor." I shift, then add, "Aiden's apartment."

He scoffs and meets my eyes. "Why the hell are you there?"

I don't want to be the one to tell him Aiden's plans, but the way he's glaring at me, I'm not sure I have a choice. I open my mouth to explain everything—the fire, the trunk, Jameson's threat, the marriage plan.

Until someone screams. It's distant, like it's not even in the same store. The familiar *pop-pop-pop* of gunfire follows. We both instinctively hunch and wait for a moment. More shrieking drifts toward us.

"That's my cue," Colin says. He jumps down and quickly presses a kiss to my forehead. "We'll get you out of there. I promise you that."

"I… don't get hurt because of me." I latch on to his arm again, stopping him. "That's why I'm doing this. Please don't do anything stupid. Go upstate and stay there."

He cracks the door and peeks out, then returns his focus to me. "Sorry, Gem. You don't get to issue orders. I'm trying to do what's best."

And then he's out and gone, and my worry ramps up. I shove my shoes back on my feet and open the door an inch.

Sam is gone from the entrance. I hurriedly pull on my shirt, abandoning the new clothes, and creep forward. Everything's gone eerily silent, then a *boom* shakes the building. I drop into a crouch. Dust and particles float down around me. This isn't just a random coincidence—this is an attack.

I make my way to the arched entryway. There are people here in the store, the tops of their heads visible between racks of clothes and displays. Mannequins have been knocked over, clothes scattered on the floor.

People are terrified, but I can't seem to find that same emotion. Someone shook my world like a snow globe, and yet…

My brother wouldn't have left me if he didn't know the danger. If he wasn't part of the plan. Whatever plan this might be…

Someone grabs me from behind, slamming me face-first into the wall before I've even made it a few paces out into the store's main room. I grunt, the impact rattling my bones.

Aiden flips me around and covers my mouth with his hand.

He pulls me down until my ass hits the floor, and he kneels between my legs. I stare at him with wide eyes and huff against his palm. I don't know what to think of his expression. His gaze doesn't stay locked on anything for more than a few seconds, and there's a dangerous energy in him.

The sort of energy I'd imagine follows death.

"Your brother," he says sharply. "Was he here?"

He removes his hand.

"Fuck you," I reply.

He scowls and leans into my space. "Listen very closely, princess. If you don't tell me the truth, someone you love will end up dead. We're going to get your brother either way—it's just a matter of if you want to see him alive beforehand."

He's messing with you.

I lift my chin and stare him down. "Go to hell, Aiden."

He drags me to my feet, keeping a firm hold on my arms, and guides me into the hallway. There are bullet holes in the floor, the walls. A dropped cup sits in its spattered, bright-blue liquid. It seems like what was once a relatively quiet mid-week day at the mall... well, at least there aren't bodies.

"Who was shooting?" I ask him. "And the explosion?"

"Diversions for my men." His voice is gruff. "Pulled focus from you."

"Sam? Cat?" I try to glance around for them, but he squeezes my biceps and drags me faster along.

"They're fine. Evacuated out a side entrance." A muscle in his jaw jumps.

He's furious. Things went from good to shit faster than I would've guessed. I'm not dumb—I know my family wants me back, even though I willingly gave myself up—and they'll do anything for me. The thought should warm my heart, but I'm worried for them. What's the point of this? Of blowing something up? Just so Colin could check on me?

My face heats when it clicks, and then dread churns my stomach.

We've been here for *hours*. Cat's dragged me around the whole mall with only Sam following us. Aiden said his men. Plural.

I try to ignore the sinking feeling. Was it a slip of his tongue—or maybe he considers Cat...? *Doubt it*. All I can do is swallow and pretend my sudden nausea is from the pretzels we ate. He wouldn't set my family up like that, right?

He wouldn't use me as bait.

We round a corner and, against my better judgement, I stop dead.

There are at least ten men—and a few women, too—with Kevlar vests and guns strapped to their hips. If they were to remove the vests, they'd probably seem like normal mall-goers. But now they're grouped, and their hard gazes give them away. They ignore me and concentrate on Aiden.

He's the heir, after all.

The one in control.

Keep reminding yourself that, I think. I can't afford to forget it. If I want to survive him, I need to be smarter.

Aiden releases me and strides forward, nodding to a man on his left. "Put her in my car."

"What—" I backpedal.

The man comes toward me. He doesn't seem to mind that I'm actively trying to get away from him. My gaze skates around the atrium, and I cringe at the blood on the floor. Broken glass from a skylight.

"You said you weren't running," Aiden reminds me. He stands off to the side, watching me. "Prove it."

"Now you're just being an ass," I say under my breath.

His eyes narrow, and he raises a hand. The man stops.

"Okay, Gemma." Aiden glances at someone else, and they disappear into one of the stores. "I was going to spare you from seeing this."

My gut churns. He smirks at my expression.

A chill sweeps down my spine, but I stand tall. Even when the man and his partner reappear, dragging a hooded man between them. Their captive is already bloody. A dark-red spot blooms in a circle from the hollow of their shoulder, and besides that, he's filthy. His light-gray shirt is streaked with dirt, his jeans are ripped.

Aiden strides forward and rips the hood off, and I'm suddenly face-to-face with my cousin.

Kai has been my brother's best friend since we were kids. He's basically another brother. He certainly was at my house enough growing up, soaking up everything my father would teach him. He's the one who stopped our other cousins from picking on me.

The one who taught me math because my mother hated the subject.

The one who helped me get Amelie away from the DeSantises.

He... He's family.

And right now, he stares at me like he knows exactly what's coming, and he pities me for not seeing it.

I can't tell what Aiden's plan is. I was blind to the fact that today was a trap in general, like the stupid little girl he thinks I am. So happy for a day out, for a shopping trip, that I neglected to spot the red flags.

"Don't hurt him." I can't help it. All these memories race through my mind of my brother and Kai, the inseparable duo. My heart has transformed into a frantic animal battering against my ribcage. "Aiden."

I catch his attention, but the man who stroked my hair

this morning has vanished. He's the cold, savage prince I heard stories about.

They force Kai to his knees, and I rush forward. Aiden steps to the side, letting me pass. No one speaks—the whole mall is silent except for my footsteps and harsh breathing.

"Kai," I breathe, stopping myself from throwing my arms around him. I sink to my knees in front of him, my hands hovering by his chest. "Are you okay?"

"Gem." His expression is closed off. A complete opposite from his general warmth toward me. "Get up."

"Kai—"

"Begging will not be enough for them." He leans forward and presses his forehead to mine. "It's okay."

"Get up," Aiden echoes.

He grabs me under the arms, hauling me back to my feet.

"This is what we do to Wests who threaten us," he says to me. He grips Kai's shoulder and digs his thumb into the wound.

My cousin grits his teeth, but his silence doesn't last long. His face turns red, and he screams. A vein pops out in his neck.

I stagger back, but I can't go far. Aiden still has my arm in his grip. I'm tethered to him.

"This is what happens to those who try to hurt us. We do this time and again, Gemma. We protect ourselves. We come out ahead. Always."

He releases Kai, and the latter sags. His chest rises and falls in the aftermath of the pain, and fresh blood runs down his chest. It leaves a wet trail on his shirt and spreads like a stain.

This is it. This has to be enough.

"Look at me, West," Aiden orders.

I shiver at the violence in just four words.

Kai's gaze stays glued to the floor for a long moment, then he meets Aiden's glare. His eyes are bloodshot. A bruise is newly forming on his jaw from a hit that must've happened during his capture.

Aiden punches him in the face, knocking him sideways.

I yelp and claw at Aiden's arm. "Stop this," I plead. Whether it's just to let him go or abandon him here—we can leave. It's not too late. "We can walk away from this right now and still... Still be okay."

Aiden's men step back and wait for Kai to pick himself up off the floor. I look around, wishing my brother would come to Kai's rescue. To save his best friend. Colin's aim is good. He could kill everyone in this room.

Kai struggles to his feet and meets my eyes. "Love you, Gem. It'll be okay."

It won't be okay. He cradles his arm against his stomach, and that pity has returned to his expression. *Poor naïve Gemma*, he must think.

"Gemma is mine," Aiden says in a low voice.

My heart aches, but the relief is sudden, too. He wants Kai to tell everyone about his claim. I can be okay with that outcome. It was going to be revealed eventually, anyway. Especially if I can't figure out a way to end this.

My family will find out about my impending marriage through my tortured cousin. They'll be furious, rightly so. This duty is going to kill me.

They know you wanted to save your brother.

In slow motion, Aiden pulls a gun from his waistband and raises it. I scramble against his hold, but I'm not fast enough. He squeezes the trigger.

The *bang* rattles my brain. I can't even comprehend it for a long moment. Just the echo of noise over and over.

Kai falls backward. He's got a hole in his forehead that I can't seem to make sense of. An eternity later, he hits the floor and blood pools around his head. His eyes are still open, though. Staring into oblivion.

All I can hear is my frantic heartbeat. A rush of blood in my ears. The horror just seems to descent like a fog over my head, moving too slow. Too fast, too slow. Time comes unraveled around me.

Kai is dead.

Aiden DeSantis killed my cousin. He shot him in front of me. I touch my face, surprised when my fingertips come away red.

That's how close. That's how terrible.

I open my mouth and scream.

CHAPTER 11
Aiden

Gemma is inconsolable.

Then quiet.

Later, she'll be furious. But for now, her tears have dried and she's lapsed into silence.

I lift her out of the car and into the elevator. Sam waits for us at the entrance to my apartment, and I toss him my keys. He unlocks it and follows us in, pausing when I go straight upstairs. He'll wait.

She doesn't say anything when I set her on the counter and turn on the shower. She's a limp doll, letting me untie and remove her boots, then socks. She doesn't react to my cold hands on her skin, skimming under her shirt and finally raising it over her head. Her blonde hair caught some of the pink mist, but it's her face that wears the most blood.

I toss her shirt to the floor. It's stained, too, probably unsavable.

Steam billows from the shower and fogs over the mirror. I undo the button of her jean shorts and wrap my arm around her lower back. I pick her up enough to slide the fabric down, then set her back on the counter. Denim and pink panties slide down her legs. She curls her fingers in her lap and refuses to look at me.

My heart lurches. She's so damn beautiful, even despondent.

I shed my own clothes. A bloody shirt, black pants. The gun and holster clipped to my belt. I step into the bedroom and slide back the fake panel next to the bed. I type in my safe's passcode and set my firearm inside, then relock it.

When I return to the bathroom, she's still in the same spot. Her gaze is unfocused, but her eyes are wet with tears again.

I sigh. There are a lot of things I want to say. That her cousin's death was inevitable. That he killed two of my men before we captured him. He had DeSantis blood on his hands, and that's inexcusable. We moved them before Gemma came into the atrium. I didn't want to traumatize her...

But then I shot Kai.

The sickly sweet affection between them made my blood boil. She's *mine*—not his. Not her family's. Her brother, her father... they all gave up claim to her the minute they left her in that house to wait for me.

"Get up," I say.

She flinches.

Flinches.

But then she stands. I drop my briefs and usher her into the shower. She makes a little noise in the back of her throat when I step in after her. I check the water and guide her back, until it soaks her hair. With more care than I thought I would be capable of, I wet a washcloth and swipe at her face.

Her hand covers mine, taking over. I watch her scrub viciously at her skin.

"It's gone." I take it away from her and drop it behind me. I shouldn't touch her, but I can't help myself. I slide my hands up her arms.

She hits at my chest. "Why did you do that?"

"You know why." I grip her chin and tilt her face up.

Her eyes are filled again. "Just let me break down in peace. Alone." She rips out of my hold and puts her face into the water.

Anger boils my blood, and I wrap my hand around her throat, dragging her back. Her shoulder blades hit my chest. "No. We've been over this before. You want to cry? Cry. You want to scream? Go ahead—no one will come running, princess, so make as much noise as you want. But I'm not leaving."

It's just me and her and all our ugliness between us.

Her pulse quickens. I tighten my grip and lean down, kissing her shoulder. There's a mark on her breast from this morning, and my lust stirs. I want her to wear my mark—visible ones. Claiming ones.

She trembles.

I shift my hips, showing her how turned on her fear makes me. Control is sand slipping through my fingers. She braces a hand on my thigh and pushes against me.

"I can't," she says, squirming. "I'm a virgin. And I'm not going to have sex with you the same day you murder my cousin. I hate you, Aiden DeSantis. There's a reason our families are enemies."

I still.

And fuck if her confession doesn't make me harder.

Angry little virgin. I knew she was, even before I questioned her the other day, because I was the one keeping the boys away. The one who killed and threatened to get my point across. If not for me, she might've been stolen away by some Lawrence West-approved gunslinging asshole.

But she's not dealing with boys anymore—just one man.

Me.

The urge to fuck her gets stronger, but I won't—not here, anyway.

If I kiss her, I'll lose control. So, I release her throat. She doesn't step away from me or release my leg. The hot water hits her in the sternum, running down her body. My cock bobs as I try to maintain my control.

I reach over her and grab the shampoo.

"You didn't even question him," she whispers. "You just... killed him."

Her gaze catches on my bruised knuckles.

"I grew up with him and you murdered him like it was nothing."

Her nails dig into my thigh again, but I like that I'm the one grounding her. She can't look at me, but she will. I squeeze the soap into my palm and set the bottle back down. She stays perfectly still when I lather it and massage it into her hair.

"It was nothing." I need her to understand that she didn't walk into a fairy tale by coming with me. "It was easy to kill him. It would be easy to kill your whole family."

She stiffens.

I turn her around and guide her back, rinsing her hair. She glares at my chest, refusing to meet my eyes—or down. She just lets me manipulate her body, and her gaze stays level on my tattoos. From her squint, it's the first time she's seen the artwork, and it holds her transfixed.

Interesting.

"Are you going to kill them?" Her gaze now snaps up, colliding with mine. "Where's your remorse?"

"Not your whole family, Gemma. Not if you tell me the truth." I step into her space again. "Did you see your brother?"

"No."

The most surprising part is that I can't tell if she's lying. I knew she'd say no, but her conviction controls her voice.

Keeps it from wavering, or her eyes from sliding away. She narrows her eyes and pokes her finger into my chest.

"No, he didn't show up to save me. If he did, I would've had him take me far, far away from you."

I sneer. "Dear Gemma, if you wanted me to believe you, you should've stuck to one word replies. And to answer your original question: I don't have remorse. That's how I survive in this world."

She motions for me to move, and we switch places. She runs conditioner through her hair with her fingers, seemingly done with talking to me. That's fine, I'm done talking to her, too. But I keep an eye on her, even as I take my turn under the water, dousing my head and scrubbing my skin.

The blood flakes off and swirls down the drain. My knuckles aren't too busted—there were a few people I punched, Kai West only one of them. There were too many Wests there, and that's a puzzle I can't seem to figure out.

Yes, it was a trap. For her as much as them.

But I expected Gemma's brother, maybe her father. Some backup to protect them.

What we got was a whole damn army of people willing to rescue her.

I watch her stand out of the water, her arms wrapped around her body. The longer we stand in silence, the more broken her expression becomes.

I rinse the soap off and switch places with her again. She takes her time with her hair, her eyes closing. It's just a moment of peace that she takes for herself, and I wonder if her whole shower would've gone like that if I'd left her alone.

But we won't find out.

I reach around her and shut the water off, then grab a towel and wrap her in it. I snag one for myself and step out. She comes along slower.

"What are you going to do?" she asks me. "Where's your empathy?"

I lift my chin. "What do you call this?"

Her lips twist. "This isn't empathy. It's pity, maybe. Or regret."

"If I regretted every choice I made, I wouldn't last long in this job." I invade her space again, loving the way her breathing hitches. I should be sensitive to the fact that Gemma is hurting.

But at the end of the day, I'm the asshole who would burn the whole world down for her. I trap her against the door. "Does that scare you?"

"It makes me want to stab you," she says. There isn't nearly enough vinegar in her voice for her to go through with it, though.

I smirk. "I'd love to see you try."

Reality comes crashing down around me when I remember Sam waits for me below. I step back regrettably and make a snap decision.

"Get dressed," I order. "You're coming with me."

Her eyes widen. "Where now? Another trap?"

I roll my eyes. "No. But I don't trust you not to do something stupid."

She marches out of the bathroom, unhooking the towel and wrapping it around her hair as she goes. I stare at her ass and smother a groan.

She's going to be the death of me.

We get dressed in relative peace—relative because she's trying to put on a brave face, and I think she's holding on by a thread. Sam had deposited her bags in the closet, and her cheeks turn a pretty shade of red when she realizes he must've been up here.

Her stomach gurgles.

"Hungry?"

"We didn't eat much." She shrugs. "I'm fine."

"Nonsense." I gesture for her to follow me downstairs and text the restaurant chef. They'll bring something up, no questions asked.

She opted for a flowing black dress covered in daisies. It's similar to the one she wore when I found her—sleeves that flare at her wrists, a high neckline, loose fit. Nothing ostentatious.

And it makes me wonder if she chose black to quietly mourn her cousin's death.

Sam sits at the table, a magazine open to an article.

"What's that?" I ask.

"The councilwoman." He slides it toward us.

Gemma peeks over my shoulder, her curiosity getting the better of her. Under the headline: *Interview by Amelie DeSantis*.

"She interviewed a councilwoman?" Gemma asks. "Why?"

"Luca had a meeting with her." She'd demanded to be brought to him. She was angry. And they sorted out their issues... or maybe not, seeing as the end result was her in a locked room. "That was before he shut her away."

She sinks into the chair across from Sam. "She didn't deserve what happened to her."

I raise my eyebrows. "No?"

"No," she snaps.

"Boss," Sam cuts in. "The councilwoman and her construction bill can wait. We have bigger problems."

I sigh. Of course we have bigger problems. The dead customs officer, for one. The fact that Gemma's brother killed mine and is still breathing. Our missing supplies.

"Coroner called, wants to discuss."

Gemma quietly closes the magazine. I hadn't realized she'd slid it closer to her, scanning the interview.

"You don't think it's weird?" She tilts her head.

I narrow my eyes. "What's weird?"

"Councilwoman White, under DeSantis influence, helps pass a huge bill that basically gives her control of what permits to approve, and now your *construction* supplies were stolen? When you were guaranteed approval."

Sam and I trade a look. It wasn't just *construction supplies* as she said—it was expensive Italian marble and a shitload of firearms. But I'm not about to open my mouth and admit that to her. It's easier to say it was just construction supplies, as insignificant as that seems.

Better than creating a fuss about high-end product going missing. If that got out, our reliability would tank, along with our credibility. What use is a powerful family if we can't keep one lousy shipping container from being broken into?

Shit, this is going to cost a lot to replace until our insurance kicks in.

"And before you go blaming it on my family, we have no interest in your construction business," she adds.

I scoff.

She just huffs and flips open the magazine again, staring at advertisements.

I return my attention to Sam. "The medical examiner wants me to come down there?"

He nods, and I glance at Gemma. I was going to take her with me wherever I went, but that... that might be too much. For all I know, her cousin's body will be on a slab next to the customs officer.

That's a breakdown I don't want to deal with.

"Call Cat," I order. "She's on babysitting duty. *Strict* babysitting duty." God, what a headache. She betrayed my trust when she took Gemma around my family—even if none of them seemed to piece together who she is.

Sooner or later, they'll find out. Especially after today's trap.

My family will be furious with the lives we lost. Kai West got too close—slipped under our radar because I was too busy watching the story Gemma was in, waiting to see if Colin would show up. *My fault.*

But they won't blame me—they'll blame her.

Fifteen minutes later, Cat and Gemma are seated at the table. I stand at the head of it. They both seem subdued, although it could just be an act on Cat's part. Sam wouldn't have told her what I did to her. She's good at reading a room, though. Sam must've talked to her about the card game—how stupid it was for her to endanger Gemma like that.

"You're on thin ice," I inform her. "Do not leave my apartment. Don't let anyone except Sam or me in. Don't talk to anyone—"

"I get it," Cat says. "Isolation. How long will you be gone?"

I meet Sam's eyes, then turn back at the girls. "I'll be back tonight."

She nods.

Gemma won't look at me—and I can only imagine it's for a variety of reasons. Annoyance climbs up my throat, and I pinch her chin. I force her head up, and her gaze follows a beat later.

I lean down and kiss her. Not just for the display, but because I want Sam and Cat to know that I'm serious. Gemma clawed her way into my heart, and I'll do whatever is necessary to keep her safe. Including killing her own cousin for his foolish actions.

She's frozen for a moment, and then she unlocks. What was meant to be a quick thing quickly derails. Her lips on mine is like a static shock, and I deepen the kiss. She tilts her head, accepting it—or so I think.

My fingers are still on her chin, dictating her movements, and I slide my other hand around the back of her neck.

Her teeth catch my lower lip, and she bites me hard. The metallic tang of blood fills my mouth, and I groan. *Fuck*, that hurts. But I press harder against her lips, unwilling to let her win. She makes a noise of frustration, but I have her caught. I nip her own lip in return, then pull away.

I smirk and press my thumb to my lip. It comes away smeared in blood, and satisfaction explodes in my chest.

She can't look at me, but her face is tomato-red.

I grin.

"Well." Cat fans herself. "Is it hot in here?"

"Shut up," Gemma mutters.

I can't keep the smirk off my face on the way out the door.

CHAPTER 12

"We're not staying cooped up all night," Cat announces. "And you're going to tell me what the hell happened today."

I sigh. "I'm not really in the mood. Not to talk, and definitely not to go out."

Not after Kai. God, I can still see his open eyes staring at nothing. It makes me wonder if he knew it was going to happen. He had pity for me, and it must've been because I didn't see it coming.

There was no way he was going to walk away from the DeSantises alive.

My mind keeps going back to the handful of seconds before Aiden shot him. I had been so fucking naïve. Hopeful, even, that things would be okay. For a West to survive a DeSantis...

I'm the only one who ever managed it.

And it wasn't like Aiden was trying to kill me. I was his hostage for an afternoon. A dumb girl who didn't realize she was being used as a ransom.

I keep running through that day—I've done this for

three years, trying to figure it out. We went to the pier. We ate ice cream. He took a discreet picture at some point, which was used against my parents. *Proof* that I was a hostage.

It was just the first in a long line of fucked-up things our parents did in the name of war.

I go into the kitchen and climb up on the counter, pushing aside the spices on the top shelf of one of the cabinets to locate the tequila. I take a peek to make sure the burner phone is still there, and to my relief, it is.

I don't know why I assumed Aiden was aware I'd found it.

But once he realizes we put a dent in the tequila, he'll definitely know I located his hiding spot. I tuck it into my bra. With the bottle in my grasp, I hop down and show Cat.

"Liquid courage?" She appraises me for a moment, then gives me a sly grin. "I'm sure he has shot glasses around here."

"No need." I twist the cap off and take a swig. The room-temperature liquor burns its way down my throat.

"Wasn't expecting that. You okay?"

"Not in the slightest."

She nods and takes the bottle, mimicking my movement. She grimaces. "I don't know how you can drink this straight. Wonder if he has limes? Or margarita mix?"

Miraculously, he *does* have a lone lime in a bowl of other citruses. She cuts it into wedges, and I slide up on the counter beside her. She passes the tequila back. Getting drunk isn't really what I was intending, but it suddenly seems like it might make the day more manageable.

Let's not discuss the idea that we're using alcohol as a coping mechanism.

She waits until I'm three swigs in to ask me what happened. And this time, I don't resist—but I do, for a moment, consider how this might affect her.

"My cousin was killed," I say. *By Aiden*. "At the mall."

Cat gasps. "Oh my god, Gemma." She squeezes my hand. "I… I don't even know what to say to that. I'm so sorry."

I swipe at my nose. "It's not your fault."

She sighs. "Obviously, but it's still traumatic. Were you close?"

"He grew up with us." I turn my attention to my nails. "Practically lived with us over the summers, and especially when Colin got older…"

They'd do jobs together. Patrol or security gigs when we were moving sensitive material. I wasn't privy to more than that, although I pieced it together. They both carried guns and practiced hand-to-hand fighting in our summer home's basement. They pulled me into it a few times, taught me to grapple, but my parents put an end to that.

There were better things I could be doing with my time. Learning the piano, to play blindfolded, or singing lessons. Horseback riding. Puzzles.

In hindsight, I should've begged for at least the tools of self-defense. Better practice with a firearm, no matter how small. *Something* to not feel like this. Guilty. Helpless.

"He was at the mall?" Cat asks. "Did you see him?"

I jerk my head to the side. I don't want to tell her that it happened two feet in front of me. "No, I didn't. I didn't know he was there until after. I just… Aunt Mary is going to be devastated. The whole family is." I cover my mouth. "How can I go back to them?"

She squeezes my knee. "It isn't your fault."

It is.

"This is war," she continues. "Casualties happen—no matter how sad. I think both of our families are equipped to deal with it."

I inch out of her grasp, taking the tequila bottle with me. It doesn't even burn as I take another mouthful. "I would've just appreciated the sympathy, you know."

She frowns. "It was meant to be a comfort."

"What, that because they were at the mall, he deserved to die?" I narrow my eyes. "That's fucked-up. I wasn't raised around this sort of violence—were you? Is that how your childhood as a DeSantis went?"

She winces. "All I know is that I was shopping, then there was gunfire. And then some sort of explosion. It *felt* like war. I was scared, and I count my blessings that my brother was already tracking me down when it started. Weren't you terrified? You were alone."

"Aiden found me," I say. "I wasn't alone for long."

I wasn't scared until I saw my cousin forced to his knees. I wasn't terrified until Aiden dug his finger into Kai's wound. And the hope in me—that I'd ever be able to coexist with these people—died the moment Kai did.

"My brother, your cousin, they're soldiers in a war—"

I shake my head sharply. "I understand who he is. *Was*. That doesn't mean I can forget. Or be okay with it. It's death, Cat. It fucking sucks, and I just want one last chance to talk to him."

Her gaze follows me to the door, and I yank it open.

"Please leave."

She blows out a breath. "Okay."

She doesn't look at me on her way out, and I slam the door behind her. The noise jolts me, even though I expected it. For the first time since Kai's death, I'm alone. And my body can't seem to decide what to do first—cry or scream.

I fall to my knees in front of the door. I set down the bottle and tip my head back, but the noise gets lodged in my throat. I can't seem to make any noise now that I'm on my own.

After a few moments, my chest burning, I stagger to my feet and grab the tequila. I pat my chest, reassuring myself the phone is still pressed against my skin, and lace my boots tighter. Cat was right: I can't stay cooped up here. Hanging out with her is off the table, and I can't breathe. It's like the dose of fresh air I got this afternoon just reminded me how much I miss it.

I can't tell if I'm more pissed or upset that Cat doesn't understand, and loneliness strikes me. I know why I'm here—I know my intentions. But it's really fucking hard to hold on to that when Aiden killed Kai in front of me. I miss my family. I miss the normalcy, my friendships. There was a never-ending stream of family in and out of our home—first the Brooklyn one, then Manhattan when we relocated. They were headquarters as much as home. But now I'm here and I don't know how to handle it.

This isn't how to calm down the war. My *intentions* have gone unnoticed by both sides.

But unfortunately—or maybe it's fortune on my side—the tequila has hit me, disintegrating my reservations.

I hunt through the kitchen until I find duct tape, then open the apartment door and peer into the hallway. I prop it open with my foot and carefully tape over the door latch.

I don't have a key—why would Prince Aiden have deigned to give me one? And I want to be able to get back inside when I'm ready. He said he'd be back tonight, and I should probably be safely tucked away *before* he realizes I'm gone.

Once I'm sure the door will open under pressure alone, I amble toward the stairwell. I go up instead of down, and maybe that's just to convince myself that I don't want to actually escape. There's a little plaque with the floor level—twenty-four—and an arrow pointing up. *Roof access*, it says underneath the numbers. Cat mentioned the roof, but I had put it out of my head. Easy to do when we consider how my night ended.

I climb what feels like fifteen more stories before the stairwell narrows, and I shove the door open. I slip my shoe off and block the door, just in case, and gasp.

It isn't just a roof. It's a mini paradise.

There's a pool lit from within, lounge chairs spaced around it. A section of tables with umbrellas—now closed—in the corner. A bar against a far wall. The railing around the edge of the building is just glass, giving an unobstructed view of the surrounding buildings. A warm breeze sweeps over me, tugging at my blonde hair. I take a deep breath, and the fresh hint of rain fills my lungs.

My voice is still stuck in my throat, so I take another sip of the tequila and kick off my other shoe. I'm glad I opted for a black bralette under the dress. Dark panties. I pull the dress off and set it on top of my shoe, along with the phone.

The world tilts a bit, and I sit heavily on the ledge of the pool. I drop my feet in the water, and it's surprisingly warm. I reach back and fumble for the cell, flipping it open and powering it on. My body tingles.

There aren't any contacts. Nothing on the phone at all, actually.

I dial by memory and wait.

"What?" a gruff voice snaps.

"It's me." My voice is hoarse, and I don't know why. It's not like I was screaming.

"Gemma?" There's background noise, loud for a moment, then it silences. My brother sighs into the phone. "My god, are you okay?"

Tears threaten to erupt, and I can't breathe around the lump in my throat.

I swallow a few times. "Yeah, I just... he didn't hurt me, if that's what you thought."

"You saw that bastard shoot Kai in the face," he growls. "He fucking made you watch."

I sit up straight. "Did you see it?"

"No, I just... heard."

The tequila is messing with my brain.

"Do you want to come home?" he asks. "Because we will storm the castle and bring you back. I promise you that. Just say—"

"Shut up, boy," my father's voice cuts him off. "Give me the phone."

My stomach flips.

"Gemma," Dad says. "Are you okay?"

"I'm alive," I say bitterly.

"We recovered Kai's body after they left," he tells me. He's never opened up about family business before. For years, I've gained my knowledge from eavesdropping. Opportunities. This is different. His whole tone is different. "Do you know if he said anything?"

I grit my teeth. Even to *him*, Kai's death is transactional.

"He didn't in front of me," I say. "But Aiden didn't question him, either."

My father grunts.

"Are you having a funeral?" I blurt out. "I want to be there. Please."

I imagine them in the den, toasting Kai's life. Or maybe at one of the bars to accommodate more people. Funerals and celebrations of life are part of the job—that's what my brother used to say. We both had to attend as Lawrence West's children. Most often, neither of us were familiar with the person who'd died. Distant cousins, men brought into the family. People who controlled the periphery, sometimes. It didn't matter. They were mourned the same way.

Colin or Kai would always stick close to me, keeping my hand in theirs. As I got older, I realized it was because they didn't fully trust anyone. And it was never long before the room dissolved into drunk adults.

Mom's funeral was like that. Grand but hushed. It wasn't

until later, at the restaurant down the street from our Manhattan home, that people broke loose. The stories stuck with me, reiterating that she was a good person. No one made me leave early from that, and everyone stayed quiet about the eighteen-year-old getting drunk at the bar.

Kai's will be the same, and I'm desperate to be part of it. To share my stories, tell my family how much Colin and I loved him. To salute his life and reminisce after burying him.

But Dad clears his throat, and my stomach twists.

"You're a soldier now, Gemma. You were the moment you volunteered." *To be the bait*, is what he doesn't tack on. "We're having a funeral, yes. One I doubt you'll attend. You're behind enemy lines, kid. I know this was tough—it was a poorly executed plan by my son." This is pointed at Colin. "Don't show them anything. But if you do, let it be anger."

I brush at my cheeks. My fingers come away wet.

He makes sense. I can't afford to be a wreck in front of the enemy. I clear my throat to speak—to agree, disagree, I'm not sure what will come out of my mouth.

"We've talked too long on an open line," he finally says. "Be strong."

The call drops.

I stare down at it in shock. He just hung up on me. And the weight of being the sacrifice slams into me. I let out a small huff, as if the force of realization is a real punch to my gut, and curl over myself. I focus on my ragged breaths.

Something shifts inside me. If I can't go to Kai's funeral, if I can't pay my respects, then I'll just... do it now. Here.

There are planters around the edge of the space, overflowing with flowers. I didn't notice them before, but I hoist myself up and go to one. I snatch flowers out, filling my grip with a makeshift bouquet. I circle the area, plucking random blooms. At one, I shove the now-off phone into the soil.

I don't know if it'll survive the weather, or being watered, but I can't be found with it.

Once I'm satisfied with the amount of flowers, I go back to my seat at the pool and drop my legs in. I toss the flowers into the water, one at a time, and then slide in after them.

I slip under the water, releasing most of the air in my lungs so I sink faster. My heels hit the smooth bottom first, then my ass. I open my eyes and look up.

It's the first time I've looked *up* since I walked outside.

The floating flowers block out the moon. They're shadows dancing on the gentle waves. I wrap my arms around my knees and open my mouth, shrieking out the rest of my air. It hits my ears in a muffled way, but it still hurts. Everything hurts.

A little piece of me died along with my cousin. It was my first taste of violent death. Never mind Wilder DeSantis's death. Or my mother in the hospital, either.

I shoot to the surface, breaking through my little tribute to Kai, and tread in the center of the pool. I heave in big gulps of air, then finally roll onto my back and let the water hold me. My chest still feels tight. At one point, I swim to the edge and retrieve the tequila. I lift myself half out of the water, up on one elbow.

The world goes blurry the next minute.

Too much, Gem.

I let out a sigh and hold on to the bottle, keeping my thumb over the top and returning to my previous position of floating on my back. I lost the cap somewhere on the journey up here.

I spread my arms out, the water caressing me, and shiver. The flower heads nudge at my skin. It's just enough peace for me to close my eyes. It must be the alcohol, or just a profound sense of exhaustion, because the world fades away.

I'm not sure how long I stay like that, quietly grieving Kai in my own way. I drift in and out of consciousness until hands wrap around my neck, forcing me under the water.

CHAPTER 13

Aiden

I step off the elevator and unbutton the top of my shirt. It's been a stressful evening in more ways than one, and I'm grateful to be back. Even if this isn't my normal space, it's still home enough. Besides, Gemma is here.

I don't like that she's a comfort. My mind kept straying back to her while I asked the medical examiner about Jimmy, questions that made him twitch with unease. In the end, all the information Sam and I digested was enough to give me a raging headache.

We didn't linger. With the bullet fragment in hand, Sam went off to have a chat with one of the local gunrunners. We let them live in peace because their business doesn't affect us, but I've noticed their involvement in more and more. It's not enough to squash them, not when we could use them to our advantage.

If the small-time gang isn't willing to talk, then we'll have issues.

Key in hand, I push it into the lock—and the whole door swings inward.

I step back quickly, drawing my gun. I palm the door and press gently, and it opens on silent hinges. I sweep through the apartment methodically, clearing every inch of space before venturing upstairs.

Empty.

I even go so far as checking under the bed, in the cabinets below the sink, the supply closet next to the front door.

Nothing. No Gemma. No Cat. No freaking *note*, either.

Still, I don't react. I can't, not yet. Not until I find her.

I yank the door open again and realize the latch has been taped over. Easy way to avoid getting locked out if someone doesn't have a key.

The box of food I ordered is off to the side. A lazy server didn't even attempt to get inside, then? Or did they listen to the part of my instructions about not talking to anyone, but disregard the rest?

I blow out a breath. If Gemma did this, it means she left voluntarily. But... with or without Catrina?

And then my heart lurches, and I grit my teeth.

I keep my gun at my side and bypass the elevator—it's too slow—going straight for the stairs. I go down a level and pound on Cat and Sam's door until she opens it. Her face pales.

"Where is she?" I growl.

She shakes her head. "I left her—"

"You were supposed to be *watching* her!" I yell.

She flinches, but I barely register it. I'll deal with my disobedient cousin later, when this churning in my gut eases. I swing around and go back to the stairs, this time heading up. My attention snags on the *roof access* plaque, and I bolt. Of course she'd go to the roof.

My heart is in my throat when I reach the door. One single shoe is in the stairwell, beside the door. I stare at it for a moment. The door doesn't lock—a safety mechanism—but she must not have known that.

I shove it open and stride out, ready to give her hell.

But what I'm *not* expecting is to see one of my lowlife cousins in the pool. He moves quietly toward Gemma, who floats with her eyes closed in the center of the water. My cousin reaches out and puts his hands on her neck, shoving her under.

Her body seems to collapse in, her feet kicking the air for a split second. She hits him with something, but it doesn't do any good. She's got no leverage.

He's drowning her.

And I. See. Red.

I let out a roar and race toward them, raising my gun. He glances over his shoulder at me. His eyes are wild, but his expression is quickly overtaken by fear.

And he has my fiancée under the water still, even as she scrambles at his forearms.

"Mistake." I squeeze the trigger three times. My first shot tears through his throat, but the second and third are cleaner, directly through his forehead. He falls toward Gemma in slow motion, and I leap into the water, swimming hard to get to them.

I yank him off her and drag her up.

She comes fighting, her eyes screwed shut. Her nails cut into my cheeks, my neck, before I capture her wrists and pin them between us. I pull her close, urging her to wrap her legs around me. We're on the slant between the shallow and deep end, water up to my chest.

"Shh, shh," I whisper, hugging her tightly. I want her closer than is physically possible. "You're okay."

Her eyes crack open, and she blinks at me for a long, slow moment. I wonder if she's debating whether or not to trust me, but my doubt vanishes when relief crosses her face. She latches on to me, her now free arms winding around my shoulders.

I back us away from the man, cupping the back of her head so she doesn't twist around and see him. He's facedown, blood mixing with the water around him. She burrows her face into my neck and clings to me.

"Did he hurt you?"

"Besides trying to drown me?" Her hot breath hits my skin. She leans back and stares into my eyes. "No. Just drunk."

I stare at her a beat, then sniff.

Tequila.

She gives me a doe-eyed look of pure innocence, and I sigh. Before I can stop her, she wiggles from my grasp and plants her feet, glancing back at the man. I expect... I don't know, disgust or horror. Instead, she's curious.

She wades toward him and rolls him over. She can't seem to tear her gaze away from the bullet holes in his forehead, the open gash in his throat.

"Did you hesitate?" She doesn't look away until I don't answer, then she glances over her shoulder. The tequila seems to be making her bold tonight. Unafraid, even though her voice is hoarse.

I narrow my eyes. "No."

"Why not? You know who he is, right?"

"A cousin," I acknowledge. "I couldn't tell you his name. Don't really give a fuck."

She grunts.

I grab her arm and guide her back toward me. "He was trying to drown you. Do you know why?"

"Because of who I am?"

I help her out of the pool and follow. My clothes are drenched, my shoes waterlogged. She shivers in her black bralette and panties. I spot her dress and shoes on the cement not far away. There's a chest of towels in the far corner, but I ignore that and focus on her.

"Because of the mall. We lost men, and I can't control everything—not when I haven't had the chance to tell them you're off limits. Do you see why I didn't want you to leave?" I grasp her chin and resist the urge to shake her.

Fuck me, I was *worried*. I was going to be delicate around her. Her cousin shot in front of her, and now another life attempt. He didn't even put up a fight—not against me, anyway. He had a one-minded mission to kill her.

And I have to wonder how many other people will try.

Keeping her locked up has clearly backfired. I should've had her out in a show of force—insinuated that I didn't give a fuck what anyone else thought. But I hid her away and thought no one would notice.

"You got lucky playing cards with Cat. *This* could've happened there, and who would've helped you in a room full of people who want you gone? Catrina has never had to fight for her life, let alone someone else's."

She lifts her hand and traces my lips. "And now I have. But I'm okay."

"You're so far from okay."

Why did I take her in the first place?

Why didn't I just shoot her in the head—like I would've done to any West who tried to stop me from finding my brother's killer—and call it a day?

She's nothing but an innocent girl.

And I've wanted her for myself for three years.

"I just don't want to feel," she mumbles, staggering back and grabbing her clothes. She can barely walk.

I retrieve my gun and shove it into the waistband of my pants, then cross the space to where she's crouched. I scoop her up, and she squeaks. Her arms come around my neck.

"What are you doing?" Her voice is hollow.

"Making sure you don't fall down the stairs," I say.

She opens the door for us, and we travel back to my floor in relative silence. Relative because every so often, her breathing hitches like she's trying to keep herself under control. My anger flares again, and I kick the door open to our apartment.

I don't bother removing the tape—if anyone wants to come in here, I'll shoot first and ask questions later. I don't put her down until we're in the bathroom, and I set her on the counter.

"This is familiar," she mutters.

I agree.

She doesn't have much to strip off this time, but then something catches my eye. The red prints of the fucker upstairs. I nudge her chin up to get a better look, and it isn't until her hand lands on my chest that I realize I've been making a low noise.

"He's dead," she says.

"I wish I didn't kill him," I admit.

Her eyes widen.

But I'm not done. "Because that fucker died way too fast."

She surprises me by laughing. Her composure quickly dissolves into hysterical giggles. She howls, rocking back and forth, and tears stream down her face. I brush her wet hair off her shoulder and slide the strap of her bra down her arm.

She goes silent just as quickly as the laugher came on.

"What are you going to do?" Her voice is husky.

And the way she stares at me, it's like she's daring me to do something. *Anything*. I'd love nothing more than to bury my face between her legs—or my cock. To rip that sweet virginity from her like a fucking caveman.

"What do you want, princess?"

Gemma smirks and leans forward, pressing her lips to mine. She pulls away—probably misinterpreting my surprise as disinterest—but I don't let her get far. I capture the back of her head and bring her forward, meeting halfway.

We slam together. Not just the kiss, but her whole body is flush against me. I'm hard in an instant.

I lick the seam of her lips, and she parts them, letting my tongue take ownership of her mouth. I taste the flavor of tequila. Her hands go to the waistband of my pants, undoing the button and dragging the zipper down.

Fuck.

She shoves the material off my hips and palms my length. I groan into her mouth as she wraps her fingers around me, sliding her hand up and down. I continue dragging her bra down and run my thumb over her pebbled nipple. I tear my lips from hers and work my way down her jaw, her throat. I nip her skin, the chlorine water a sharp taste, and she arches into me.

I try to erase the marks that asshole left on her skin. Claim her with my teeth.

She tilts her head and lets out a soft groan, squeezing my cock.

"Aiden," she whispers. "I want to feel you." Her thighs tighten around my hips, and only the scrap of material covering her pussy separates us.

She releases my erection and urges me closer, her legs locking around me.

She's drunk, some part of my mind screams. It echoes around, nagging at me, until I pull away. All the way away.

I turn sharply to catch my breath.

"What—"

"I won't fuck you when you couldn't even walk straight." I can't believe I'm saying that—but I want her present. I want her plainly, not hiding behind liquor. Hiding from trauma. The thought slips through me like poison.

She scoffs. "Since when have you ever been the bigger person?"

I wheel back around. "Don't test me."

She hops off the counter and steps toward me. "I don't want the bigger person. I want whatever you can give me."

I reach over and flick on the shower, leaving it icy cold, and lift her into it.

She screeches, but I step out of the way of her swinging hands. I glance at myself in the mirror and note the scratches she managed to inflict. A long gouge in my cheek, a few more on my neck.

It brings a smile to my lips.

Steam billows out of the shower now, heating the room.

I shuck off the rest of my clothes and wait for her to finish moping, but the other side of the frosted glass is silent. Eventually, she peeks around the wall and meets my eyes.

"Are you joining me?" She bites her lip.

My control is already fraying, so I nod once and step forward. The hot water is heaven on my chilled skin, and Gemma steps aside so I can be in the direct stream. She leans against the tiles, arms banded around her stomach.

"What are you thinking?"

She shrugs.

I squint at her.

"I just want to know where this is going," she murmurs. "How the hell you're going to convince your family not to murder me any time your back is turned. Why you even told your father you'd marry me..."

Ah. A plan has seeded in my mind, but I'm not ready to reveal it to her. "You'll see."

She sighs and inches up next to me. "In that case..." She twists the water to the coldest setting and rushes out of the shower.

It goes from pleasantly hot to ice in an instant, and it effectively kills my hard-on. I swear, forcing the showerhead away.

"Payback, DeSantis," she calls, disappearing with a towel into the bedroom.

I smirk. "You'll need to do a lot worse than that, sweetheart."

CHAPTER 14
Gemma

I wake up plastered to Aiden. Again.

A lump forms in my throat at how close we are. The night before, it was his choice. His arm over my waist, his legs tangled with mine. But this is very clearly *me*. My head is tucked under his chin, my hand splayed out on his chest. My leg... my leg is thrown over his, and I don't have to look to know he's hard. His erection presses against my thigh.

My core pulses, and before I fully realize what I'm doing, I roll my hips. I only had one experience of *almost* giving myself an orgasm. My core brushes his thigh, but the relief isn't enough. I've been turned on since last night, when he abruptly stopped touching me.

God, that was definitely liquor-induced stupidity.

I bite my lip and, when he doesn't move, I do it again. The friction just drives my need higher.

"Let me help you." His voice is soft and low with sleep. He doesn't wait for my answer, though, just slides his hand down my side. His fingers maneuver beneath my sleep shorts and panties and finds my clit.

I squeeze my eyes shut, but I can't help the hand on his

chest. I dig my fingernails into his skin, and he huffs under his breath.

His fingers continue on their path. "You're soaked."

I shift again, into his palm. His touch is too light. Teasing. I don't know what I want, but this isn't it.

"Look at me," he orders.

I lean back so I can meet his hot gaze. Any trace of sleep that clung to either of us a moment ago burns away. He doesn't duck down and kiss me, but instead watches as he pushes a finger inside me.

I gasp.

He strokes a spot deep inside me that I didn't know existed. One I had never bothered to truly find on my own. But he knows, and within moments I'm a mess. I just want *more*, but all I have is the feel of his finger.

"Do you regret last night?" He raises his eyebrow.

I blush. I don't feel a headache—probably compliments of the lack of sugar—and I remember most of it. My makeshift funeral, being drunk, the man who tried to kill me. In the same day Aiden murdered my cousin, he saves me from another DeSantis.

I hate that it puts his life in perspective: he doesn't really give a shit who he kills.

But kissing him, driven purely by desire? Touching *him*? It's no different than kneeling before him and opening my mouth, is it?

"No." It comes out on a whimper.

He withdraws his hand, and I think that maybe I said the wrong thing. Am I supposed to regret it?

He suddenly rolls us so I'm pinned under him. He sits back and peels off my shorts and panties. I let him move me, dropping the light fabric to the floor, and then return between my legs. He only wears shorts, his erection tenting it. I let myself look, my cheeks getting even hotter.

Aiden parts my knees wider, placing a kiss on the inner corner. He works his way up, a trail of kisses. Anticipation rushes through me, but nerves, too.

His breath hits my core, and I jerk.

He meets my eyes, giving me a devious grin before descending. His tongue sweeps up my center, but I barely register that before he latches on to my clit. I gasp, arching, as electric shocks flood through me. I bury my hands in his hair, but even I can't tell if I'm trying to shove him away or press him closer.

The same but different.

The first time, my ass cheeks were sore from his palm, and anger lit us up. Anger and lust. It's different in the hazy, warm light of morning. I scrape my nails along his scalp, and he hums against my skin.

There. It's just a flicker. An instinct that something greater is coming. A tightening in my abdomen.

His thumb skates over my clit then down. He inserts two fingers inside me and sucks hard on my clit. His fingers curl. His teeth find my sensitive bud, and it's the pain mixed with intense pleasure that pushes me over the edge. An orgasm explodes over me, and I scream. He takes it all, until my muscles relax and I sag back into the bed. I release his hair, and slowly, the mortification takes over.

He kisses his way up my body, and I watch him through heavy lidded eyes. He pushes my shirt higher, exposing my breasts.

I should stop this, but... I'll be selfish for once.

He bites my breast. I gasp and drag him up. Our lips meet, parting, and I taste myself on his tongue. It should be weird, but it isn't. I deepen the kiss and wind my arms around his neck.

"If you don't want me to fuck you right now, we should stop," he mutters, barely leaning away.

I open my eyes and stare into his. The implication is clear.

"I'm trying to be the good guy." He grunts.

I hesitate.

He sighs, dropping his forehead to my chest. I accept his body weight on top of me. It's grounding, and I wrap my legs around his hips again. Dangerous, given how easily he could disregard my non-verbal *no*.

"I need a cold shower." He lifts off of me.

I pull my t-shirt back into place and watch him go.

The water turns on, and I press my fingers to my lips. There's a part of me that must still be in shock, because it takes too long for me to register what just happened. And what I *wanted* to happen.

I step into the bathroom and peel off my shirt, dropping it behind me. Aiden makes a small noise when I step into the shower with him and drop to my knees.

"Gemma."

His cock bobs in front of me. The water is lukewarm, and he blocks the spray with his body. It mists over his shoulder, and droplets cling to my hair, my eyelashes. I open my mouth, licking his shaft, and look up.

He groans and braces his arm on the wall. I use my hand to help, guiding him into my mouth. It's all an experiment, but I'm beginning to love the little noises he makes when I do certain things. And he's letting me keep the control.

I take him deeper and swirl my tongue. He thrusts into my mouth, his hips jerking. I open my mouth wider, relaxing into the movement. Tears prick the backs of my eyes. I cup his balls, and he lets out a guttural groan.

"Fuck, Gemma." His fingers knot in my hair, holding me as he takes over. "I'm going to come."

I suck hard, and he shouts. His hot seed fills my mouth, and I swallow around him. I don't know what it is about him, but I'm impossibly turned on. He pulls away, and his gaze sweeps down me. My pussy clenches in response.

He hauls me up and slams his lips to mine, backing me against the wall. He nips my lips, my tongue. I give it back to him, my teeth scraping his lower lip, then step back. I wish we could stay like this, but...

There's a line I'm not willing to cross.

Not yet.

So I shift toward the door and let myself out.

Alone in the closet, I let out a ragged sigh. I sweep my damp hair back and braid it. It falls straight down the center of my back. The closet is a mess, but I make quick work ripping off tags from new items—brought in yesterday by Sam and left on top of the dresser in here—and hanging them in a corner gives me an ounce of satisfaction.

I dress quietly, a better bra and panties, another dress. This one is short-sleeved, navy blue, and hugs my curves. It felt sexier when I tried it on at the mall, and it got Cat's seal of approval.

Thinking of her, I wince. We ended things badly yesterday, and after what happened in the pool... I can't afford to make more enemies. Not when I'm living in the hornet's nest.

Aiden steps into the closet in nothing more than a towel. I eye his abs, then the scratches on his neck and cheek. I did that to him.

He winks at me and drops the towel, and my face burns. Call me crazy, but it's a different vibe seeing him naked *not* sexually. More intimate? Either way, I can't deny my flaming hot cheeks. I scoot past him, out the door, and his laugh follows me into the bathroom.

We make breakfast in silence and sit on the couch. We're closer than we might've been even yesterday. I don't know what's shifted between us, except the realization that Aiden will do anything to keep me alive.

Maybe not safe, but... not dead, either.

If anything, I should be strong in my resolve that the DeSantises need to be stopped. And on some level, I still agree with that. They've had it out for my family for years.

The hate runs deep.

But he's saved my life more than once. That's what's confusing me. What was once black and white—West vs. DeSantis, good vs. evil—is now murky gray.

"Eat," he prods. "You're staring like you've never seen toast before."

I scoff. If there's one thing I *don't* have a problem doing, it's eating. Sure, chocolate chip banana pancakes sound better than toast, but I'm not about to be picky. In no time, we're both done, left only to finish our coffees.

It's quiet in here.

When I was alone, I tried not to dwell in the silence. I kept the television on low to be a steady hum of noise. I didn't want to go insane.

But now I glance at Aiden and think I might be there, anyway. What else would explain not one, but multiple orgasms at his hands... and tongue? Or how desperately I wanted his dick in my mouth just moments ago?

The front door opens.

Aiden bolts to his feet, withdrawing a gun before I can even blink. When he registers who it is, he lowers it and grunts.

I crane around him, then wish I hadn't.

Jameson strides in like he owns the place, casting a look around in disdain. "Care to explain?"

Aiden hauls me up by my arm. "Wait for me upstairs."

"No, I think she stays." Jameson's brow lowers. "I'm sure she's caught up in the mess."

Aiden keeps me behind him. I don't mind—his father terrifies me. Not just how he acts, which, yes, is intimidating.

It's more how he sees me. In his eyes, I'm disposable. Just another sacrifice in his war.

We edge out into open space, the stairs to the bedroom behind us.

"Did you think I wouldn't find out my son shot Leon?" Jameson sneers. "You're smarter than that."

"I didn't really give a fuck if you found out," Aiden says. "I told you Gemma is mine."

His father makes a noise of disgust in the back of his throat. "And, what, you caught them together? I suggested she be put with the other girls—it's not too late to change your mind. A just punishment for a West, don't you think?" His eyes gleam. "I can only imagine what her family would think."

I shudder, and Aiden squeezes my arm. His hand slides down until he finds mine, then squeezes again. I lace our fingers together and take a deep breath, then step out next to Aiden. Not fully—I'm not an idiot—but enough to see his father.

"Ah, there's the little mouse." Jameson's gaze bores holes into my forehead. "Come to rise to your own defense?"

"No need," Aiden grits out. He's practically vibrating with fury. "If anyone lays a hand on Gemma, I will kill them. No questions asked. Last night was just a message I'm happy to repeat."

His father eyes us like he's never seen anything like it. I don't know what we are, but I feel more firmly planted on Aiden's side than I did before. Even if it's tenuous. Even if it's temporary.

"Now, with all due respect," Aiden adds. "Get the fuck out."

Jameson laughs. "Fine. I cleaned up your mess, by the way. And we have a lunch date. Be ready at noon."

"With who?" Aiden demands.

His father just smiles and heads to the door. He pauses

and runs his finger over the latch. Aiden removed the tape before we fell asleep, but maybe there's a residue? He implies that he knows what I did.

"I'm getting a deadbolt," Aiden says as soon as the door clicks shut. "Fucker. Of course he has a key."

I cover my eyes with my free hand. "You just left him there?"

He gently pulls my hand away. "No. I had my guys clean it up. He was spewing bullshit, like usual."

My eyes widen. "You have guys?"

He chuckles and ducks down, kissing my temple. "Yes, princess. More than just cousins. Friends. Guys who have my back."

Over his father's? But apparently, he has a leak in his ship if Jameson found out.

"You're capable of friendship?"

His chuckle turns into a full-blown laugh. "Some would say no."

"Well, I need to meet them. Find out everything I can about you." I yank my hand free, stepping back and clearing my throat. For a moment, it seemed like we were getting too close. My stomach flips, and I raise my hands to my hot cheeks.

"You'll meet them soon enough." He nods to himself and turns away. "Apparently, we have a lunch date that can't be missed. Until then, I have to do some work. Should I send Cat up?"

I wince.

He eyes me but doesn't say anything. If Cat already told him... she must've had a good excuse, right? To not be watching me?

"I'll be fine on my own. I won't leave."

He sighs. "Yeah, I don't believe that. You're coming with me."

My stomach twists again.

"Do you have an office?" I don't need prompting this time to follow him out. We wait for the elevator, and I pick invisible lint off my dress.

"I do. One I don't use too much, but today..." He sighs. "Luca handles permits, but with *him* gone, it's fallen to me. All sorts of things on my plate. I just need to get shit done for the next few hours."

I cross my arms. "And what will I do? Stare at you?"

"Maybe."

Turns out, Aiden's office is nearly on top of Jameson's on the twentieth floor. The latter man gives me a withering glare when we pass his open door, but Aiden doesn't release my hand. Once we're locked in his office, he motions for me to go to the chair in front of his desk.

I can't, though, because I'm fixated on the view.

Finally, I'm pretty sure this faces south. We're higher up than the restaurant. Aiden's question the first night he brought me here resurfaces: *Do you recognize this?* It's been nagging at me. I squint at the building across from us.

It doesn't look too familiar... but all I can see is the glass reflecting our building back at us. It's a bright morning, the sun already high. I glance back at Aiden, who watches me with an inscrutable expression.

He circles his desk and sits, pulling a laptop from one of the drawers and opening it. I go back to staring out the window as he types, and I wonder who, exactly, my would-be killer was.

Jameson mentioned his name was Leon, but that doesn't explain anything. And to get access to the roof, he was obviously someone familiar with the building. A DeSantis, even. In my drunken state, I didn't question it. I didn't question *Aiden*.

I'm an idiot.

Someone tried to kill me, and in the moment, I accepted it. I mean, yes, I fought, but I didn't *question* the attempt. I know they all hate me. He said it was from the mall, but it's deeper than that. More ingrained. They see me and think I'm... what? Going to pick up an automatic weapon and shoot them all down?

I twist back to my so-called fiancé. The marks on his cheek and neck are still red, standing out against his tan skin. I approach and sit on the corner of his desk, right next to his laptop, and cross my arms.

A corner of his lips tips up, but his focus stays on the screen.

I automatically shiver. What is it about him? Why is he a magnet for me?

His phone rings, and he sighs. He answers it, bringing it to his ear, and his other hand inches up my leg.

I consider shoving him away, but I'm curious as to what he'll do.

"Just spit it out," he demands. "I've got shit to do."

The person on the other line squawks. I can't make out the words, just the tone. Frantic, it seems. I part my knees, letting Aiden's hand creep under the hem of my dress. He traces the edge of my panties and meets my eyes.

I open my mouth, but he shakes his head. There's a devilish glint to his gaze, and he pushes the fabric aside. I bite my lip and grab the edge of the desk. My back arches when his finger dips inside me. My muscles tighten.

He makes a noise of affirmation on the phone and answers them. Something about... I don't know. Permits, territory. My heart pounds. There's an extra level of danger here, in a semi-public space.

He rubs my clit with his wet fingers while their conversation drones on. All I can do is try not to combust. He pinches the phone between his ear and shoulder, his other hand now free. He grabs my ankle, spreading my legs wider. My dress rides up, and he smirks.

"Don't make a noise," he mouths.

Like I'd risk anyone hearing me.

But a second later, he pinches my clit, and I gasp, my sudden climax taking me by surprise. I hadn't known I was riding that edge, so close I could burst, until he pried it out of me. He thrusts his fingers back inside me, prolonging my pleasure. I clench around him and throw my head back. I bite my lip to keep any sound from escaping.

"I'll call you back," he says to whoever's on the other end of the line.

He tosses his phone down and rises, looming over me. He pulls out of me and licks me off his fingers. My breath hitches. I'm captivated by the way his tongue sweeps around his fingers. His hand cups the back of my neck, and his thumb traces my throat. My pulse hammers.

His kiss this time is sweeter. Not quite gentle, not when his teeth nip my lower lip, then travel down my jaw. Each nip reels me farther into his web.

"On your knees, princess," he says in my ear. "If I can't claim your cunt, I'll fuck your mouth."

My eyes widen, but I do as he asks. I slip off the desk and almost fall to my knees next to his chair. He sits back down, and my gaze goes to his pants. I undo his belt, the button and zipper of his pants, and free his erection.

I lick my lips.

In truth?

I've dreamed about doing this. Taking his cock in my mouth. It started when I was seventeen and accidentally walked in on Kai watching porn. The girl on the screen was enthusiastically sucking the guy off, and I was transfixed for a moment. Up until then? Totally innocent.

Kai then noticed I was there and threw something at me, effectively scaring me away.

But... I went to bed that night thinking about Aiden.

Ridiculous, really, that he implanted himself in my mind and stuck. We knew each other for one day. A blip in time. But all that dreaming... maybe it was just easing the way for *this* to happen. And even though I've done it before, heat curls low in my abdomen.

"Gemma." His hoarse voice brings me back to the present. "Tell me what you want."

"I want to suck your cock." I shake my head once. That isn't quite right. "No, I want you to fuck my mouth. Choke me with it. Don't go easy on me, if that's what you think I need. Not like this morning."

I rise on my knees and lean forward, taking him into my mouth.

He groans, and his fingers fist through my hair. I swirl my tongue around his head, smearing the bead of pre-cum on my lips. His hand on the back of my head is light, guiding—but not for long. His grip tightens, almost painfully, and he jacks his hips up. I gag and relax my throat. My eyes burn, and my core clenches, as he does exactly what I asked. And I just kneel there and take it. He slides in and out of my mouth, and I imagine that's what he'll do to my pussy when I'm ready. The thought only turns me on more.

I should be afraid of this. But I'm not.

"Fuck, baby, I'm going to come."

My core pulses at those words, and he spills into my throat. I swallow around him and sit back on my haunches. I touch my swollen lips and meet his gaze.

He yanks me up onto his lap and kisses me. His tongue slips into my mouth, and I feel claimed all over again.

"What was that for?" I ask, pulling away.

He smirks. "Do I need a reason to kiss you?"

I shrug and glance away.

He grabs my chin, pulling my gaze back to him.

"Don't do that," he says. "Don't put up more walls. We're making progress."

I shift. "We're not making progress. This has just been..."

"A reprieve." He exhales. "You'll let me all the way in one day, princess. Body, mind, and soul."

I shudder and rise, putting distance between us. I already feel vulnerable, like he's managed to flay me open. I'm sleeping with the enemy—just sleeping, I guess, but still. I should feel gross. But in the back of my mind, I have to ask: what else did I think was going to happen?

Aiden wasn't going to kill me.

Even if he should've.

He tucks himself back into his pants and goes back to work. I sit back down on the window ledge and stare outside. The sun on my face is a nice contrast to the air-conditioning.

Someone knocks on the door. I keep my eyes on the tiny people below, ants on the sidewalk, and ignore when Aiden unlocks it and ushers someone in.

"Jack," Aiden says. "This is Gemma."

I twist around and frown. I don't bother to tell him we've met—if Aiden had stuck around at the card game, he would've seen Jack. And my husband-to-be would probably put much more space between us.

Not that Aiden has anything to worry about... just because he's a possessive asshole.

But maybe Jack realizes this, too. His eyes are wide, locked on mine. He must've truly believed I was Cat's friend, not Aiden's... plaything. Fiancée. Hostage. There's a flash of hurt in his expression, but he masks it.

He strides forward and reaches out his hand to shake mine.

I start, and Aiden's jaw clenches.

"Jack." He regains his friend's attention and motions for him to sit. "What did you have to discuss?"

I can't hide my relief when Jack turns around and sinks into the chair across from Aiden's desk. Aiden takes my hand, guiding me away from the window and back onto his lap. His hand lands on my hip, and his thumb circles the spot.

Jack eyes us. "Sam took me to meet with Rubert."

What kind of name is Rubert?

Still, I keep my mouth shut.

"And?" Aiden prods.

"They've made a deal with the..." Jack's sweating. He rubs at his forehead, the back of his neck. His gaze is suddenly glued to the desk instead of us.

"Jack," Aiden warns.

"Lawrence," Jack mutters, wincing. "Rubert and Lawrence made a deal already."

I try to straighten, not really understanding the half of it, but his hand keeps me down.

"Stop," he hisses.

"If it's my father—"

"Give us a minute, Jack," Aiden says evenly.

He scrambles up, more than eager to be out of the office. The door slams behind him, and it's just us again. This time, though, the air is thick with tension. I can't figure it out, though. It's like trying to solve a puzzle blindfolded, and no one will tell me anything.

I shove off Aiden and stride back to the window. "What's going on?"

"Your father is in the weapon smuggling business."

I cross my arms and refuse to face him. The truth of the matter is that I *knew* that. I never was invited to be part of the business side of the family, but... well, how is a girl supposed to prove herself if every door is shut?

My answer: break the fucking windows.

"Rubert is a small time gunrunner. An asshole who's been supplying New Jersey, little shipments down south. Nothing too crazy. We were leaving them alone."

I whirl around, contemplating him. "But something changed."

"A dead customs officer killed by an unusual bullet."

It clicks. The accusation.

"You think Rubert's guys supplied the gun that killed your customs officer. The one who must've been killed when your shipment was stolen." I glare at him. "I already told you, we don't have shit to do with construction, or whatever else was in your stupid container."

He doesn't believe me.

Why would he?

"We didn't kill him," I grit out. Some days it seems I'll die defending my family—but I refuse to believe we had anything to do with this. I'm reminded of the politician in their pocket, the one with the power to approve—or deny—any construction permit they might need. How interesting it is that no one seems to give a shit about the councilwoman.

Amelie did. Or her mother, the owner of that stupid magazine. They might've seen through the watered-down crap the DeSantis family is feeding everyone.

He stalks forward and wraps his hand around my throat, shoving me back against the window. "*You* didn't, Gemma. You can't speak for your whole family."

I sneer through my fear. "Fuck you."

His face darkens. "Try me."

We stay locked in our stare-off until his office door opens. Aiden's lips press together. Without releasing me, he pulls his gun and points it at the door.

"Leave," he orders.

"Charming," Jameson drawls.

I wince. Second time in one day—I wonder if this is

normal, or if it's a new record for them? I've never hated anyone more than I do Aiden's father, but this is a timely intervention. I'm pretty sure Aiden was a few seconds away from going caveman on me. Although, even just thinking of that, my body tingles.

Aiden watches my reaction and smirks. But he releases me and slides his gun back into the holster, shielding me from his father while I discreetly tug my dress farther down my legs.

"We're going to be late." Jameson is positively gleeful.

Dread pools in my stomach. If he's happy about this lunch, something truly awful must be about to happen.

CHAPTER 15

Gemma

We climb into Aiden's car. It's a dark-blue Porsche that he seems particularly eager to drive. I eye him, then the light-pink air freshener hanging from the mirror.

"Whose car is this?"

Jameson is in the vehicle ahead of us. He doesn't do much driving, apparently, preferring armored SUVs and bodyguards. We follow him onto the street. I suspect neither of us knows where we're going, so Aiden sticks close to his father's black vehicle.

"Aiden, come on." I flick the air freshener. "Unless you're into pink..."

"It's Amelie's." He chuckles. "She said I should drive it occasionally to keep it running."

"Uh-huh."

He grins. "I'll show you her speed on the open road. But fair warning, it's addictive."

I snort. "We need to survive this lunch first. Any ideas?"

His smile drops. "No. But whoever it is, stay alert. My

father always has a plan... unfortunately, I think Wilder's death has unhinged him a bit."

Great.

We cross into Queens, one of the few boroughs not covered by West or DeSantis shadows. It used to be considered a safe place. Neutral ground. But now... I have a feeling all bets are off.

We finally roll to a stop at an Italian restaurant. I don't recognize it—I can't say the last time I've been in Queens, actually—but my stomach flips. Something about the area seems familiar. Like another punch of déjà vu.

I hop out of the car and wait for Aiden at the curb. He circles around, taking my hand in his and leading me toward his waiting father. The three of us enter. The hostess doesn't ask for a name, just glances at Jameson and blushes. She leads us through the empty restaurant to a table in the back.

My heart skids to a stop.

Dad rises from his seat, narrowing his eyes at Jameson. His gaze flicks to me, taking me in, then returns to the danger in the room.

"Sit," Jameson orders Aiden and me.

I take the chair across from my father, trying to shoot questions at him with my eyes. Jameson and Aiden claim the two remaining seats facing each other. We sit in silence for a moment.

It's only a matter of time before all hell breaks loose—Jameson is smug, there's no denying it. But neither Dad nor Aiden open their mouth to ask what's going on, so I do it.

"What is this?" I ask.

Jameson snags my wrist, yanking it across the table and twisting it so my forearm is exposed. Aiden and my father do great statue impersonations, but I catch the worry on Aiden's face. Dad has had far too long to control his reactions, but Aiden... Aiden's never had *me*.

"I called this meeting because I sense a bluff," Jameson explains. "So we're going to play a little game of Russian roulette."

I narrow my eyes, refusing to feel scared in front of him. "What's the bluff?"

"That you and Aiden are in love."

"Well, that's a fucking riot, because we're *not.*" I yank at my wrist. "Aiden's possessive. He takes what he wants—and he wanted me. You should understand that."

"You misunderstood my compliance, DeSantis," Dad says. "The whole point of my attendance was so you *wouldn't* harm my daughter."

I shudder. Why would Dad even trust him?

"Let her go," Aiden says. His hand is under the table, but the audible *click* of his gun's safety switching off is unmistakable. He glares holes in his dad's face.

"Aiden and Gemma will be married in three days, or I'll slit her throat." Jameson is unbothered by the threat his son makes and runs his finger up my arm, tracing the bluish purple vein under my pale skin. "Aren't you happy for our blushing bride-to-be?"

"Thrilled," Dad answers. He leans back and crosses his arms. "Release her."

Jameson does, and I retract my arm quickly, cradling it in my lap. Aiden's foot presses down on top of mine, gently. Like he's checking to see if I'm okay—which doesn't make sense, because he's the reason we're in this position.

If he had killed me, then this war wouldn't be happening. This *lunch* wouldn't be happening. But now, apparently Jameson is going to take my life himself.

"Three days," Jameson repeats. "I don't think you need to attend, Lawrence. After all, we're not under the guise of a truce. Not when your boys are killing mine in the streets."

I bite my tongue to control my reaction. I've been stuck in

the ivory tower while our families spill blood across Manhattan?

Dad lifts his chin. "A war is a war, DeSantis. Did you not expect casualties on your side?"

Aiden grimaces. "We're here to celebrate, right?"

"No," Dad and Jameson both snap.

I get the impression that this is a standoff between the three of them, and I'm powerless to stop it. Who would stop Jameson from killing my father in front of us?

Not a damn person.

I glance around, trying to find Dad's angle. Why he'd come here without backup. Why he'd show at all.

But Aiden presses harder on my foot, and I swivel back around.

Food we didn't order is brought over—a salad with grilled salmon for me, sandwiches for the rest of them. My mouth waters at the smell of the fries on Aiden's plate.

"That's all," Jameson says to the waitress. "Leave."

She gives him a wild nod and rushes away. The kitchen door swings shut behind her. The whole restaurant has cleared out—not just empty of patrons, which it was when we arrived, but the staff, as well.

"Eat," he orders his son.

Aiden leans back in his chair and places his gun on the table, facing his father. It sits between him and I—it would be so easy to grab it and just *end* this. Until Jameson's gaze flickers over me, and he smiles.

"Would you like to know what I found when researching you, Gemma?"

Not particularly.

"You went through a lot of tutors for the last few years of high school. Before your little incident that required home-schooling, you were... adventurous."

Was I? I would disagree. A lot of students called me the

quiet one. It was Colin who was outgoing, dragging me straight into trouble. Kai supervised.

My stomach twists at the thought of my fallen cousin. Dad's here, looking perfectly normal, when I know the whole family is probably anything but that. I wonder if most of the women are still out of the city.

"It's no surprise that you'd take on this new adventure," Jameson adds.

Dad goes still.

That should be my first clue that things are about to go wrong.

"What the fuck are you talking about?" Aiden snaps.

"She's a spy."

We all stop, and I stare at Aiden with wide eyes. I want to say I'm not, to automatically deny it, but... I still am loyal to my family. It's just that he's given me *nothing*. I've seen the inside of Aiden's bland apartment, a restaurant, the roof, and a handful of other places.

To spy would be to actively seek intel and pass it along... right?

Jameson stands and circles behind me, lowering his face until it's right next to mine. The knife comes up under my chin and touches my throat.

"Didn't we prove ourselves?" I grit out.

"As I said—I'm calling your bluff." His hot breath touches my cheek as he turns his head slightly toward me. "You have two men who would do anything to save you, Gemma. But what would you do to save just one?"

My blood runs cold. "What?"

"Pick one to save, Gemma, or it's your blood that will stain this table red. You're a survivalist. Adventurous. So, who do you want to save?"

"Stop this," Aiden demands.

His father laughs in my ear. "He's afraid you won't pick

him—or maybe he's worried that I'll disregard your choice." He grabs my hair and tilts my head to the side.

"You'd kill your son?" I dig my nails into my palms and try not to panic. I can't seem to focus clearly on either Aiden or my father. "If I chose to save Dad, you'd hurt Aiden?"

He shrugs and digs the knife deeper into my throat. "Let's find out. This is a game of roulette, after all. Is that your choice?"

"Gemma," Dad snaps.

My gaze flies to him.

He stares at me, and... it feels like goodbye. I just saw the same look on Kai's face before Aiden shot him yesterday. There's pity in there, too, because he knows the guilt will keep me from ever finding peace. But Aiden can't be safe, either, not with Luca still in the mix. I can only imagine how far Jameson would go to bring back the last son, ensuring the DeSantis line continues.

Lawrence West has always been an enemy to them.

There's acceptance in Dad's eyes, and he nods like he knows the way my thoughts run. We could've spent more time together. He could've taught me better. Mom always kept me away from that life, but then she died. Everything else fell to the wayside, anyway.

There's no time to stall. I get the sense that refusing to pick one of them would just prompt Jameson to drag the knife across my throat, and he's waiting for that moment. Dad clearly doesn't think I should say his name, even though my heart aches for it.

"Not enough motivation?" Jameson whispers. He drops the knife, and it clatters on the floor.

It's the only noise for a handful of seconds, then silence. Aiden and Dad's eyes bore into me. Jameson pulls out his gun, running the muzzle down my temple. I suck in a breath.

"Are you trying to figure out if I'd shoot my own son?" He

aims at Aiden's head. His other hand, in my hair, directs my attention to my fiancé. "I like that you're trying to figure me out. You're a smart little girl—but don't try to outsmart me."

He squeezes the trigger.

I scream, lurching against his hold.

But Aiden isn't dead. He sits there with a shocked expression, and a hole in the sleeve of his shirt. Blood seeps out—the graze might've been accidental, but I still can't tell.

"Please don't kill him," I babble. The violence has me talking, and as much as I want to reel my voice in... I've lost control. "Don't kill them. Please. There's no point—"

Jameson presses the muzzle into my throat. It sears my skin, and tears spill down my cheeks.

"Jesus, women talk a lot," he mutters. "Back to the question at hand, Gemma. Will you pick the son you claim not to love? Or old daddy dearest?"

I choke on a sob.

"It's okay, Gemma," Dad says.

"Shut *up*, West." Jameson shoves me forward, pressing the hot metal into the back of my head. "Choose who to save. Right now, or I'll blow your brains out."

I don't think about my decision. I can't. Instead, I go with my gut—and what Dad seems to be screaming at me to do. "I pick Aiden."

Jameson laughs, ripping my head back. "Consider this your wedding present, then. Don't say I never gave you anything."

He points his firearm at Dad, and my heart lurches.

He squeezes the trigger.

Not once or twice. He empties the rest of his magazine into Dad's chest.

I don't scream this time. I can't breathe, I can't move—not with his fist still curled in my hair and his other arm framing me in. Dad falls backwards in his chair, toppling to the floor. There's hot liquid on my face, and I blink a few times.

This has to be a dream.

A fucked-up nightmare.

But then Jameson DeSantis yanks me up by my hair. He drags me around the table and throws me to my father's side. I take one look at Dad's pale face and force my gaze away.

Jameson plucks his napkin from the table and dunks it into a water glass. He dabs at his face and holsters his gun. His attention goes from me to his son, who hasn't moved.

"Clean this up," he says. "You know what will happen if the Wests discover this."

And then he just... leaves.

We let my father's murderer stroll out the door.

I turn back to Dad. His shirt is shredded, blood pooling under his body on the tile. My hand hovers over his chest, and I'm caught between wanting to salvage... salvage *what?*

His chest moves slightly, his gaze sliding to mine.

I grab his hand and press closer. "Oh my god. Dad. I'm so sorry. I don't—"

"It's okay." Blood comes up on his lips with his words, staining his lips red. "Love you."

"Aiden. We have to save him." I clutch Dad's hands. My vision goes blurry, wet drops falling on his shirt. I don't know what to do. Put pressure on the wounds? "Call an ambulance."

Aiden kneels on the other side of my father, but he makes no move for his phone.

"Please, Aiden, I can't lose him. *Help* me." My plea comes too late. "Dad. Hang in there. We're getting you help, it'll be okay. I'll make sure Colin is okay."

Dad squeezes my hand once, maybe acknowledging my words. Maybe it's a spasm. Our skin is slick with blood. He closes his eyes and exhales, and he doesn't take another breath.

I don't know where we go when we die, but I hope it's somewhere peaceful.

I sniffle, running the back of my hand under my nose. Mom died only eighteen months ago—but I was spared *seeing* it. This... this is so much worse. Worse than Aiden shooting the DeSantis who wanted me dead. Worse than Kai's death. I open my mouth and babble apologies to my father for every little thing I can think of—every atrocity, in my mind, that I committed.

The grief wells up in my chest, but just like in the apartment, none of it wants to come out. I lean forward and press my forehead to Dad's bloody shoulder. My disbelief almost hurts—it seems to bang around my skull, waiting for absorption. But what I don't feel is sadness. Not yet, anyway.

Someone comes in the restaurant. Minutes later, hours. I don't know. Hands haul me back, onto a lap. Aiden. He's on the floor, too, and he clutches me to him. I watch as two men come over and lay out plastic, then lift my father's body onto it. They begin to roll it, and my stomach heaves.

"Stop—"

"Let them," Aiden says in my ear.

I wriggle free and bolt to my feet. I step in front of one of them and shoot him my worst glare. "I said stop!"

"You heard her," Aiden says.

The one I stand before and my fiancé exchange glances, then the latter motions for them to put down the plastic.

"Give me your phone." I hold out my hand to Aiden.

He rises and watches me carefully, then retrieves his cell from his pocket.

I snatch it before he second-guesses himself and swipe it open. I dial Colin's number and pace away from them. I focus on my anger toward Jameson—that's the only thing from keeping me together.

"What?" Colin snaps.

I suppress my irritation. "Colin."

"Gemma? What—"

"Do you know where Dad went today?"

He's silent for a moment, then audibly swallows. "He got a call from Jameson DeSantis. The lunatic wanted a meeting. He threatened to kill you if he didn't show."

"Why did you let him go alone?" I whisper. I immediately shake my head. "I'm sorry. I don't know why I asked you that."

He makes a frustrated noise. "Tell me what's going on. I swear, Gemma, I tried to follow him. He lost me going into Manhattan this morning. Where is he?"

"He's dead." I close my eyes.

Aiden's arms wrap around my waist, pulling me back into his chest. "Gemma."

"Listen to me, Colin. You cannot act out against the DeSantises for this." I want to reach through the phone and make sure he's hearing me. First Kai, now Dad. How many hits can our family take? "Let me handle this."

"Jameson," Colin grunts. "That bastard killed our father? Did you see it?"

I suck my lower lip between my teeth. I refuse to tell him the details—it'll just incite him.

Aiden takes the phone from my hand. "Colin, it's Aiden."

He strides away from me before I can even open my mouth to protest.

"Miss?" One of the guys who had moved Dad's body comes over with a towel. "Sorry we're meeting under these circumstances. I'm Ford."

I nod once.

"I thought you might like to clean up…" He extends the towel.

I take it and stare down at my hands. "One towel might

not be enough." I glance up. "Are you with Aiden or the family?"

"Aiden," Ford says firmly. "My boys and I don't see eye to eye with the DeSantises. We leave them to their business."

"Then clean up their mess," I finish.

His brows draw together. "For what it's worth, no one's ever outright targeted Lawrence before—especially not Jameson. We couldn't have predicted..."

"Maybe it was because we showed up at Wilder's funeral." I scrub at my hands, staining the white fabric pink. "He probably took it as a direct insult. Then my engagement to Aiden... I don't know. That bastard deserves to die for this."

Ford nods.

Aiden returns and loops his arm around my shoulders, holding me into his side. I go willingly and let him hold some of my body weight.

"What did you say to Colin?" I ask him.

"I explained what happened. We'll go meet him and return your father's body."

I exhale. "He'll try to kill you."

"He won't. Temporary truce for bereavement." He kisses my temple. "Come on."

He leads me through the kitchen and out the back door, where an SUV idles. He guides me into the passenger seat. I stare straight ahead, and he leans over me, buckling me in, and then closes my door. A moment later, Ford and his partner carry out the plastic-wrapped body. They slide it... *him* into the backseat. They shake Aiden's hand and return to the restaurant.

"Where are we meeting Colin?" My stomach twists.

"Outside the city." Aiden buckles and starts the car, the navigates out onto the quiet street. "I know better than to ask how you are, but..."

"I'm fine."

He glances at me.

It's a bright, warm afternoon, like New York just wants to send another *fuck you* to my emotions. I shove everything down and focus on the road ahead of me.

The DeSantises have taken *everything* from me—and I suddenly wonder if Aiden wants to finish us off by killing Colin. I grit my teeth against the sudden surge of panic.

"Don't hurt my brother," I say, turning and grabbing Aiden's leg. "I know you think he killed Wilder, but please. And I know begging doesn't help anything. It's pointless—"

His hand covers mine. "I meant what I said. We have a truce. For the afternoon."

I nod shakily and try to withdraw, but his grip tightens. I roll my eyes and stop trying to fight it. He relaxes as soon as I do.

"How did your mother die?" he asks me.

I flinch. Dig my fingers into his thigh. "Why are you asking me?"

"You never talked about it. No one does." He shrugs. "And I don't want you retreating into your head."

I inhale sharply. It's exactly what *I* want, though: to hide away in my mind so I can stop processing this awful week. But instead, I open my mouth and talk. I don't start with her death. I start with her life with Dad. Me. Colin.

CHAPTER 16
Aiden

She sits beside me, her hand on my leg, and tells me stories about her family. I don't know any other time she'd volunteer this information, but we've opened the floodgates, and it all comes pouring out.

Family trips, the way her mother and father would swing her as they went down the sidewalk, riding horses through Central Park. They got as close to normal as a Mafia family could get, it sounded like. She lived carefree until the day I came along.

After that, everything changed. I can hear it in her voice.

No more spur-of-the-moment outings. Guards followed them through Central Park, accompanied them on trips. They moved Gemma to their Manhattan home and homeschooled her. She was the vulnerable one, she guessed. While Colin got to learn how to shoot and fight—her cousin, Kai, taking him under his wing—she was pushed toward academia.

And probably, eventually, marriage.

I didn't expect to care—I didn't expect to be hanging on her words. I wanted her to talk so she wouldn't slip into a numb shock—talking keeps her present. But it's grounded me in the present, too. Here we are, driving toward Hillshire County, and I want to know everything. I crave it.

"You don't want to hear about her death," she says quietly.

"I do."

It was eighteen months ago. She was already gone and buried by the time the newspapers got wind of it. A nice little tribute in the *New York Times*, a professional photo of her from her wedding. It gathered a lot of sympathy around the city. Even if she wasn't very well known, she was a West.

Her impact was clear by her last name alone.

Faith West just had something about her.

"I met her once, before the feud between our families got out of control," I tell her.

Gemma stares blankly ahead. Maybe she knows this already, or maybe she's trying to hide her surprise.

"I was pretty young. I don't know why my parents insisted on bringing Wilder and I to a charity dinner. She caught me drawing on the underside of a table with a permanent marker." I chuckle at the memory of her lifting the tablecloth, trying to suppress her grin. "She treated me with kindness."

"She had an aneurysm," Gemma says. "Doctors said she was born with it, and it was a ticking time bomb in her head waiting to go off. I was with my tutor, and Colin was out. I don't know where Dad was. By the time we realized it wasn't just a migraine she could sleep off, it was too late."

She quickly brushes a tear from her cheek.

"It wouldn't have been my play to take away your remaining parent." I feel... agonized over it. And I don't know why. Lawrence West has been a thorn in our family's side for years. His family loves to cause trouble. Yet the guilt rides through me in steady waves.

"You just sat there." Her voice is barely audible. "You sat there and let Jameson hold a knife to my throat, then a gun. A *gun*, and you had one on the table. You threatened him with it, and he still did exactly what he wanted."

She twists to face me.

"Would you have killed him?"

I grit my teeth. "I *should've* killed him."

"You should have."

"He won't lay a finger on you again." I will her to believe me. I managed to keep a lid on my anger—it wouldn't have done any good in that room. But now, it seems to flash through my blood like lightning.

He threatened me, too. Shot at me.

The worst part? I couldn't tell if he was serious. If my own father would kill me just to spite Gemma or Lawrence. If she had chosen her father, he might've killed me and then her, just to make the Wests suffer.

I pull onto a narrow road. It leads to one of the forests surrounding Hillshire County. We pass the main parking area for hikers and campers. Soon, it turns to gravel. Then just a two-track path through the grass.

We park on the side, and I kill the engine, tipping my head back. I tilt so I can see her. "Can I ask you something?"

She huffs, but I take it for a *yes*.

"Will you go back with Colin?"

I've surprised her. She yanks her hand off my leg and curls into herself. Her reaction isn't what I expect—I guess this, too, is a test.

"You'd let me?"

I scowl. "No."

"Then, no," she answers. "I'm not stupid."

I highly doubt it's stupidity keeping her with me. She knows we've still been searching for Colin—who has remained elusive over the past two months. I never lied to her about stopping.

Something else keeps her at my side.

Another car coming up behind us catches my attention. I watch it in the mirror until it stops next to us, and Colin rolls down the passenger window. He doesn't even spare me a glance, just leans forward to see Gemma.

His face pales.

Yeah, there's still a good amount of blood on her dress. Her face and neck are covered in spatter, too. She cleaned her hands off, but sometimes blood just sticks.

"You okay, Gem?"

She nods and shoves her door open. Colin meets her in the front of our cars, wrapping her in a hug. She tucks her head to his chest.

I unholster my gun and keep it low. If he so much as moves back toward his car with her...

But then he releases her and looks her up and down.

I step out of the car, slamming my door.

Colin West and I have a lot more in common than he might think. Both not entirely sure we were meant to run our families, but suddenly having that thrust upon us. Because I have no doubt he's going to return home and pull his family up by the straps.

And then they'll come for us—harder than they've already been. The attacks my father has been keeping under wraps will explode into the daylight. No more one-offs. We're trucking toward a fully fledged war, and honestly? I'm not sure if the Wests will survive it.

My father is ruthless. And he has a plan.

He always has a plan.

Colin eyes my gun and laughs. "Really, DeSantis? Don't trust me?"

"Just making sure you don't manhandle my girl." I narrow my eyes.

His gaze swings between me and Gemma. "Your girl?"

"She's mine," I affirm. I try to keep the growl from my

voice, but it's damn near impossible. I don't bother telling him the only reason we're both alive is because she picked me over her father—some things should be kept to ourselves. But I file away that information for later, in case he turns out to be a bigger dick than Lawrence.

Colin sighs. "Fine. I hoped..."

"He'd still come after you," she whispers. "Dad didn't kill Wilder. We both know that. He was just waiting for a moment to murder him."

I grip my gun tighter. She's right—he didn't kill Wilder. My brother's murderer stands right in front of me. But what did my father gain from Lawrence's death? That's the question I need to chase down.

Because he has a plan, and it will backfire on Gemma and me if we're not careful.

Gemma steps in front of him and walks toward me. I glare over her shoulder at her brother, tempted as hell to just... get it over with. Pull the trigger. It would be no less than the vengeance my brother deserves.

She puts her hand on my wrist.

"Trust me." She keeps tugging until I meet her gaze. "We're just going to keep shedding blood until there's no one left. Stop this."

Her side has seen two deaths inside a week, more, if the situation on the street is as bad as I'm starting to think. There's pain in her eyes, and I've never wanted to be a DeSantis less than I do right now.

I nod and holster my firearm. "Wait in the car, princess."

She heaves a sigh. This is the part where Colin and I do the dirty work. We can't make him disappear, but Colin can deliver his body to the morgue. Everything can be done quietly. No fuss. No disaster. Some money will change hands, but the police won't be called. Just like when Faith, Gemma's mom, died and the hospital staff was bribed to keep things quiet for a month.

Gemma sits rigidly in the front seat as Colin and I get his trunk open, laying down another layer of protective plastic. Then we lift Lawrence's body out of the car and carry him the short distance, sliding him inside.

Colin and I pause next to each other, staring down at the body.

"I'm sorry," I offer. It's the only apology he'll get from me, because the rest of them? I don't feel remorse. Not for killing his cousin or whoever else has crossed our path since I learned how to shoot. I wanted the apology to lessen the guilt. Gemma was completely right: I didn't stop it. I couldn't.

The family would turn on me if I killed Jameson without a good reason—and saving Lawrence West would *not* have been a good reason. I grit my teeth and force myself to keep a straight face. I should just drive south and not stop.

Abandon ship.

"Get my sister out of here," he says, like a mind reader. "It's the least you can do. Remove her from the line of fire—because it's coming for you."

I nod. "I'll consider it."

He eyes me. "I'm going to say goodbye to her."

"Okay."

He steps around me.

"We're getting married in three days." I guess I can't let him have the last word. Or... I'm trying to lessen the guilt. *Again*.

He freezes. His shoulders bunch up, like he's trying to contain himself.

"So declared by my father," I finish.

He whirls around. "You hurt her, I'll make it my mission to end you."

I roll my eyes, but I don't bother to make promises. This sort of life is destined to hurt us one way or another.

"I expect nothing less, West." At least someone is looking out for Gemma's best interests. Because it definitely isn't anyone in my family.

He goes to say goodbye to Gemma, and I slam his trunk closed.

"Rest in peace, old man."

CHAPTER 17
Gemma

Cat waits for us outside Aiden's apartment. Her eyes widen when she sees us step off the elevator. My legs buckled on the way in, and Aiden has yet to put me down. I study her but don't lift my head from his chest.

This day has been bone-crushingly exhausting, and it's catching up to me. Eventually, my numbness will break and all I'll be able to do is *feel*. I'm dreading that moment.

Aiden tosses Cat his key, and she unlocks the door for us.

She follows us inside. "Gemma, I—"

"This is really not a good time," Aiden says.

I sigh. We're due a conversation, and it may as well be now. "Put me down, please."

His gaze meets mine, and all I can see in his eyes is concern. Little broken Gemma. Still, he sets me on my feet and stands so close behind me, I can feel his body heat. He winds his arms around my waist and pulls me against him.

I guess this will happen in front of him.

"I'm sorry," Cat blurts out.

"Me, too." I step out of his embrace and grab her hands. "I wasn't thinking."

"No, *I* wasn't thinking. I should've just been there for you. It's fucked-up what happened, and I… I let myself just fall back on how I was raised. But it isn't right." Her gaze rises and drills into Aiden. "Can you give us a minute?"

"Fine." He strides upstairs.

We don't speak again until the bedroom door swings shut.

"I shouldn't have said Kai was a soldier," she whispers.

Following her lead, I keep my voice hushed, too. "It gets worse."

She leads me over to the kitchen and wets one of the dish towels. "I take it your lunch was… not pleasant, judging from the blood on your face."

My gaze hardens. "Jameson killed my father in front of Aiden and me."

She drops the towel. When she bends down to retrieve it, she stays down. I crouch beside her and grip her arm.

"Cat."

"This family is so fucked-up." She squeezes her eyes shut. "Please tell me your father… he did something to deserve it, right? Attacked Aiden? Tried to take you back?"

My laugh is hollow. "No."

"Sam told me Aiden was the one who killed your cousin," she whispers. "And I just feel so much worse about everything. How are you still standing?"

"I don't know." I choke on a laugh, sliding backward to sit on the floor beside her. "Someone tried to kill me."

"What?"

"After you left yesterday, I went up to the roof. I guess someone in the family wasn't thrilled that I was around, because he tried to drown me."

Cat grabs my hands. "I… don't understand. *You* haven't done anything."

"I exist." I lift my chin and meet Aiden's gaze over her shoulder. I didn't hear him come down, but his presence is enough to prickle awareness across my skin "Sometimes existing is enough of an offense."

"I thought it was," Aiden says. "But it isn't."

He comes over and helps me to my feet, then Cat.

She hands him the damp towel and steps back. "I'm going to go. But tomorrow, or maybe the day after—you and me, okay?"

I nod. Now that we're back on the same page, some of my guilt eases. She makes a hasty exit, and I turn carefully in Aiden's arms.

"You're a mess." He runs his hands down my arms.

"That's harsh."

He finds the hidden zipper under my arm and drags it down, pushing the blue fabric off my shoulders. It slips past my hips and pools at my feet. My breath hitches when he lifts me onto the counter.

"It's not harsh when you're covered in blood," he says quietly.

"This is just becoming our new thing."

He cracks a smile. "Well, glad to see you're adjusting to Mafia life."

I snort. "I've been in the life."

"Not to this degree." He cups my cheek.

"Are you going to take me away from this place?" I put my hand over his.

He begins to clean my face, my neck. I even have blood on my legs that he sweeps the wet cloth over. He rinses it a few times, warming the water before returning it to my skin. I let him maneuver me like a doll because I'm fascinated with the way he's staring at me.

"I want to," he says. "I've never wanted anything more."

Heat curls in my belly, and I'm struck with desire. Foolish, really, to want someone when I should run screaming in the opposite direction.

"Aiden?" I whisper.

He meets my gaze.

"Make me forget?" I don't wait for his answer—or his protesting. I put my hands on either side of his head and pull him closer. I kiss him softly, hesitantly. This isn't me—I'm not the instigator. Well, I am today. I press deeper, willing him to react.

He inhales and straightens, tossing the towel into the sink. His hands slide up my back, drawing me closer, and our kiss deepens. When our tongues meet, sparks ricochet behind my eyelids. I wrap my arms around his neck and lock my ankles behind him.

Aiden picks me up off the counter and carries me upstairs, managing to do it without breaking our kiss. He drops me on the bed and tugs my shoes off. Then my panties. Bra. By now, I can't deny that I like him. Saying I don't would just be foolish. It's my heart's problem that I *do* like him so much, and my brain's biggest dilemma.

I lie on the bed completely naked, and he's still fully dressed. I lick my lips, waiting for his next move. In this area, I'm still unsure. A naïve girl.

He removes his t-shirt. I sit up and yank his pants down, his briefs going with them, and I stare for a moment at his erect cock. It bobs in my face, and I automatically reach for it. *This*... this I can do. I don't know why it grounds me so much, having something familiar between us.

He groans when I wrap my lips around his head, pumping him with my hand.

His fingers tangle in my hair, and I take him as far into my mouth as I can. His tip hits the back of my throat. I swirl my tongue, sucking hard, until his grip on the back of my head smarts.

It only goes on for a few moments, then he pulls me up to him. His kiss is bruising. My teeth snag his lower lip, biting hard enough to draw blood, and he growls.

He guides me back to the bed and hovers over me. His cock is lined up at my entrance, and my breath catches. His eyes bore into mine, then he leans down and kisses my cheek. Jaw. Little nips that send electricity flooding through me. His fingers find my clit. I gasp, clawing his shoulders.

"Say what you want, princess," he demands, pushing two fingers into me.

"I want you to fuck me." I arch into his fingers. "I want... *you*. Aiden, please."

He lowers himself, latching on to my nipple. He works magic on my clit, and there's too much sensation. My orgasm shatters over me, and a metallic taste fills my mouth when Aiden's lips return to mine.

Before I've come down from my high, he thrusts into me.

I gasp and grip his neck. He isn't gentle about it—I don't want gentle. I didn't ask for lovemaking, and he doesn't give that to me. If he had, I don't think I would be able to go through with it. This is more about how I don't want to feel everything else brewing behind the lust.

He rocks forward, fully seated inside me, and the sensation is a mixture of pain and a foreign type of pleasure. I want both.

He doesn't wait for me to be okay with it. He pulls out and slams back in, and I scream. I leave marks on his skin as he fucks me, hitting a deep spot inside me. I raise my hips to meet him and turn my face into his neck. I kiss his jaw, down his throat. My teeth catch his skin, biting hard enough to draw blood again.

I feel like a wild animal.

"Fuck," he growls. "You feel so fucking good."

He withdraws suddenly, and I yelp. But he isn't done—far

from it, I'd guess. He flips me onto my stomach and yanks my hips up. My ass is in the air, my face pressed to the mattress.

"Hold on," he says.

I reach forward and curl my fingers around the mattress lip just as he thrusts back into me. I scream again, my body unaccustomed to his cock. My eyes shut of their own accord. He pounds into me, and all I can do is hold on. He reaches around and finds my clit again.

"Aiden," I moan.

"Fuck, Gemma," he replies. His pace increases. The whole bed shakes, the frame slamming into the wall.

He slaps my ass with his free hand, and I tip over the edge. It's different this time, continuing on and on. My pussy clenches around him, and he lets out a roar before stilling inside me.

Holy shit.

He immediately slides out and rolls me onto my back, coming down on top of me. His gaze takes in my expression, and his finger slides inside me again.

"Do you feel my cum inside you?"

Panic whips through me. "Aiden—"

He massages it into my clit, and his lips attack mine in a kiss that makes my heart skip. His other hand glides up my side, stopping just under my breast. I shudder and shove at his wrist. Two orgasms have me feeling weak—another isn't possible.

"You're perfect. Another day, I'll wrench three from you." His lips move on mine, our breath mingling. He lays on his side and takes me with him, wrapping his arms around me. "But we need to clean you up."

I hum, satiated and exhausted. My mind has already skipped to pregnancy, even though I've had the implant for almost six months. Obviously, I haven't had a need for it, and there's a part of my brain that doubts it actually works. As if he can read my mind, his thumb brushes over the inside of my upper arm.

I go still. "How did you know that was there?"

He smirks. "I know more about you than you'd think. Like, that you got your wisdom teeth out a year ago. They got infected. And then you had a hospital scare—was it your appendix?"

My jaw drops. "You're a fully fledged stalker."

"I knew I wanted you, Gemma West." He runs his thumb over the implant in a lazy way. "I won't apologize for it. Although this will have to come out at some point."

"I—"

"I want you pregnant," he says, his gaze dropping to my stomach. "Someday."

There's nothing I can say to that. Nothing I want to say besides an automatic denial... yet, I keep my mouth shut. My face is probably a shade of red close to a tomato, but he doesn't seem to mind. He hops out of bed and helps me up. My core aches, and for the first time I look down. Blood is smeared between my legs, mixing with his cum as it seeps out.

I shiver.

"You okay?"

I eye him. He's gloriously naked, the twisting skull tattoo on his chest capturing my attention. He's handsome enough that it hurts. There are new scratches on his neck and chest that stand out against the old ones, but he doesn't seem to mind. In fact, he seems rather smug.

And he's waiting for an answer.

"It's just a lot of blood for one day," I manage.

He nods. "You're right."

"Music to my ears."

The tub sits in its own corner, away from the standing shower we usually use. It's a mammoth, and for a split second,

I wonder why I didn't take advantage of it before. Maybe it's because I hate baths—*oh, yeah, that's why*.

I balk when he pulls the stopper and the basin fills. But he ignores my look, and it fills in record time. He tests the water, then steps in. He's got a firm grip on my wrist, keeping me from running, but I don't expect him to sit.

"What are you doing?" I ask.

"Enjoying your discomfort." He grins. "Get in."

"I..."

"Get in the water, Gemma."

"Fine." I step in and lower myself. The water is almost too hot, but my muscles immediately loosen. I let out a sigh and lean back opposite him.

He takes my foot into his lap, and I jerk back. The water sloshes, but he holds fast. I stare at him as he rubs the ball of my foot, massaging it. I can't stop staring, even when I relax farther into the water. It's up to my chin now, and I can't say I have much worry.

I close my eyes.

My mouth and nose dip below the water, and I surge up with a gasp.

"Come here." His expression is filled with light. Not happiness, but something closer to contentment. In this moment, anyway.

I glare at him like it's *his* fault I almost drowned. But he seems nonplussed, and in fact, there's a spark in his gaze. Like he can see through me. Sex has *not* broken down all our barriers. I refuse to believe in the cliché that sex would make us closer.

Physically, yes. Emotionally? Not so much.

Still, I crawl into his embrace and wrap my arms around his neck.

His kiss on the corner of my lips is tender.

"We can't keep doing this, you know," I whisper.

"Which part?"

"The sweet part."

He scoffs. "My temporary truce extends to you, too, princess. That's what today is."

He turns me until my back is against his front. I rest my head on his shoulder and close my eyes again, trusting that he'll keep me above the water. He grabs a washcloth and squirts soap onto it, then sweeps it down my front. He cleans my thighs, my stomach and chest. The cloth swirls under and around my breasts.

"When will it end?" The truce, I mean, although I'm not sure I have to clarify it to him.

He's quiet.

"Aiden," I prod.

"After."

I suck my lower lip between my teeth and chew on it. *After what?* I want to ask, but on some deeper level, I don't want to know. This sort of affection is completely new—and I *like* it. I like the way I feel when he touches me like this.

Something must be wrong with my brain.

But maybe we'll go back to normal tomorrow. We'll get up and remember that we're supposed to be on two different sides of this war.

My family...

My throat closes.

What must they be doing right now? Did Colin tell them?

"Breathe," Aiden says in my ear.

"I can't." There's a weight on my chest, and a yawning black hole in front of me. I'm on the edge of it, teetering above the dark. My parents are gone—snuffed out. My cousin.

It's just Colin and me left. Yes, there are others. Aunts, my uncle in prison, others who fight for the West name. We're a relatively small blood family. It was our connections and lifelong friendships that secured us.

Will they drift away now that Dad is gone?

Has Jameson succeeded in decimating the Wests?

Aiden holds me upright and rubs my back. I cover my face with my hands and let out a ragged exhale.

"I'm fine," I argue. "No need to pity the orphaned princess."

"I'm not pitying you."

I turn back, ready to reply, but his expression is sincere. He's concerned, maybe. I don't know because I've never seen that look in his eye before. The one where he might just set the whole world on fire because I'm upset.

"I imagine I'll catch a lot of pity in the next few weeks," I mutter. "Not by your family, of course, but... others. Outside."

"Maybe."

"What do you think the headlines will read? '*Head of the West family found dead*' or maybe '*West orphan married to her family's enemy*?' I can't decide." I need to focus on something else. Anything else.

I press my lips to his. He obliges me for a moment, then breaks away and tips his forehead down to rest against mine.

"We'll keep you busy tomorrow." He lifts me out of the water and puts me on my feet, then wraps me in a towel. He takes his time rubbing it over my body.

"I can do it." I try to take it from him.

"I know." But he doesn't stop until he's dried every inch of my skin, then he quickly towels himself off and leads me to bed.

I pause at the blood spot on the sheet.

He rolls his eyes and removes the offending sheet, folding it and setting it aside. He throws on a new one, then drags the comforter back into place and motions for me to get into bed.

It's barely evening. But I don't complain when he slides in behind me and hits the button on the sheer version of the shades, rolling them up. We stare out the windows at the sunset. The sky is a mix of cobalt blue and bright orange.

My stomach growls.

Aiden's lips touch my shoulder, and he types something one-handed on his phone. I raise my eyebrows but say nothing. I don't have anything left to give—and that includes curiosity. We stay in our embrace until his cell chimes again.

"Stay here," he orders.

He rises and grabs his pants from the floor, sliding them on mid-motion.

I watch his ass as he rounds the corner and disappears downstairs.

His cell is right there, and I've never wanted to grab it more. I could call Colin again, see if he's okay. At least check on him, at any rate. But before I can make that decision, Aiden returns with a bag and two beers.

"The restaurant made us grilled cheeses," he says.

I smile.

"And the beers are to take the edge off."

He climbs back into bed beside me and pops the tops off the bottles. I examine mine before I take a sip, immediately wincing. It's not the greatest taste. Bitter. But it's cold, and I'm suddenly parched. I swallow another big mouthful, then set it aside.

He opens the containers and hands me one.

We dig in, and my hunger roars out of nowhere. I eat quickly and then lean back, nursing the beer. Aiden finishes his and wipes his mouth, leaning back, too.

"I had the opposite reaction when Mom died," I tell him.

He squeezes my leg.

"When she..." I swallow. "I was a mess. I screamed and cried. Threw stuff. Threatened to burn down the hospital." I choke on my laugh, remembering my father's appalled face.

"For seventeen years, I followed their rules. And suddenly I was acting like..."

He presses a featherlight kiss to my shoulder.

"My brother was the quiet one. I don't know if he was in shock, or I was just being too loud for him to have his own reaction. I do know that in the last eighteen months, he's dove deeper into the family businesses. The legal ones," I add, eyeing Aiden. "He took over some of the clubs we own. He got quiet, but I thought he was okay."

I stare at the ceiling.

"But now I feel like the quiet one, and I don't think I'm okay. If I'm like this now... why did Colin suffer in silence back then?"

Aiden brushes a tear from my cheek. "He might've been talking to other people. Blowing off steam... productively."

I turn to him suddenly. "Your mom. Where is she?"

"Out of the picture."

I bite my lip. Aiden narrows his eyes until I release it, and he sweeps his thumb over my mouth. He's been much more touchy lately.

I don't have a problem with it. *That must be my trauma talking.*

He doesn't say anything else, instead pulling me onto his lap. I curl my arm around his neck and meet his gaze.

"What?" I ask.

"I'm just wondering how you're not falling apart." He raises one shoulder. "You're tougher than I gave you credit for, princess."

I roll my eyes. "Just keep me distracted. But honestly? I could sleep for a week and not come up for air."

"Okay."

He clears off the takeout containers and returns to the room with bottles of water. I take a few gulps and then hunker down, facing the windows again.

He fits in behind me, draping his arm across my bare stomach. Was it just a few days ago that I didn't want him to touch me? In our temporary truce, I seem to crave his touch. I would crawl inside his skin if he let me.

But no—he's dealing with death, too. There's a pang in my chest at that realization. *Foolish girl.* I've been so fixated on my own issues that I never stopped to think about Aiden's grief. Only his revenge. Only how it affected me.

I stifle a sob, covering my mouth with my hand.

I'm horrified at my own selfishness.

He misinterprets me, though. He kisses my bare shoulder, up my neck, until my body relaxes back against him. I let out a slow breath of tension, but I can't get the words out. What would I say? An apology for Wilder?

It doesn't seem good enough.

"Sleep," he whispers.

I close my eyes and follow his command. And I'll deal with death tomorrow.

CHAPTER 18

Gemma

I wake alone and promptly burst into tears. There was a handful of seconds right before this moment where I *forgot* that Dad was gone. And then the tragedy of it came rushing back like a tidal wave, knocking down my defenses before I could fortify myself.

It takes me too long to get ahold of myself, and I sit up. My eyes hurt.

Aiden isn't here, but he kept the shades pulled down for me. Even still, the sky seems gloomy.

I reach over and hit the button. The shades retract, revealing rain-streaked windows. A flash of lightning illuminates the sky, followed quickly by a crack of thunder.

Suddenly, the mattress is too... comfortable. I can't sit here while my father is on a cold slab in the county morgue. I slide out of bed and grab Aiden's shirt from the floor. Once it's on, I crawl toward the window and lean against it. My forehead touches the cold glass.

Goosebumps break out down my arms, and I pull my legs up to my chest.

"You were crying in your sleep," Aiden says.

I glance over my shoulder. He's in the doorway with two mugs. His black t-shirt clings to his chest, and the gray sweatpants make my stomach swoop. He seems to absorb my mental state in one look, because his expression softens.

"It's okay to cry." He sets one mug in front of me, then sits beside me. He leans his back against the window. "I used to cry. Right after Mom left. In the shower, where my brothers couldn't hear me."

I reach out and take his hand.

"Wilder was upset, but it wasn't a strong emotion. It's like he knew exactly why she left and just used it to fortify himself. Luca—well, she wasn't his mother. I was the only one who really seemed to give a shit."

"Where did she go?" I whisper. I don't want him to stop talking.

"Away." He shrugs. "Doesn't matter. I moved on from crying to hitting things."

I flip his hand over and brush his knuckles. The bruising has faded a little, the split skin scabbed over. "Then killing?"

"That came later."

I lift the mug and take a sip, surprised by the chocolate flavor on my tongue.

"Hot chocolate?"

He nods.

I take another sip. It's almost too hot to drink, but it warms me from the inside out. "I haven't had hot chocolate in years."

"I figured. It's a good comfort drink." He watches me with a steady gaze. "What's your plan?"

"For what?"

He just raises his eyebrow.

I sigh and shift, eyeing the dark clouds. "Maybe just stay up here all day." I turn back to him. "You could distract me."

"I could. Are you sore?"

I shift and contemplate that. I should, at the very least, be hesitant about sleeping with the enemy again. It's like my brain has been put on pause and my cunt is in charge. And the pain will ground me in reality… or prolong my fictional world where everyone I love is still alive and happy.

His gaze darkens. We both set our mugs aside, and I pivot onto my knees. He doesn't object when I climb onto his lap, straddling him, and lean forward. This is my show—for now, anyway. I hook my fingers under his shirt and pull it over his head. He raises his arms, smirking when I toss it away. I mimic the movement for myself, throwing my shirt over my shoulder.

He runs his hands up my sides, cupping my breasts.

"So fucking beautiful." He rolls my nipple between his fingers.

I tip my head back and close my eyes.

His hot mouth latches on to my other nipple, and his teeth scrape my skin before his tongue darts out. I dig my nails into his biceps while his hands ghost up my spine. He winds his fingers into my hair and tugs my head back farther, while his lips travel up my chest.

"I love my marks on you," he says, nipping my throat.

I open my eyes and run my finger down the scratches I left on him, and my stomach flips.

"Me, too." I'm so hot I might combust. I roll my hips against his growing erection, seeking some sort of relief. "Aiden."

"Patience," he admonishes.

There goes my control.

He flicks his tongue against my earlobe, and I groan. I reach between us and palm his length, gripping him through his sweatpants.

"Are you going to turn me into a sex addict?" I blurt out. Because that's how I feel. Crazy for it—him.

"Would that be the worst thing?" His breath hits my ear. "Shirk all our responsibilities and stay in bed forever?"

He doesn't let me answer. His lips press to mine. My grip tightens on his cock, and he groans into my mouth. Our lips part, his tongue sweeping into my mouth. He tastes like coffee, and he kisses me like I'm his breath.

I drop my other hand to his lap, pulling his cock out. He doesn't protest when I shift closer to him, on my knees. I didn't put panties on—didn't think of it when I first got out of bed, and now I'm grateful for that.

He growls when I run his tip through my folds, pausing at my entrance. He breaks our kiss to look down.

"Impale yourself on me," he orders.

I take him in an inch at a time, bringing my hands to his shoulders. He stretches me, and it's a mix of pain—different than last night—and pleasure. He palms my hips, guiding me down until he's fully inside me.

This isn't the fast fuck I was hoping for. Instead, I meet his steady gaze, and my heart skips a beat. I don't feel... *alone*. Like here, naked, he can see me—and he isn't running away. If anything, he bares his own demons to match mine.

I rise a little and lower myself, and my eyes nearly roll back. He watches me figure it out. How to move. What feels good.

I'm a quick study.

"Touch yourself," he whispers.

I suck my lower lip into my mouth and shake my head. "I can't."

"You did before. What feels good?" His finger finds my clit, rubbing small circles. "Show me."

I hesitantly cover his hand with mine, replacing his finger. He stops thrusting inside me, watching my finger move with dark eyes. I keep my gaze locked on his face, one hand curled around his neck. He groans when I lean back slightly, creating more room, and the tension in my abdomen creeps higher.

He pinches my nipple again.

I gasp and arch my back. I lift up and come back down, fucking him and getting off at the same time. He grunts and grasps my sides, but he doesn't take over. Not until my orgasm crashes over me, and I still.

He thrusts up, milking every last drop from me. I see stars, my vision spotting white. Then he grips my hips and moves below me. I hold on, my breasts bouncing with each slap of our thighs meeting, until he suddenly comes with a groan.

We sit like that for a moment, still connected, and he cups my cheek.

I will away the emotions, but they blindside me. Tears fill my eyes again. My attention snags on the white bandage on his arm—something I'd stupidly failed to notice until now.

"Your own father shot you."

He lifts his chin. "If he wanted me dead, I would be."

"Why even take that risk?" I rise, and he slips out of me. The loss is a keen emptiness, but I squash it.

He watches me stand and cross to the bathroom. I just... I need a minute. But a minute of silence, sitting on the toilet, turns into two. I don't want to move and face the day again.

Why would Jameson even point a gun at Aiden? It's stupid to risk his whole empire like that. Even crazy, Jameson would have to acknowledge that there's only one son left after Aiden—and he's on the other side of the world.

Virtually untouchable with Amelie.

I finish my business and wash my hands, trying to work out the *why* behind Jameson.

It's impossible. It doesn't make sense.

Risk for no reward, besides torturing me.

Wait.

I spin slowly toward the closed door. I go and yank it open, hiding my surprise that Aiden's right on the other side of it.

"Is the endgame just to torture me?"

Aiden raises his eyebrows.

"Your father. That's why he made me choose. But it's not just him, right? You wanted me to suffer when you killed Kai in front of me." Forget grief—anger blazes through me.

"No," he says.

I shove at his bare chest. "Stop lying."

He doesn't even move, but his brow lowers. I'm provoking him. I need him to understand that this isn't a joke for me.

"I started to trust you," I continue. "I trusted you to at the very least not want to hurt me—"

"And why would you think that?"

I freeze.

He steps forward, boxing me in the bathroom.

"You were your father's sacrificial lamb, baby. Your family is the one that gave you to the wolves hoping to save themselves. What the fuck did you expect?" He laughs. "Guess our truce is over."

I cross my arms and narrow my eyes, ignoring my pounding heart. "Guess so."

He reaches out and touches my collarbone, tracing the edge of one of the bruises he left on my skin. He presses into it, eliciting a hiss from between my teeth, and chuckles at my response. I stay stock-still as he walks me backward. My ass bumps the counter, and he frames me in.

Caught.

"What do you think that means?"

I grimace. "Will you lock me up for real this time?"

"Because you deserve it?" He sees too much.

"I do," I bite out. "I let you kill Kai. I chose you over my father—that's the worst thing I could've done. I played right into your hands." Why did I pick Aiden? Jameson was eager to kill Dad.

His hand moves up, wrapping around the back of my neck, and he pulls me forward. His lips capture mine.

Why is he kissing me?

When I don't respond, he leans back just the slightest bit, nipping my lower lip. He kisses me again, softer. Little presses, his tongue slipping along the seam of my mouth.

I'm confused, and I grip the countertop so I don't give in to him. I can't.

"I'm not torturing you, Gemma." His voice is low, right in my ear. "You're the one torturing me. The only way you'll play into my hand is by coming on my fingers."

My abdomen clenches, and his hand dips between my legs.

"What do you want me to say? That you don't deserve what's happened to you?"

His teeth graze my earlobe, and I automatically tilt my head to give him better access.

"You're a West."

"And you're a DeSantis." My words come out breathless. "We're not supposed to be happy."

"Glad that's decided." He hoists me up on the counter and plunges two fingers inside me. "Let's be miserable together, then."

And we are… at least, until we're not.

CHAPTER 19
Aiden

I stride down the dark hall. Sam waits for me outside a door, and his expression is carefully blank.

Great.

"What?" I snap.

"Jameson has ordered the whole family to attend a wedding in two days," he says. "I thought this would be a drawn-out thing."

I resist the urge to rub my eyes. "He's impatient. He can see the end of the West family on the horizon."

"Marry Gemma, kill her brother?"

"You think that's a bad idea."

He shrugs. "I didn't say that."

He never says anything—he waits for me to guess what he's thinking. It's how he stays safe and off Jameson's shit list. It's how Ford and my other guys operate, too. Discreetly. Father dearest might suspect I have my own men, but he's never come out and said anything about it.

There are very few people I trust in this world.

"How's he fairing?" I jerk my head at the door.

Sam makes a noise in the back of his throat. "He's not used to the big league."

"Did he say anything?"

"Nothing we didn't already know."

I nod once and motion for him to move, tugging on my black leather gloves. He grins and opens the door for me, then steps aside. I take in the scene: our hostage stands in the center of the room. His hands are bound above his head, attached to a chain suspended from the ceiling. It's loose right now, letting his feet touch the floor. He lifts his head and stares at me, revealing a face full of injuries.

Busted lip, black, puffy eye. His cheekbone might be broken, the angle all wrong compared to the other one. And that's just his face.

I cross to the wall and jerk on the chain, wrapping it around another peg. It hoists him up until just his toes scrape the concrete.

"What do you want?" he growls. He's got a bravado, even still.

It's because I'm the new face. He's dealt with Sam, but now he needs to know how I operate.

I draw my knife and stop in front of him. He flinches when I cut through the collar of his shirt, dragging it down. The fabric slices easily, revealing a litany of bruises across his torso. He's been here for less than a day, but Sam works quickly.

I dig the tip of the knife between his ribs and twist. Not deep enough for serious injury, but it gets my point across.

He grunts, trying to get away from me.

"Just making sure you're awake." I grin and pat his injured cheek.

I pull the blade free and wipe it on the tatters of his shirt, then flip it in my hand. I confiscated it from Gemma when she first arrived. She had it in her boot, but I doubt she realizes I kept it close after she tried to use it on me. It's well-balanced, not some cheap thing she could've got from her kitchen. Besides, I like that it's hers.

"What the fuck?" He shoves away and swings wildly, spinning around.

I step back and let him go, folding my arms over my chest. Sam snickers in the corner.

Rubert's small-time gang is trying to make a run for the big time. But unfortunately for them, *big time* lands them directly in DeSantis territory. And no one is allowed to get away with encroachment.

"Do you know who I am?" I ask.

Rubert's second-in-command wouldn't have heard of me —just rumors. But it's the rumors that I bank on, and for a moment, he simply eyes me. But then his mouth slackens. His struggle intensifies, jerking on the chains. They rattle, but he doesn't get anywhere.

"I don't know anything, man." He twitches. "Seriously, what the fuck? Your family always treated us well. We—"

"Your little gang is making a bid for Manhattan." I shake my head, disappointed. "Cut the shit. You're Thomas McCreery. Thirty-two years old. Born in Pittsburgh and moved here with your mommy and daddy when you were sixteen. Fell in with some interesting people. Dropped out of school a year later. Married, although she's not really a looker, is she? How do you fuck her without cringing?"

"A hole is a hole," Sam says behind me.

McCreery snarls, lashing out at me. I laugh, slapping away his foot and plunging Gemma's blade deeper into his side. He squeals like a pig. I yank it out, and blood spills down, collecting in the waistband of his pants. It drips onto the floor.

"You fucking asshole," he yells.

"So much fight." I step closer and wrap my hand around his throat. I cut off his air—and the noise. "You're going to tell me what I want to know, or I'll go find your ugly wife and drag her here. I'll take my time carving her up in front of you. If that doesn't work, maybe your mother would do the trick?"

He's turning blue in the face, so I release him and immediately drill my fist into his stomach. I hit him again then retreat, taking a cloth from Sam's outstretched hand.

"We heard the Wests and DeSantises were going to war," he rasps.

I tilt my head. "And?"

"And that leaves an opening." His chest heaves, and his eyes are wild.

There's some part of him that knows he's not getting out of this room—but there's a bigger part that will sing when I ask. That bigger part is my worst enemy: *hope*. It's a dirty word in my brain. But it serves its purpose now, giving McCreery that spark of incentive to spill secrets like blood across the floor. If he just *talks*, then we won't kill him.

Wrong.

He was dead the minute Sam grabbed him from the street.

"An opening," I repeat, drawing it out to get him to continue.

"Lawrence West is dead, ain't he? Can't be a coincidence that this is all starting after they took a shot at your brother. It's about time the city's most self-important families imploded on each other."

My laugh is cold, and I have to stop myself from gutting him.

He's not done. "And you've got Gemma in your—"

The knife is at his throat before I can stop myself. I wrap my other hand around the back of his neck, holding him still. At this angle, we're eye to eye.

"Think very carefully about what you say next," I say in a low voice. "Your life depends on it."

He swallows, and the bob of his Adam's apple causes the blade to nick his skin. He winces. "I only meant everyone heard of your upcoming wedding," he blabbers. "And that can only mean one thing, right? Consolidation. We saw an opening."

"To partner with the Wests?"

"What? No."

Jack and Sam met with Rubert, who supposedly confirmed it himself. And then, hours later, Lawrence is full of bullets. Maybe Jameson was going to kill Lawrence either way because of that stupid deal.

It doesn't matter now. Unless there's a paper trail, Rubert's gang will deny, deny, deny. All to save their own skin.

I narrow my eyes and slice a little further. "Tell me about the shipyard."

"Fuck, man, I don't know anything—okay, okay." He lets out a strangled sigh when I step back. "Rubert got a contract. It was just the damn money. Easy in and out, hit the customs guy and loop the security feeds."

Shit.

Why the hell didn't I think that was a possibility? We were operating under the assumption of a brutal show of force—not a carefully thought-out plan. But of course it was thought out. How else would they have slipped past the cameras undetected?

They hacked the feeds.

It was the middle of the night. No change in lighting, no people.

"Did they hire you to steal from us?"

His eyes bug. "Steal? We ain't got a death wish. It was a simple job, man, I promise. We wouldn't have done it if we knew he was protected."

I grunt. The customs officer *wasn't* protected. Wasn't even on our radar.

"Who hired you?" I ask.

"He didn't say—"

I yank my gun from the holster in the small of my back. I shoot him in the fucking face and turn away before his body even stops twitching. I'm so done with this day—but it isn't over. He might've given me everything he knew, or he might have had more to spill.

I glare at Sam to keep him from opening his mouth. Yes, I realize there are inconsistencies in the stories we're being told, but my patience snapped.

I call Breaker, gritting my teeth until the call connects.

"Boss," his deep voice booms.

"Find Rubert," I order. "Don't move in—just call me when you've got his location."

"Done."

My next call is to Ford, who answers on the first ring. I give him our location and then turn to Sam. He'll put McCreery's body back inside his house, probably position him in the living room—or worse, their bedroom. When the wife finds him, she'll go crying to the gang.

I'm stoking another fire, but there's one person who can tell us who contracted Rubert's guys to mess with us. I cross the hall and step into another room, where the harbormaster waits. His accommodations are slightly better than McCreery's. Sam gave him a padded mattress on the floor, a bucket. I step over a fast food bag and soft drink cup, glaring at the man hunched on his mattress.

"What's your relationship to Rubert Willis?" I ask.

He lifts his head. His shocked expression is nothing new—he seems to be constantly surprised at whatever comes out of my mouth.

"Martin," I say patiently, crouching in front of him. "I've

got no more use for you, so let me put it plainly: you can tell me how you know Rubert, or I can put a bullet in your brain and ask your wife."

He sucks in a breath, his chin wobbling. If he fucking pisses his pants again, I'm going to kick him in the balls. My patience is fraying.

"He's my wife's cousin," he finally says. "Came around wanting to learn the ropes of the yard, you know? That was a few weeks ago—he's got nothing to do with—"

I press the muzzle of my gun to his temple. "Don't tell me what he has nothing to do with, Martin."

He bursts into tears.

Tears.

This big man sobs in front of me, ignoring the gun. He's probably decided he's going to die. There's no information left for him to give, and that damn hope has popped, leaving him... *this*. Messy.

"Get up," I growl.

When he doesn't move, I stow my firearm and lift him by his upper arms, then let him go.

"Take your family and get the fuck out of my city," I say. "If I so much as hear a whisper of you warning Rubert, I will hunt you down."

He doesn't need any more prodding. Sam stands by the open door and lets him pass. He breaks into a jog once he's in the hallway, and we watch him navigate his way through the maze of corridors.

"You don't think he'll tell someone about this place?" Sam asks.

We don't usually let people just walk out of here—but the man is virtually untouched, save for the fear and adrenaline he's been building up over the past few days.

"Wife's cousin," I muse. "He didn't think to mention that relation."

Sam grunts, and we head up to the ground floor. This building is one of our safe houses, but it's about time we let it burn. I don't think the harbormaster would squeal, but then again, Rubert probably didn't think McCreery would give him up, either.

Anything can happen.

"Clean up and close it down," I say to Sam.

My thoughts shift to Gemma. Two days until our wedding. She's with Cat right now, *hopefully* in our apartment. They had a dress designer bringing a litany of wedding dresses for her to choose from. If she's not in our apartment, I might have to resort to more drastic measures.

A tracker under her skin.

A chain around her ankle.

Welding the door of my apartment closed.

That last one might prove to be a challenge when I want to return, but as I said, it would be a drastic measure. It would keep her safe. And in one place for longer than an hour.

Ford pulls up beside the house, and I climb in the passenger's seat. He eyes me but says nothing. As always.

"My house," I tell him.

Halfway to Rose Hill, where our summer estate is, my home is situated in a tiny neighborhood of people who like privacy. There's a gate to get onto a narrow winding road lined with giant oak trees. My house is toward the front entrance—slightly more traffic, but if I ever had to escape in a hurry, it's best to not get boxed in. Besides, the cluster of houses along the cul-de-sac in the back is just a cesspool of children. It takes us about a half hour to get there, and Ford follows me inside.

"Does the girl know?"

I raise my eyebrow. "She knows I don't live full time at the tower."

She's smart, though. She may have already guessed.

He grunts and keeps moving toward the kitchen, his gun

drawn at his side. I leave him to sweep the downstairs and head up, my weapon also drawn. No one *should* know about this place, or know when I'm headed here.

But Gemma and I *will* be coming here after the wedding, and so Ford will periodically make sure it's secure. This place has more of my personality in it. My office on the second floor has framed photos of my brothers and me, a portrait of my mother.

Above the fireplace hangs a painting I commissioned of Gemma—it's abstract but undeniably her. The slope of her nose, her golden blonde hair. Her blue-gray eyes. The rest is unique to the artist, flashes of colors and lines that blend with the stand-out *Gemma* features.

I stare at it for a moment, then pour myself a drink.

"All clear," Ford says in the doorway. "You... okay?"

I glance at him, then back to the painting. "The wedding will be trouble."

He exhales. "Probably."

"We should call in Hart." I swallow my whiskey in one go and relish the burn down my throat. It has a smoky aftertaste that sits on my tongue.

Hart is Ford's brother—in spirit, not blood. Although it may as well be blood. They served in the Marines together, fought beside each other... No better bond than that. So I hear, anyway. I picked up Ford when he was fresh off deployment and looking for work. Hart tagged along, but the city can be too much for him.

He does better in quiet settings, which is why he's working in upstate New York doing security. It's peaceful up there—precisely what he needs.

However, he offered his services if we were ever in dire need, and I'm sure this qualifies.

"I'll see what his schedule is like, but it shouldn't be a problem."

I'm unconvinced, with my father being a fucking wild card and Gemma... and her family. I've been left in the dark on how this wedding ceremony will go. But at least I learned one thing: the whole DeSantis clan is going to attend.

If that doesn't spell danger for Gemma, then I'm illiterate.

My phone buzzes, and this time it's my father. My chest seizes. I don't trust him with Gemma—so why the hell did I leave her there alone?

Just two more days, I tell myself. Then we can get out of dodge.

Well, *I* can't, but Gemma can. And if she's safe, I can do my damn job without worrying about her. That's what I tell myself, anyway.

The truth of the matter is, I can see why Luca and Amelie abandoned the family. Luca never felt like part of it, what with his mother being different from mine and Wilder's. Dad didn't really care where they went once the Pages—Amelie's parents—wired him the money.

A deal with the devil turned out all right. Who would've thought?

But now I have the same longing to leave it all behind, even as guilt and duty fasten me down tighter to the city. Without speaking with her, I imagine Gemma feels the same. Perhaps less, having not been brought up knowing she'd take a position of power.

"Go," I finally tell Ford. "I've got the bike here."

I settle at my desk and pull out a stack of paperwork from the drawer. Three years ago, I opened a corporation that has been acting in my interest, purchasing property in Hell's Kitchen and surrounding neighborhoods. Hart is the acting CEO, and he signs off on all decisions. He emailed me updates on our accounts—it funds Ford and Breaker, as well as an offshore account for myself.

An escape plan I now don't think I'll get the chance to use.

After an hour of poring over finances, signing off on Hart's proposals for new contracts, and generally exhausting my eyes, I rise. I give myself another second to take in the painting, and then lock up my desk.

Everything else is in order, and I've given the girls long enough to try on dresses.

My phone buzzes in my pocket. I glance at it, then do a double take.

This isn't the dress she picked, but isn't she fierce?

I load the image, and my heart stops. Gemma stands on a stool in the center of the living room, holding back her hair. The dress is sexy—the sort I'd expect on a vixen or seductress, not Gemma. It hugs the curves I've been learning intimately, the lace nearly sheer. The neckline plunges to just above her bellybutton, and the designer must've fastened a heavy necklace for the effect.

I adjust myself in my pants and grit my teeth, then dial the designer.

"Mr. DeSantis," she answers, her voice high. "How can I help you?"

"Are you still in the tower?"

"I was just heading to my car. Ms. West found a lovely dress. It fit her—"

"I don't want details." Call me superstitious, but I'd rather be surprised. There's still *some* element of a real wedding happening—right? If not, then all of it would be a sham, and I can't bear to think that way.

I want this to be real.

More than anything.

Gemma is *mine.*

I tell the designer what to do and end the call. My leather jacket is hanging from a peg in the garage, and I slide it on over my black shirt. I zip it up and secure my phone, then pull on my helmet. My bike is like an old friend. One I haven't been able to see in a while—not with the craziness happening in Manhattan.

She roars to life under me, and I can't stop my grin from spreading.

Just two more days.

CHAPTER 20

Gemma

"It's going to be perfect." Cat bounces on her heels, holding the black dress bag in her arms. Inside it is *the* dress. The perfect one.

I didn't think it existed. I'm still a bit skeptical about the whole wedding—a forced charade, honestly. But there's a deeper part of me that wants to take it seriously.

"What about the rest?" I ask.

She tilts her head.

"Something borrowed, blue, um... old?"

"Oh!" She grins. "I'll take care of it. And I'm going to store this bad baby in my closet so Aiden isn't tempted to peek. I'll talk to you later?"

I nod. It's dark out, and my stomach lets out an unfortunate growl. Once I've locked up behind Cat—a new measure of protection is a deadbolt that only Aiden has the key for—I get to work cooking.

And, let's be honest, *cooking* is a stretch. I find pasta and an assortment of cheeses. It can't be too hard to make homemade macaroni and cheese, right?

Wrong.

Twenty minutes later, my pasta is an odd blend of some overdone, mushy pieces and a few crunchy ones. They're all stuck together, either way. And the sauce has clumped and attached itself to my spoon.

I toss the curdled cheese mess into the sink, pan and all, and groan. Inexplicably, tears blur my vision. It's stupid—I was fine when he was gone. I make a mean grilled cheese and soup—but *pasta* has conquered me.

Aiden walks in with a helmet in his grip, and his gaze immediately finds mine.

"What's wrong?" he demands.

I shrug, but the burning behind my eyes intensifies. It's made worse when I remember the first meal he made me: *fucking pasta*.

He circles the island and comes up behind me, peering into the sink.

"If you laugh, I'm going to knee you in the balls."

His hands slide around my waist and pull me back into him. I release a sigh and tip my head back. *Damn it, body, why are you relaxing against him?*

"Cheese sauce is at least intermediate level," he says in my ear.

"And the pasta?" I point to the bowl of shells.

"When we have time, I'll teach you."

I rotate in his arms and meet his gaze. "Is that a promise?"

He smirks. "Yes. But for now..." He maneuvers me sideways, to the counter beside the sink, and lifts me onto it. He wraps his hand around the back of my neck and guides me forward, our lips touching.

All too soon, he pulls away, a mischievous glint in his eyes. I pout and draw my leg up, resting my chin on my knee. And he proceeds to go full Italian chef on me. Chicken, a creamy pesto sauce, sautéed spinach, gnocchi. *Gnocchi*. I haven't had that in years.

My mouth is watering by the time he's done. Neither of us have spoken a word, instead opting for a smooth instrumental soundtrack to play over the speaker half hidden by the citrus bowl. And it's actually nice.

We're coexisting.

Today is weird.

We spent most of the morning exploring each other's bodies, until Aiden got called away. It was the distraction I needed, but I still feel untethered.

And then the dress shopping after lunch, Cat and the designer fawning over different fabrics. She had brought a whole wheeling rack with her stuffed with garment bags, a wide selection of styles.

Aiden steps between my legs and wraps his arms around my back. I loop mine around his neck, then lock my ankles together behind him.

"We could stay like this," he says, tilting his head back. "Or we could eat."

I nod. "After all your hard work, I won't turn down the meal."

He smiles and releases me. I hop down, and together we build plates. He pours me a glass of wine, setting it on the table for me. I die of happiness when I take my first bite. All of the bites. I let out a groan, and his expression darkens.

Another groan, but I can't help it. I'm in awe of the meal he made. Whether it's a talent he keeps a secret, or a well-known fact, he's impressed me. Then again, the easiest way to a girl's heart is through her stomach—so the saying goes, anyway.

He shifts in his seat, eyes on my lips. "I won't be held responsible for my actions if you keep making those noises."

I wink. "I'll make up for it later."

"Where did you come from?" he asks, but it seems more of a rhetorical question.

I get it—I feel different. Like someone new has slid into the driver's seat in my brain. Maybe that'll end and I'll go back to feeling all sorts of hatred toward the DeSantises, but I can't muster that same energy of anger toward Aiden.

And the sex...

Who knew it would feel like this?

I've woken up, when my family wanted to keep me asleep.

"Thank you," I say to him.

His brow lifts. "You're welcome. But, for what?"

I glance away. "I guess... all of this? It could've turned out differently." *Worse*, I don't add.

"No," he says simply.

"What?"

"It wouldn't have turned out differently. I was coming for you regardless." He leans forward, his tone serious. "I told you before, you were mine since you were sixteen. Nothing was going to stand between us."

"Just our families." My voice is a whisper.

"And look what happened to them."

I rise and go to the window. "We aren't Romeo and Juliet."

"I should hope not. Their story ends in death." He comes up behind me again, and this time his hands don't slip around my waist. He just gives me his presence. "We aren't going to die. We're going to make it through this wedding, and then..."

I exhale. "That's the problem. You can't promise we won't die."

He grunts.

"You can't. Life and death don't work like that."

He sweeps my hair off my shoulder, and his lips touch my neck. "*I* work like that, princess. Get used to it."

I sniff against the sudden pain in my throat. His hot breath travels higher, to my earlobe. His teeth catch it, and I tilt my head to the side even as tears fill my eyes. It's stupid, really, that I'm worrying about an *us* with everything else happening.

"Crying won't save you," he says.

"I don't want to save *me*." I swipe the wetness on my cheeks away.

He grabs my fingers and brings them to his mouth, licking the tears away. My lips part, and heat unfurls in my chest. It's too much. There's too much hope and grief and anticipation inside me, threatening to burst out.

And the loneliness... the unbearable loneliness ebbs when he's around.

I twist in his arms and bury my face on his chest.

"You've been cooped up here all day," he says suddenly.

I don't answer.

He steps back and draws me with him, eyeing my clothes. Light-washed, high-waisted jeans. Bare feet. The bottom hem of my rust-colored cropped top—a hand-me-down from Cat—just brushes the top of the jeans. If I lift my arms, it reveals my stomach. It has bell sleeves, but they're rolled and tied above my elbows with little ribbons.

"Boots," he mutters, shaking his head as if to clear his vision. "Go on."

I step past him, and he slaps my ass.

I yelp and leap forward, tossing a glare over my shoulder. He smirks at me, and his gaze is hungry. But I want to go wherever he's thinking of taking me, so I hurry upstairs to grab my shoes and ignore the way my stomach flips.

Aiden's phone rings downstairs, only once before he answers with a sharp greeting.

My curiosity piques.

I grab my boots and creep forward on the landing. I don't need to see Aiden to know he's almost directly under the stairs.

"You found him," he says. It sounds like he's repeating it back to whoever's on the other end of the line. "Where?"

I slide my socks on, then lace my boots. No use sitting here doing absolutely nothing—that's the easiest way to get caught.

"Follow him. Don't engage until I get there—he's fucking mine."

My heart turns to ice.

He's found Colin.

Their truce ended. Of course it did. And the hunt resumed, while I tried on pretty dresses and thought Aiden and I might survive this.

I pull myself up and rush downstairs, furious at myself. Aiden steps toward me, stashing his phone in his pocket, and I shove at his chest. He goes back a few steps. Confusion flickers over his features.

"How could you?" I shove at him again. "What, were you going to take me to watch you kill my brother?"

He scoffs. "You think so little of me."

"You *killed my cousin*," I shriek. I go to push him again.

He grabs my wrists, dragging me into him. "I did. He killed three of my men. Men who had families at home. Wives. Children. Not everyone is like us, Gemma, with no attachments."

I shudder. "I have attachments."

"You have a brother you're not entirely convinced is innocent," he snaps. "You had a cousin who was known to cause trouble between our families. Your father—"

"Do not talk about my father." I glare at him. "Your family is so fucking flawed, too, Aiden. Your charming, sociopath older brother. Your psychotic dad. And the bastard brother who abandoned you in this hellhole."

He grips my jaw and squeezes. *Now* I've pissed him off. Oddly enough, I love the rush. My face may burn, but arguing also fuels the fire in my blood, too.

"Did Colin kill Wilder?"

"No," I snap. "Fuck off."

He laughs hoarsely and kisses me. I fight against him, but he's still got my wrists in one hand, sandwiched between us, and my chin in his other. If he sticks his tongue in my mouth, I'm biting it off. I keep my jaw locked, but he seems content with what I give him.

"Eavesdropping on half a conversation will give you the wrong idea." He releases my face. "Now, come with me."

His hand on my wrists slides down, lacing through my fingers. He hands me a jacket, and I pause. It's one just like his, supple black leather with silver zippers, but it slides on like it was made just for me.

Wait.

"Did you buy this?"

He adjusts it and drags the zipper up. It's off center, cutting over my breast and ending under the collar. His gaze runs down me and back up, and he nods to himself. He retrieves his helmet, and nerves swoop in my chest.

I follow him into the elevator, and we stand in tense silence while we descend. The doors slide open on the parking garage level, and I jolt. I don't know why I assumed he wasn't taking me... *out*. Rather to another floor, or the roof again.

But a cool breeze sweeps through the garage, and I suck in a deep breath.

"I want you to know that I learned my lesson from Luca," he tells me, leading me down a row of vehicles. We stop at a black motorcycle.

"What lesson?"

My mind flicks back to Amelie.

"I won't keep you locked up." He gives me a half-grin. "Unless you're into that kind of thing."

The scar on Amelie's forehead—and the haunted look in her eyes—was enough to give me nightmares. I'd never been so grateful to be able to *do* something. To have a task, a challenge, hell, a mission. And it was successful.

"Do you hold it against me?" I ask. "The fact that I helped her escape?"

He shakes his head and traces his finger over my knuckles. "No."

"Why not?"

"Because Luca was acting out of fear."

I eye him. "And what are you doing?"

"I'm not afraid." He raises another helmet and slides it on my head. He latches the strap under my chin. The visor is up, so I don't miss the dark gleam in his eyes. He watches me like a predator would watch prey. "I don't scare easy, princess."

I laugh. "Right."

He puts on his own helmet and smirks. "Ready for some fun?"

Am I ever. But I'm not nervous. Shouldn't I be? Shouldn't I be... I don't know, afraid? I've never been on a motorcycle before, but I mimic him and swing my leg over, sliding down until my front is flush with his back. He reaches back and flicks my visor down, then does the same for his own.

The engine turns over with a mighty roar. I wrap my arms around his waist—I'm not one of those girls who will need to be told to hold on tighter. Pretty sure I've got a death grip.

Not nervous, just smart.

His laugh rumbles his chest over the bike's vibrations, and he pats my hand.

And then we're off, speeding into the night.

The wind whips my hair back, billowing out from under my helmet. I have the urge to throw my arms out wide, but we weave between cars to get out of the city. The way we lean is terrifying at first, and I squeeze Aiden hard the first few times.

I can't risk losing my balance—or worse, falling.

But it gets easier the farther we go, making our way

through late-evening traffic. It isn't too bad on the quieter roads, but we hit a stretch that has too many restaurants and clubs, and I think we might suffocate on the number of vehicles in our way.

Soon enough, it thins out again.

He guns it, and we fly through an intersection, and my stomach is suspended for a moment. I'm breathless until we're clear of it, then up a ramp and onto a deserted highway.

I lean slightly to the left to see around Aiden. We cut west, over one of the many bridges connecting Manhattan to the rest of the world, then south. It isn't long before we cross into New Jersey. I take in a deep breath and force myself to relish this moment. It would be so easy to disregard it. To think that this is something I should expect.

It's not—it's a gift.

How easy would it have been for Aiden to keep me away in his apartment until the wedding? And even after?

Luca did it with minimal grief to Amelie... at least, until *after*.

I can't imagine loving someone so much to forgive them. To allow them the power to hurt me again. Aiden's hurt everyone around me, but he treats me like I'm precious. My mind can't reconcile it.

Isn't every transgression against my family against me, too?

The bike slowing distracts me from my worrying, and I glance around. We turn onto a dirt road, off the beaten path, and stop. He kills the engine, then removes his helmet. I follow, undoing the buckle and dragging it up. I can't see it, but my hair *feels* like a rat's nest. I quickly smooth it and ignore the blush working its way up my neck.

We dismount, and he takes the helmet from me, then my hand. "Do you trust me?"

I swallow. "Why?"

He narrows his eyes.

Okay, then. "I trust you as far as I can throw you," I mutter. "I don't trust you not to kill the rest of my family."

He chuckles. "Fair enough."

"Why?" I repeat.

He squeezes my hand. "Just stay silent, okay? No matter what happens."

I grimace. Staying silent is not my strong suit. I used to have to pinch myself whenever I snuck around the house to eavesdrop on Dad's meetings, a painful reminder of my penchant to just... *react*.

"Is this like a life or death sort of silence?" I whisper.

"Not *your* life or death," he says.

My stomach rolls, but at least the fear of him murdering me in the woods is... probably not realistic. He could kill me anywhere and get away with it. This is too much effort. We step off the dirt road and onto a narrower track. It leads us through the woods, to a small cabin. The windows have been painted black, and the only sign of life is a thin stream of smoke out the chimney protruding from the roof.

He leads me to the door and unlocks it, then gestures for me to go inside.

I glance around at the rather unimpressive cabin. One room. Sink and fridge and tiny counter against the far back wall. A lamp on a table against another—the only illumination.

The real star of the show is the trap door in the floor.

"What is that?"

He just shakes his head and raises his eyebrows.

Right.

Silence.

I mime zipping my lips closed.

He lifts the trap door, opening it completely. I inch forward and peer down into the darkness. It smells like sweat and something more sour. Metallic.

Blood?

"If you don't want to see, you can stay up here." He crosses to the one and only door, clipping a padlock across the deadbolt. He tucks the key in his pocket.

"What is this place?"

"Where I get information," he says. "Stay up here or come down and satiate your curiosity—it's up to you."

He descends a ladder. I watch him disappear into the gloom, and I swallow.

You can do this. My curiosity is at an all-time high. And part of me isn't convinced I won't find my brother in Aiden's death chamber.

"Shut up, Gem," I whisper to myself.

And then I step into the hole.

CHAPTER 21
Aiden

Gemma comes down slowly, muttering to herself. She's cute when she's scared. Her foot slips off one of the rungs, and she loses her balance. I catch her before she hits the floor.

"Thanks," she says, then her eyes widen at our surroundings. We're in a tunnel that extends into the gloom in one direction. The other way has a metal door blocking access to the room where my guest awaits.

"Put your hair up." I hand her a hair tie.

She quirks her lips but does as I say. She's brimming with questions—they're on the tip of her tongue. Wisely, though, she doesn't voice them. While the sound won't travel too far, it's better to be safe than sorry.

I could warn her... but I'd rather not.

According to Breaker on the phone, things changed rapidly.

Rubert changed the game—and we have no choice but to change it back. She finishes tying her long blonde hair back in a low ponytail. I reach around her and tuck the long, silky strands into her jacket, then pull a cap over her head. She makes a noise in the back of her throat.

I ignore it and hand her a black surgical mask. It will cover her nose and mouth and block most of her face.

"Incognito," she mumbles.

I wink.

She grabs my arm and tugs the mask down, kissing my cheek quickly. I catch the strawberry-pink blush on her cheeks before she adjusts the mask and hat. I love her reactive skin. The way she turns pink—or, if she's truly embarrassed, red.

"Ready." She nods once.

I lead the way inside.

Breaker leans against the wall beside the door, and he eyes Gemma. Rubert is in a chair in the center of the room, his forearms strapped down. His ankles are bound together. There's a ball gag in his mouth, and even in the low light, spit is streaked down his chin. He makes a noise low in his throat, a wail that fills the room.

"Nice touch," I say to Breaker.

My old friend grimaces. "Short notice."

"Yeah, yeah, you kinky fucker. Did you even clean it before shoving it in his mouth?"

He glares at me. "No one tastes my girl except me."

I grin.

Riling him up is too easy. Still, he's been down here supervising our hostage for an hour. I hook my thumb toward the door, and he slips past Gemma. My girl takes up Breaker's position against the wall while I stride forward.

I take a moment to acknowledge the unexpected nerves in my gut. She could react to this side of my life poorly. I only showed her a taste of my violence—once directed at her cousin, and another at her would-be killer. This is different.

This is malice toward someone she doesn't know.

A stranger.

He deserves it—he fucking deserves worse than he'll get from me tonight—but she doesn't know that. I've left Gemma purposefully in the dark. I hate that I'm testing her like this, but I can't get her hatred out of my mind.

Rubert glares at me. The noise that first came out of him faded, leaving silence in its wake. He knows better than Thomas McCreery what happens to those who cross us. Who make a bid for power they don't understand.

And simple intimidation won't work on a man like Rubert.

I rip the gag out of his mouth and drop it into his lap. He coughs, jerking his arms against the rope restraints.

"You bring your slut along to torture me?" he wheezes.

I tilt my head. He wants a reaction out of me—any sort of anger will just... justify his words. My weakness is standing behind me, and he can't know that. Especially if he leaves here in one piece. The mask and cap were a ridiculous idea, anyway. Anyone with a brain would know who she is.

When I don't respond, Rubert's gaze swings to her. "Gemma West, the princess with daddy issues. How's he looking, these days? A little ashen?"

She shoves off the wall and punches him in the throat. He didn't see that one coming, I'd bet. He chokes, gargling, and she glares at him while returning to her position. Her eyes flick to mine, and she offers me a glare, as well.

I can interpret it to mean, *You said not to talk, and I didn't.*

I smirk.

"You're off to a good start," I tell Rubert. "Pissing off a West... *and* a DeSantis. How's that working for you?"

He grunts and gasps, leaning forward to cough. "Fucking bitch."

I drive the blade into his leg, just above his kneecap.

Rubert screams, thrashing in the chair. "What the fuck," he yells. "You fucking asshole!"

I shrug. It's not my fault he's dumb. I thought he might not be, what with figuring out who Gemma is, but it's been five minutes and he should be dead twice over. My hands ball into fists.

"Let's play a game," I say, dragging a chair from out of the shadows and placing it backward in front of him. I sink into it and rest my forearms on the back. "For every question you dodge, or answer dishonestly, I'll twist this little blade." I reach forward and tap it, and he lurches.

"Fuck you."

"Now, Rubert, you don't even know what I want."

"The whole town is talking about your precious fucking Italian marble," he spits.

I lean back and raise my eyebrows. "Continue."

"We didn't have shit to do with it. Just bad timing."

He shifts, and I narrow my eyes. I hope he lies to me, because I'd love nothing more than to cut his whole goddamn leg off.

"Who approached you to kill the customs officer?"

"I don't know."

I sneer. "Sure." I reach forward, grasping the knife.

"No, no—"

I twist, and blood spurts up from the wound I create. He screams until he gags, gasping for breath. The pain must be bitter, but it will return to a new baseline as soon as I release it.

"It came through the grapevine," he moans. "Guy didn't want any connection to us, so a messenger delivered the contract and photo. Money was wired into our account as soon as it was done."

"What did you do with the product?" Gemma asks. "You can say you had nothing to do with that, but if you were in the area, why wouldn't they use you for that, too? No offense, dude, but your explanation is fucking dumb."

She's right. I was operating under the assumption that there were two separate parties: Rubert's gunrunners who killed the customs guy and looped the feeds, then whoever contracted them went in and stole our shipment. But it would make *more* sense for the contract to be for all of it.

The staging, the feeds, the hit. Less mess. Fewer bodies in the shipyard. A smaller risk of getting caught.

He jerks, like he'd forgotten she was there. "A warehouse," he stammers. "Hell's Kitchen."

Fuck. I've never wanted to kiss her more. Not just for the fact that she's participating—*against my orders*—but because she's a genius. And I can put aside that she was supposed to observe.

She's helping.

"Be precise." She circles us, stopping beside him. She pulls the mask down and twists the cap backward on her head. Her attention fastens on the handle of the knife—*her* knife—then flickers to me. Her eyes stay on me as she leans down, her mouth next to his ear. "Where?"

Rubert's expression is pained. "I don't remember."

Lie.

Gemma leans forward and yanks the knife out of his leg. She idly wipes his blood from it and flips it in her hand.

She examines the clean blade for a moment, then presses the tip into her own thumb. A drop of blood wells there, and Rubert is transfixed. Hell, I am, too. She sticks her thumb into her mouth, then meets his eyes.

"Try again," she urges.

Fuck if I'm not turned on by this dark side of her. She doesn't seem perturbed at all by the scene playing out before us. The scene she's now fully in control of. I'm happy to let her steer the conversation, because she's already caught on to what I want.

The *who* and the *where*.

Why and how can come later.

"Do you have children, Rubert?" She runs the blade up his arm and down his front, letting it dangle over his crotch.

The implication is clear, and he flinches. "Fine, fine, I'll tell you," he says. "I never wanted any trouble, okay?"

"McCreery seemed to think you wanted to move in while Mommy and Daddy fought," I say.

He pales. "No, no. I mean, yes, if the Wests—"

Gemma digs the knife into his uninjured leg, and he hisses.

"We thought you were joining forces. It left an opening."

"You're mistaken," Gemma says. "An address. Right now, or say goodbye to the family jewels."

She's bluffing. Her jaw tics, like she's fighting to stay in control, but she doesn't admit defeat. She doesn't want to permanently disfigure him—and she definitely doesn't want to go anywhere near his balls.

Rubert doesn't know that, though. And when he talks, he sings.

The name of the messenger company that delivered the contract. The details of the hit. How much fucking money he was paid, even. And finally, the address.

Gemma twitches. Rubert finally stops talking, and I meet my fiancée's gaze. She stares back, conveying nothing, then tosses the knife back to me.

I catch the handle on reflex.

"I'll wait upstairs," she says.

Her voice is tired and a million miles away, but I don't stop her from hurrying out. Breaker comes down a minute later, and I nod to him.

"Have fun with him, Breaker. And Rubert, just know—all

of this pain could've been avoided had you not fucking double crossed us."

"Wait," Rubert yells. "What the fuck? I thought you were going to let me leave..."

"That's the thing about hope," I sneer. "It always disappoints."

I leave, the door swinging shut behind me. Gemma is at the sink, scrubbing blood off her hands.

"That was impressive," I say.

She whirls around, water droplets arcing off her wet hands. "Was it?" Her voice is faint. "Seemed stupid to me."

I approach her and set her knife on the counter, then box her in. Her face is pale, and she automatically clutches the front of my jacket. I can't decide if it's to keep me from getting closer or farther away. Part of me would prefer if it's the latter, but realistically...

She rotates toward the knife, lifting it. "This is mine."

"Yeah."

"Why did you keep it?"

I press a kiss to her temple. "Why did I keep you?"

Her cheeks heat. "Can we leave?"

"Yes." I give her space and unlock the door.

Before we go outside, I hand her the small sheath for her knife out of my pocket. She grins and bends down, quickly attaching it to her calf. She'd have to remove her boots and draw up her jeans to pull it, but it doesn't matter for now. Her unspoken message is that she thinks—*knows*—I'll keep her safe.

The night air is chilly, and she sucks in a loud breath. We make it back to the bike, but she pauses before climbing on. She gives me a rare grin, then tips her head back and stares at the stars.

Wonder fills her expression.

I could look up and see what she sees—the sky exploded

with pinpricks of light. A sight to behold, especially for a girl who's lived in Manhattan for most of her life. The city never darkens enough to see the stars. But here...

And let's not forget that I've kept the princess trapped in her tower for weeks.

So yeah, I could look up. But then I'd miss the beautiful joy written in her features.

My heart thumps. I lean against the bike and just... watch her. She shrugs out of her jacket. It falls to the ground beside her. She throws her arms out wide and breathes deeply, rotating in a small circle.

"Dance with me," she says.

I tilt my head and don't say the obvious—that there's no music.

"Aiden. Live a little. Dance with me."

I rise and stalk toward her. Her teeth catch her lower lip, but she releases it when I stop just shy of touching her. She raises her eyebrows in challenge.

Well.

I take her hand and put my other one on her waist, pulling her flush against me. Her free hand settles on my upper arm, just below the bandage. Whether she knows she avoided my injury or did it subconsciously, it still does something to me.

We begin to move, following a beat that plays out between us. Maybe it's our heartbeats, or the wind, or adrenaline. I spin her out and reel her back in. Luca and I used to party downtown—we frequented one of the clubs the Wests owned, among others—and dancing was always one of my favorite things.

She comes back into my arms and grins. We move across the dirt road, dust kicked up by our boots. Another twirl, her fingers light on my palm, and when she comes back, I dip her low. She shrieks and clutches at me, but there's no need. I've got her, although her cap falls off.

When we come back up, we both regard each other for a moment.

Until I can't take it any longer.

She must feel the same urge, because our mouths meet halfway. We clash together, a hot new eagerness between us. My erection strains against my zipper. She unbuckles my jeans, wasting no time to slide her hand in and wrap it around my cock. I back her into a tree.

She grunts at the force and nips my lip. Her hand leaves me for her own jeans, shoving them down. I spin her around and kick her legs wider, guiding her hands to the rough bark. My cock slides against her, teasing her slit. The need to be inside her might kill me, but the little noises she makes when she's on edge is sweeter.

"Aiden," she says, shifting her hips back.

The head of my cock finds her entrance, and I push in the smallest bit. I exhale sharply and hold on to her waist, stopping her from taking me in further.

"Princess," I reply. I reach around her and rub her clit. I want to bury my face in her pussy and taste her—and I will. Later. When I can watch her expressions.

"Split me in half, DeSantis."

I smile at the order, still working her clit. I thrust inside her fully, and she automatically clenches at my length. She's slick and hot. I draw out slowly and slam back in. Her whole body jolts, only her grip on the tree keeping her upright.

"Come on," she growls.

I give her what she's asking for. I slap her ass, and she gets wetter around me. *Fuck*. She groans, her own fingers taking over on her clit. I bat her hand away and pinch. Hard.

She screams. The orgasm takes her by surprise, and it's only my hand on her stomach that keeps her upright. She pulses around me, and I see stars. I pump twice more, then come inside her.

We stay like that for a moment, both breathing heavily.

"I fucking love you," I say.

She goes stock-still.

I move inside her, my dick still semi-hard, and she whimpers.

"Did you hear me?" I pull her back against me and bite her earlobe.

"Aiden, I can't—"

I wrap my hand around her throat, fingers on her jaw, and direct her mouth back to mine. I claim her lips, *telling* her that this is happening. She can't run from me. She won't.

Love will destroy us both, but it's already done. There's a Gemma-sized hole in my chest.

She steps away, and I slip out of her. The loss of her heat is unsettling, but I try to shove it away as I pull my briefs and jeans back into place.

She does the same, dragging her jeans up from where they rested around her ankles. My cum will seep out of her on the way home, dampening her panties. That thought does dangerous things to me.

I wait for her to face me, but she doesn't.

"You already knew," I say to her back. "I told you that you were mine."

"Being possessive and being in love are two different things," she whispers.

I have the urge to throw her over my shoulder and take her home. Not to the tower—fuck that. *My* home. It's funny: I just promised I wouldn't make Luca's mistake and lock her up. But now I consider it.

"It's not different." I turn her around and cup her cheek. "Part of me fell in love with you that day—but you were sixteen. I wasn't going to do that to you."

Her eyes are wide.

"I stayed away," I reiterate. "You were a teenager. Now

you're legally an adult, and you're really fucking easy to love. So just deal with it."

She winces.

"What?"

"I'm not easy to love." She glances away. Tries to, anyway.

I redirect her gaze back to me. "You are. You won Cat over. And Breaker. Ford, too, probably. Maybe even Sam." I narrow my eyes. "Not that they'll ever touch you."

"Is it because I stabbed that guy?"

I tip my head back and laugh. "Not totally. Although it was a fucking turn-on. And you're smart. You take no shit from anyone. You disobey orders when you think they're wrong. You speak up. You're kind."

"I can be mean."

"You can be," I acknowledge. "And I enjoy that, too."

Her cheeks turn red.

The moon is high, casting slight shadows on the ground. I hold out my hand and guide her back to the bike. She takes one last look back at the sky and lets out a huge breath.

"I can't say..."

"I know," I interrupt. "I didn't tell you just to hear it back."

She's quiet. I've freaked her out after an already stressful day. But she needs to hear it—she needs to know that I've always been all-in with her. Some part of her doesn't believe this is real. That the wedding in two days is a sham, that I'm only marrying her to make her family suffer.

That's not it at all.

And once she knows the whole truth, everything is going to change.

CHAPTER 22
Gemma

My thoughts are a jumbled mess on the way to Manhattan. Before we leave, he tucks my hands inside his jacket—a thoughtful gesture to keep my fingers from freezing on the road.

Still, our ride home is slower. It's close to midnight by now, and I tip my head back to watch the stars. They fade before my eyes as we cross into the city.

I let out a sigh.

There are so many questions brewing in my mind, I don't know where to start.

Maybe the first and most important is that *Aiden loves me*. He's not shy about admitting it, either. Even more worrisome. And the way my body reacted... my heart nearly stopped dead.

But then there's the whole secret-interrogation-house-in-the-woods thing. Rubert's confession. The information I extracted from him.

I can practically feel the puzzle pieces sliding together, but it's like creating the image blindfolded. I don't know what I'm building—but I'm desperately trying to figure it out. It pulls my focus like an itch I can't reach.

The DeSantis construction business is only a part of what they do, but it's one of their most solid legal businesses. It funds the illegal part—much like our restaurants and clubs fund other such ventures. Drugs, in our case. Weapons in theirs.

Huh.

It wasn't too long ago that Sam and Aiden were discussing the empty container while I scanned an article about Councilwoman White's new bill in the Pages' magazine. Back then, in my mind, there was a connection.

However.

Italian marble is a hell of a lot more expensive than whatever I was picturing. And... it can't just be *marble*. I know how this family probably operates, if it's anything like mine. There had to be weapons in that shipping container, too.

Which creates a bit more urgency behind this witch hunt.

Worry tugs at my gut.

We slow to a stop at a red light, and I flip up my visor. "Are we going to the address Rubert gave us?"

He raises his, too, and twists around to meet my gaze. "Are you up for it?"

I grimace. "We should check it out."

He hums. The light changes, and we both put our visors back down. He revs the engine and rockets forward, following the car ahead of us. We reach the middle of the intersection when another engine roars.

I turn my head toward the bright lights, and my grip automatically tightens around Aiden's waist.

He shoots up next to the car ahead of us, still accelerating until we're alone on the road. Maybe he feels my nerves, because he releases a handle and pats my hand. I appreciate the gesture, although my heart is still in my throat. We fly through the next intersection a block down. The wind whips my hair back, and I take a deep breath.

The truck comes out of nowhere, and there isn't time to avoid it. My hollow scream rings in my ears. The headlights are blinding.

Metal screeches against metal, and the bike jerks out from under us. I lose my grip on Aiden and hit the ground hard. My head bounces on the asphalt, but my helmet protects it from the worst damage. I squeeze my eyes shut as I slide, unable to stop my forward momentum. I hit the curb and roll up onto the sidewalk, finally stopping on my side.

Aiden's on me in an instant. He presses me flat on my back, his helmet off and looking like he's ready to rain fury down on the person who hit us. I grab his wrist, but he just shakes his head. "Stay down."

I glance over at the truck, which has blocked one of the streets. Two men climb out, weapons drawn, and my heart lurches into my throat. My whole body hurts, and it reacts sluggishly to my desire to stand.

Aiden straightens, giving me his back, and strides toward them.

The way we fell, they're almost twenty yards away—and closing.

I grit my teeth and shove myself up. I recognize the truck who hit us, and the two men, too. My stomach flip-flops with dread because they won't hesitate to kill Aiden. Hell, I'm sure they knew it was him, with his fancy motorcycle and the way he acts like this city is beneath him.

It *is* beneath him, but sometimes the city pushes back.

"Wait," I call. I start forward, but my leg won't hold my weight.

Any minute, they're going to kill each other. I can feel it more than I feel my own body—just a sense that something is going to go terribly wrong. Didn't I feel it at the last intersection?

The two men are West soldiers. They provide security for

our family's illegal activities—transporting imported goods from private airports, debt collectors, guards. These two drive drugs into Manhattan for dispersal at the clubs.

In other words, they're scary motherfuckers.

But not to me.

One picked me up from a friend's house, once. That was just after Aiden abducted me and my parents were paranoid. Another shadowed me and my mother at my seventeenth birthday party. Those were my only direct interactions with them, although I've seen them in and out of my house plenty of times.

Turner.

Marius.

They're targeting DeSantises.

Does my brother know?

Is he condoning this behavior?

Belatedly, I realize my helmet is still on, obscuring both my face and voice. I yank it off and quickly limp after Aiden. He stops suddenly, and I almost slam into his back. I dig my fingers into the waistband of his jeans. His breath hitches, but he doesn't look behind him.

"DeSantis," one of them sneers. Turner, probably.

I have to do something.

I slide my hand under his jacket and yank his gun free. I sidestep him and show my face to the two men.

They both jerk to a halt.

"Gemma?" Turner asks. He lowers his firearm and stares at me.

"What the fuck?" I yell. "Were you just going to kill him?"

Marius scowls. "He's a DeSantis. And after Lawrence—"

"Don't." I stow the gun—it's better that I have it, but I don't plan on killing my own men. I march up to Marius and shove him back. "I was there. It was *my* father's blood on my face. And Kai's."

Their gazes flick up to Aiden.

There's a little distance between us now, and I glance back to gauge my fiancé's reaction. He wears a blank mask, betraying absolutely nothing.

Turner scoffs. "What the fuck are you doing with him, Gemma? We've been searching for him—and now that we've found him, you're here?"

"If you try to kill him, you won't see till morning." I keep my voice light. Conversational. We just interrogated a man, and now we're standing in an empty intersection. I've lost it—I'm trying to stop a war.

A wildfire that Aiden and these two would gladly feed.

"His people won't find us," Marius reasons. His voice is pitched low to keep Aiden from overhearing us. "They took you—but we can save you. Come back with us."

I tilt my head. They weren't in the loop—no one was, beyond my father and me. Colin and Kai came later, I'm sure. Once I was already gone. It's why they wanted to see me in the mall. This terrible secret plan between me and my father was supposed to keep everyone safe.

It's done the opposite. Everything that's happened between Aiden coming to me at Aunt Mary's house in Rose Hill and today is on my shoulders.

So, yeah, I could just hang up my hat and go with them. Let them shoot Aiden—or worse.

But my body seizes up when I think about that scenario. Aiden strung up in a basement, tortured as retribution. It wouldn't end there.

"No." I swallow my guilt and square my shoulders. There's no escaping this path I've chosen. I don't *want* to escape it—or *him*. "You wouldn't see the light of day because I would put a fucking bullet in your thick skulls."

My words echo in my brain, bounce around.

"You—"

"My father and I had a plan." My voice comes out harsher than I intend, and I belatedly remember the weapon. I withdraw it and raise it at Turner, who has taken a step to the side. Like he'd love to go for Aiden and couldn't seem to stop himself.

"You and everyone else targeting the DeSantises on the street are fucking everything up. Spread the word—no one touches them. The feud ends my way." I sneer. "I've got no problem emptying this thing into your gut if you keep moving toward him."

There's no way they're going to listen to me—I'm... *me*. Gemma West. The princess, not the queen. Not a leader. Not respected.

"She's got more balls than her brother," Turner finally says.

I level them with a glare.

"Fine," Marius says. "We'll spread the word."

He reaches into his pocket for his phone, then shoves it into my hand.

I stare at the smartphone, then back at him.

"In case you decide you want backup." His voice is gruff. Pity fills his expression.

I shake my head and toss it back. "You don't want your phone in DeSantis possession." *Or the pity.* I can't take anything from them, not when I'll be asking for more sacrifices soon enough.

He gives me a weird look and rests his hand on my shoulder. "Your father's celebration of life is in four days. We'll all be wanting you there."

Don't fuck this up, in other words.

I nod curtly and step back. I don't relax until they've climbed in their truck and driven around me. Their engine guns, and their taillights disappear around a corner.

Aiden steps up behind me and wraps his arms around my waist. I lean back against him, exhaling.

"I didn't expect you to ride to my defense."

I twist so I can see his expression, but his attention is on his mangled bike.

"I..." What can I say to that? I would've been more than horrified if something happened to him. "Yeah, well. We go way back."

He grunts and pulls out his phone, making a quick call. I recognize the name he says, *Ford*. The one who helped clean up my father's murder scene. One of Aiden's guys—not a DeSantis.

Exhaustion nudges at me. Now that the adrenaline is wearing off, the pain is coming back. My whole left side aches like I was rubbed with sandpaper. I put more of my weight on Aiden.

"You're shivering." He doesn't run his hands up and down my arms, but he does turn me and hug me tightly.

I tuck my head under his chin. We stay like that for a few minutes, just breathing, and I try to contain my panic.

"We almost died." My teeth chatter. "They were surprised to see me, obviously, but they knew exactly who you were."

He grimaces. "My bike isn't subtle. You were the wild card, it seems."

If they've been hunting DeSantises, of course Aiden would be the white whale catch. Everyone would be pinning for him.

A wave of dizziness hits me, and I squeeze my eyes shut.

It isn't just that he's in danger—he isn't hiding from it.

He continues to go out like normal. He's still searching for my brother. Still trying to figure out the theft. He's just like Colin and Kai, refusing to hide when it would be good for them. It will get him killed.

I take a step out of his embrace, and my leg buckles.

Aiden swings me up into his arms. "You're hurt."

An accusation.

"You are, too." I loop my arm around his neck, and the other curls in his jacket.

He sighs.

Eventually, a car turns into the intersection and stops close to us, followed closely by an SUV. Ford and a new guy hop out, and they both appraise the situation.

"No bullet wounds?" Ford asks. He goes over and picks up my helmet, inspecting the damage. It's severely scuffed but not cracked. "A fight?"

"Gem's a negotiator," Aiden answers.

Gem. My heart does a weird skip, and I grip the back of his neck tighter.

The new guy gestures to the SUV, and Aiden tries to set me down in the backseat. My fingers won't unlock—okay, maybe I'm not handling this the best—and Aiden lets out a soft exhale.

"It'll be okay." But he doesn't try to put me down again. He slides himself into the seat, arranging me on his lap so we both fit.

New Guy closes our door and confers with Ford for a minute, then hops into the driver's seat. "We called Dr. Matthews," he tells us. "He's meeting you at your apartment."

Aiden grimaces.

"We can't go to your place, boss," New Guy says quietly. "Jameson was asking about you."

"Fuck," I whisper. I don't care about what place Aiden has—another safe house, perhaps—but it's Jameson's name that steals the breath from my lungs. I haven't seen him since he killed my father, and I don't know what I would do.

Kill him myself?

It's tempting—*too tempting*. Aiden didn't take his

handgun back, and I'm not particularly inclined to remind him about it. Or the knife in my boot.

Today has been a weird day.

Aiden's lips press to my temple.

Is Jameson going to twist this into a definite act of war? Not one DeSantis heir targeted, but *two* in the past two and a half months. Never mind that he and Aiden have dripped West blood all over this city in the past few days. Never mind that we didn't kill Wilder. Jameson wants war—and he's going to get it.

Unless I can think of a way out of this.

Double fuck.

We get back to the DeSantis tower within minutes and unload into the elevator. New Guy doesn't get out of the car —he seems edgy, actually, and puts the car in reverse the moment we close the door.

Aiden hasn't put me down, either.

"It's just my knee," I say. "I can walk."

"Stop talking."

I press my lips together and try to decipher his expression.

Anger, sure. Frustration? Concern pulls at the corners of his eyes.

We ride to the twenty-fourth floor in silence. Dr. Matthews waits outside the apartment, and he casts a disconcerting eye over both of us before snapping back into professionalism. Aiden sets me on my feet by the kitchen table. He carefully unzips my jacket and eases it down my arms.

"You don't have to be—*ow*—" I glance down at my arm. Dark-red scrapes cover the outside of my left forearm, elbow, and part of my upper arm. They ooze blood in a few places. Where it isn't scraped, blue and black bruises bloom.

"Road rash," he says carefully. "Your leg..."

I finally look down.

Gravel clings to the denim, but that's not the worst. The

left leg of my jeans is shredded. The frayed edges are dark red. My leg appears to have gone head-to-head with a cheese grater. He kneels and unzips my boots, carefully peeling them off. My sheathed knife comes next. Then the gun in my waistband. He sets everything on the table in a row.

The doctor makes a noise of disbelief behind us.

Aiden sheds his own jacket, placing it over mine on the back of a chair. He's less beat up than me, but I think he's got more experience falling off a bike. I didn't know what to do, so I did everything wrong.

"He might have a concussion," I say to Dr. Matthews.

The man narrows his eyes. "Sit, both of you."

"Gem first," Aiden demands.

"Did you black out?" the doctor asks him.

"*Gemma first.*" Aiden slams his hand on the table.

The doctor jumps, but he recovers quickly and unzips his bag. He retrieves a pair of trauma sheers and motions for me to sit. "I'm going to cut your jeans off."

Aiden growls. "You want her to take her pants off?"

"I want to be able to treat her to the best of my ability," Dr. Matthews says stiffly. "If you have a problem with that, I suggest a hospital."

I've never seen someone stand up to Aiden and... well, not *die*, at the very least. I hold still as he slices through the ripped fabric, all the way up. Aiden watches the doc while I slide it down my other leg and kick it away. It's less torn up, just a greenish bruise and scrape on my knee.

I zone out while he treats me, then Aiden. My eyes drift shut at one point, and it isn't until I nearly fall off my chair that Aiden puts an end to the ministrations.

"We'll check base in the morning," Aiden says, showing him the door. He flips the deadbolt once Dr. Matthews is gone and comes to me. "Sore?"

"It'll probably be worse tomorrow," I say.

He nods and offers his hands. I take them. He helps me to my feet, and we walk upstairs. From wedding dress shopping, to interrogating a gang leader, to intercepting a hit on Aiden... I'm ready to sleep for a week.

We shed the rest of our clothes, replacing them with soft t-shirts, and climb into bed. I keep my injured side up, and Aiden drags me backward into his chest. His arm settles over my waist, and his lips brush my shoulder.

"Thank you," he says in my ear.

"For what?"

"Deescalating the situation." He pauses. "They listened to you."

That's the worrisome part. "Have you heard anything about Colin taking over?"

"Not so much. I'll check with Sam, though. He has his ear to the ground more than most."

I grimace. "You didn't say how bad it was getting between our families. Has this been going on for a while? Random... hits?"

"From both sides," he confirms.

"I don't want to see your father tomorrow." A small fear.

His grip on me tightens. "I don't know how much of a choice he'll give us. But perhaps I can spirit you away with Cat for the afternoon to prepare for the wedding..."

I suck my lower lip between my teeth. Jameson was willing to shoot at Aiden—what else would he be willing to risk? Nothing is adding up. Just pieces of a puzzle that don't line up. Again and again.

"Italian marble and firearms?" Suddenly, I can't close my eyes without hearing the screech of metal in my ears, or the bright glow of the truck's headlights. I reach out and hit the button for the light, encasing us in darkness.

"Yes."

"Who would want that?"

"You mean, besides your family?"

I scoff. "I told you—"

"Yeah, yeah." His teeth find my skin, and my abdomen clenches. "I'm starting to take you at your word, Gemma West."

"You should." I twist so I can see his face, faintly illuminated by the lights outside.

I press my lips to his softly.

His arm slides up and wraps around my throat, bringing me back to him. I don't object when he guides me flat on my back and hovers over me. His knee edges between my thighs. He keeps his fingers on my throat while his elbows take his weight, one on either side of my head.

"I love you, Gemma."

My heart skips a beat—and he must feel it, because a grin creeps across his face.

"I don't think I'll get tired of that reaction."

I pull him down to me, and our lips meet. Our mouths open and tongues tangle, but he doesn't make any move beyond that. Finally, he flops onto his side and exhales.

"It's nearly dawn." His voice is gravel in my ear. "Sleep, princess."

Somehow, now, *princess* doesn't feel like a bad word. I smile and flip back onto my uninjured side. We resume our positions, and in no time, I'm asleep.

CHAPTER 23

"Choose," *Jameson says in my ear.*

My gaze flickers between a gagged Aiden and my unconscious brother.

The cold muzzle of the gun against my temple is familiar, and I exhale. I can't—I won't pick. I've already played this game. I meet Aiden's eyes, and he narrows them at me. If he weren't gagged, he might mouth, "I love you" at me again. My heart aches.

"Your silence is answer enough."

Jameson circles the table and presses the gun to the back of Aiden's head.

I squeeze my eyes shut as he squeezes the trigger, and I let out a scream.

"Gemma, wake up."

Hands haul me upright, into something solid and warm.

"Shh," Aiden whispers.

I burst into tears.

Seems to be a new thing for me—when I'd prided myself on not being much of a crier before. Now I can't seem to stop the waterworks from erupting, and I clutch Aiden's shirt as I sob into his neck. It felt real.

And I couldn't pick, even though it cost Aiden his life.

He killed you. The words are on the tip of my tongue, but I can't voice them. I can't put that energy out into the universe, even though my subconscious seems convinced that Jameson will do anything to win.

"I'm sorry," I say, wiping at my nose with the back of my hand.

"Don't apologize."

"I—"

"Princess, you've been through hell. I'd be more worried if you *weren't* having nightmares."

I sniffle and lean back, meeting his gaze. He's more put together than me—dressed in jeans and a fitted gray t-shirt, his thick dark hair swept back off his face.

"Do you think your father's lashing out because he's upset about Wilder?"

Aiden freezes. "What?"

I shift. "He's been acting crazy. Do you think it's grief?"

"I think he's... I don't know. Maybe you're onto something." He rises. "Coffee?"

I lick my lips and let my attention wander down his body. The t-shirt covers his tattoos, but he still gives off a dangerous vibe.

"Maybe something else?" His voice is husky.

I automatically squirm. "Now that you mention it..."

He nods once and circles around to my side of the bed, his expression hungry. He flips the blankets off my legs. His gaze lands on the gauze wrapped around my knee. His expression closes. I wait, uncertain if he'll just storm away, or...

He swings my legs around, until they hang off the bed, and kneels between them. I shift, suddenly hot.

"You don't—"

His glare stalls my breath. He places a kiss on my inner thigh, his eyes locked on mine. I prop myself up on my elbows to see him better, at the way he slowly moves higher.

"I wanted to do this last night," he says.

His lips move against my panties, over my clit, and I let out an involuntary moan.

"I'm crazy for your taste. Your smell." He runs his nose along the hem.

"Aiden," I breathe.

He tears through my panties. The noise is harsh in the quiet room, and I yelp. He tosses the discarded fabric away and bands his arms under my thighs, gripping my ass. He yanks me closer, and then his mouth is on me.

I let my head fall back. He works my clit, sucking and nibbling. I rock against his face—I can't help myself. He blows on my sensitive nub, then latches on to it again. I moan and slide my hand into his hair. His mouth dips lower, and I scream when his tongue pierces me.

He tongue-fucks me until white spots dance in front of my vision. He replaces his tongue with two fingers and returns to my clit, and it's not long after that I see stars. I scream his name, clamping my thighs around him. I only relax once I've ridden the wave of pleasure and can breathe again.

"Holy shit," I mumble.

He grins and rises, leaning over me. I accept his hot, open-mouthed kiss. I taste myself on his tongue. He undoes his belt and drops his jeans, his mouth still fastened to mine. He thrusts into me in one smooth motion, and I whimper. He leans back and hooks his arm under my right knee. He puts my ankle on his shoulder, and my eyes roll back when he hits an all new deep spot inside me.

"I'm going to combust," I pant, raising my hips to meet him.

He pushes my shirt up to my neck and palms my breast.

My fingers slip toward my clit, and I rub small circles as he fucks me. His eyes darken, flicking between my face and my hand. It isn't long before the stimulation is too much, and another climax sweeps through me. I tense around him, and he lets out a groan before pumping twice more. He stills, buried in me, and releases my leg.

He falls forward. I grab his face and kiss him again. My whole body buzzes with bliss, and my core pulses where we're still connected.

"To chase away the nightmares," he says.

I flinch.

He draws back ever so slightly, and for a moment I wonder how perceptive he is. But then he just hoists us farther back on the bed so he's not on his feet anymore. He kisses the corner of my lips, up over my cheekbones. He nips my earlobe, and I clench around his cock again. A throaty chuckle rumbles in his chest.

He pulls out and thrusts back into me, just a bit, and I dig my nails into his jaw. I haven't released his face. He repeats the motion, and we both let out a low moan.

"Again?"

He snickers and rotates his hips. "I can't help that you feel like heaven."

My face heats. I don't know why him being nice sits weird in my chest. Compliments from guys usually have strings, and I can't help but think his are no different. He wants me to ignore that he wants my brother dead.

They put aside their hate for an afternoon, but it wasn't enough for him.

I wrap my legs around his hips.

"Do you hate that I won't say it back?" I ask.

He meets my eyes. "No."

"Why not?"

"Because your reaction to me saying it is enough to tell me what you won't admit." He steals a kiss—steals my breath, too—then works lower. And he shows me exactly what he thinks of me.

"Isn't it bad luck to see the bride before the wedding?" someone drawls.

I cringe. The voice is immediately recognizable, but I refuse to look at the door. Aiden drapes himself over me, blocking most of my body, and I bury my head in his neck.

Because really—*kill me now.*

"You thought it was a good idea to let yourself in?" Aiden asks his father.

Jameson scoffs. "You weren't answering your phone. She's not supposed to be a distraction. Or have you forgotten where your loyalties lie? Certainly not in her cunt, sweet as it might be."

Aiden grunts and pulls out of me. He quickly flips the covers over me and stands, ignoring the mortification on my face. I drag the blanket up, hiding my face. Call it cowardice, but this is the *second* time he's seen Aiden do dirty things to me, and I want to claw his eyes out. Never mind the anger his presence invokes. I won't look at him and give him the satisfaction of seeing me with anything less than armor on.

"Fuck off, Dad. I'll see you downstairs."

His father's irritation is clear in his tone. "Blue balls will be good for you, and we're late for a meeting. Come with me. *Now.* Or I'll drag your pretty bride-to-be with me... as is."

Aiden makes a noise in the back of his throat. He moves around the room, clothes rustling, and then a weight dips the bed. He slowly folds back the blanket back from my head, his face hovering over mine.

Regret fills his features.

"I'll have Cat come distract you. I'm sorry."

I shake my head. "It's..."

He kisses my quickly, then hops off the bed. He follows his father out, down the stairs, and the front door slams.

I don't move for a long moment. My legs are still open, his cum and mine seeping out. We were in the middle of a *moment*. Of course Jameson saw an opportunity to ruin it. I sigh and go straight for the shower, scrubbing the undamaged skin until it's bright red. Once I'm out, I apply the ointment Dr. Matthews left.

The burn on my back is almost fully healed—I forgot about it with everything going on, actually. It seems like a lifetime ago that Aiden set Aunt Mary's house on fire. How foolish that I wanted to save it. Weeks with him have solidified my knowledge that some things just aren't salvageable.

"Gemma?" Cat calls. "You in here?"

"Upstairs," I yell. "Come help me pick out clothes."

She steps into the bathroom and immediately winces. "Damn. Sam said you guys were in an accident, but he convinced me you were okay."

I shrug. "Just a few scrapes."

My knee feels better today. Keeping it stable overnight must've done the trick.

"Your leg..." She winces. "Well, only the scrapes on your arm will show, and those don't look too bad." She straightens my arm to examine it. "I mean, painful as fuck, but the photographer can probably edit it out."

I snort. "They won't have a photographer. Jameson is just doing this to be an ass."

Her eyes go wide. "Um, I hate to break it to you, but Aiden's sort of taken over."

I freeze. "As of when?"

"Yesterday, I think?" She grins at my expression. "Don't shoot the messenger."

"I..." I shake my head to clear my thoughts. "No, no, it's fine. I mean, I don't really have any idea what I want, and it doesn't feel real. You know, it's a sham wedding."

Her eyebrow tics up, then smooths.

I cross my arms. "You don't think it's a sham."

"Sorry, babe. I might've agreed with you before I saw you and Aiden interact, but he's totally smitten. And I think you like him, too."

I stare at myself in the mirror and sigh. I *do* like him, and that's the problem. "The whole world is against us," I whisper. "The chances of us working out are..."

"Pretty damn high," Cat finishes. "Seeing as how you two are both smart and tough. Anything is possible."

"There's a meddling father to contend with, though."

She grimaces. "Fair."

I turn away from my own reflection. "Okay, what's on the agenda today?"

She perks up. "Spa day! The wedding ceremony is at the church down the street—unlike Wilder's, this should be a lot more contained. We're starting early, and then we'll have all day to party. *But*, that means you need to be all ready for like, nine o'clock."

I sigh and nod. She trails me into the closet, and I give her my back to drop my towel and pull on underwear. "Okay, well, I can do my hair fairly fast—"

"No! God, Gemma, you're getting the works. A hair stylist is coming, along with the dress designer, and a makeup artist." She grins at my shocked expression. "It'll be fun."

"They're going to get here at the crack of dawn?"

"Well..."

"Great." I move to my little section of clothes. "So, spa day. I don't need to be fancy?"

She flips her dark hair over her shoulder. She's in leggings and a long, loose blouse. Her hair is down, and she's not wearing much makeup. A chunky turquoise necklace completes her casual outfit. There's probably a car downstairs with our name on it, unless the spa happens to be in the DeSantis building.

Which, actually, makes a lot more sense.

She waits for me to slip a silky baby pink dress on, then sandals on my feet. I'm running out of things to wear, but this will do for now. We head downstairs, and I pause at the paper on the kitchen counter. It's pinned in place by a cup of coffee made the way I like it, and a keycard beside it.

So you don't get locked out today, it reads. *Love, A*.

"Love, huh? I totally called it."

I roll my eyes and palm the card. I don't know what it'll open, but I can test it out later. It's a piece of freedom I didn't have yesterday... and I won't look a gift horse in the mouth.

Cat grins and gestures for me to try the card once we're in the elevator.

I swipe it, and the little light turns green.

"Which floor?"

"Eighteen," she says. "They offer it as a perk to clients who come up to their offices on the twentieth floor—like, hey, you're coming in for a meeting, do you want a facial?"

"That's a weird perk," I mutter.

She shrugs. "Politicians, you know?"

"I guess." *No idea*. I never had to navigate that part of this world.

Mom did, though. She was good at it. She and my father...

Pain lances through me, and I reflexively rub my chest. It's old wounds merging with new grief. They're both gone. What I wouldn't give to see either of them again. To hug them. I should've hugged my father when I saw him at the restaurant. Kissed his cheek, told him I loved him. Now it's too late.

The elevator doors slide open. We take a left and walk

toward a wall of frosted glass. Cat opens the door for us, gesturing me ahead, and the receptionist immediately rises.

"Gemma, Cat," she says.

Is it me, or is she nervous?

She gestures for us to follow her. "You've got a few minutes before your appointments, so you're welcome to relax in our sauna or the hot tub area. Lockers are here. Towels and robes are inside, as well."

"Thanks," Cat says.

The employee hightails it away from us, and I raise my eyebrows at Cat.

"She's probably never seen a West in real life before. You've got a reputation."

I laugh. "Yeah, right."

"Well, Aiden has a reputation," she amends. "And you have one by association. The only girl who's stood up to him... People have been talking about the card game nonstop. They liked you, but when you didn't shirk away from Aiden flinging you over his shoulder like a caveman? Respect."

That's... hard to swallow.

"Soon after that, someone tried to kill me," I remind her.

She waves my words away. "Some people are too hot-headed. You impressed the ones who matter."

"Who matters?"

We shed our clothes and replace them with soft terrycloth robes. I tighten the belt and wait for her answer.

"Mac, for one."

I eye her. "Your uncle." *And Jameson's brother.*

"Yep. He had a soft spot for my mom. Thinks my dad's a fucking dumbass." She knots her hair on top of her head and winks.

The door cracks, and a new woman sticks her face into the locker room. "Gemma?"

I nod.

"You're up first," she says. "Marta will be over to grab you in just a moment, Catrina."

I follow the woman down a hall and into a private room. It smells like lavender, and the air is warm. She points to the raised, cushioned table, motioning for me to shed the robe. I hesitate, then do as she says.

She sucks in a sharp breath when she takes in my new injuries. "We'll avoid these," she murmurs. "Just relax, honey. I'll take good care of you."

And she does. She loosens knots I didn't know existed, and my anxiety funnels out of me. I close my eyes.

Minutes or hours later, I wake up to a dimly lit room. It's empty.

I hoist myself off the table and look around, trying to remember what happened. The too-good-to-be-true massage happened.

Right.

I grab my robe and open the door, peeking into the hall. It's similarly deserted. No one stops me from finding my way back to the locker room. Cat's stuff is still in her locker, although I don't know how long she could be. Just in case, I check the sauna and hot tub.

Empty.

Wait a second. We're on the eighteenth floor... just two below Jameson's and Aiden's offices.

I shouldn't, but now that I realize, my curiosity is too strong to ignore. I bypass the shower and get dressed quickly, the keycard clutched in my hand.

"If Cat finds you, we can abandon this," I reason aloud. A deal with myself.

And yet, I encounter no one when I trace my steps back to the elevator, then the staircase beyond it. No one stops me from going up and quietly slipping into the office space.

My heart steadily climbs into my throat, but I need answers.

I need the full picture to this puzzle I'm solving. I have no idea if I'll find it in Jameson's office, but if he's distracted by Aiden... Now is as good of an opportunity as ever.

CHAPTER 24

Aiden

Sandra White, the councilwoman, rises from the table. It's been three fucking hours of... nothing other than Dad's flirting, really. I didn't have to be here for this. I certainly never wanted to witness him being friendly to a woman and make subtle innuendos.

Your job is hard? I'll show you what's hard, sweetheart.

Instead of scoffing, like I'm sure she'd do if any other bastard said that to her, she giggled.

Fuck my life.

Anyway, we're done here. I learned a few pieces of information that were of interest: that Sandra has had pushback from her fellow councilors about the construction permits she's been passing, and donations are on the rise. The two seem to show opposite interests on the surface.

But really? Donations are a way to nudge a government official one way or another. Donate to their organizations, to the charities they support—and sit on the board of, and take a cut from—and they're more likely to get what they want.

Except these are anonymous under a company, and

Sandra's team hasn't been able to suss out the owner. Or their agenda.

She brought it to our attention because she's worried it'll force her to act in one way or another, if the donor ever steps forward.

And I'm sure it will. These things don't get overlooked, especially in Manhattan. New York City politicians are brutal, but the lobbyists are worse.

They can destroy a person's career in days.

"It was so good to see you both," she says, stretching her hand out toward me.

I take it and shake, then retreat as soon as is socially acceptable. I've always preferred to avoid anything to do with politics, but this is my new life. Luca met with her. Amelie forced me to bring her because she was on a warpath, and that's how that stupid article in her mother's magazine came about. The councilwoman made sure to mention how flattered she was about that, too.

"Likewise, Councilwoman," Dad says smoothly. He shakes her hand and places his other on top of hers.

She blushes. "I've told you to call me Sandra."

I bite back my gag and turn from the table. They finish their conversation, and Dad meets me in the SUV we rode in together.

"Well?" he asks.

"I'd be concerned with the donor."

Dad scoffs. "It's only a problem if she bends to their will. Or if she's using that as a ploy to get us to donate more."

"Is that how she would play it?"

He shrugs. "Never assume anyone is acting in your best interest. People are inherently selfish."

I don't respond. There's truth to his words. I know people are selfish. I've caught men trying to weasel their way out of trouble by any means necessary. Too many of them are willing to give up anything for escape. Their families. Their employers.

All to scrape themselves out of a hole, or to chase freedom.

How far would I go for such things?

How far would Dad?

Or Gemma?

I shake off those thoughts as the SUV enters our parking garage.

"Join me in my office," Father says. "I have an assignment for you—something more in your wheelhouse than wining and dining."

I arch my eyebrow. "Really."

He grins.

The SUV parks, and I follow him to the elevator. My phone chimes on our way up—a text from Cat.

Gemma finished spa day early—I think she's back upstairs.

I slide my phone back into my pocket. The elevator doors slide open on the twentieth floor. Dad leads the way down the hall, and I try to put thoughts of my beautiful girl out of my mind. My father has a knack for detecting when my head isn't in the game.

Years of experience dealing with other people's bullshit has given me a similar talent.

I pause and glance in my office. The door is cracked, when I could've sworn I closed and *locked* it.

He opens his door and flicks on the light, then turns and glances back at me. "You stalling?"

Over his shoulder, I see a flash of blonde.

My stomach bottoms out. Too late, he steps farther into his office and gestures impatiently for me. I grit my teeth and walk in, closing the door behind us.

So help me God, Gemma better not be in this fucking office.

I try to be subtle when I glance around.

There aren't too many places to hide. He's got two walls of windows, and his large chestnut desk takes up most of the space front and center. When he sits, he faces the door. It's an old ingrained habit—I don't like putting my back to the door, either, even though sometimes it's necessary.

Like when the move is a power play.

There's a couch and two chairs off to the side. *That* part is a sham—I don't think he's ever offered a visitor to sit on that couch unless she was a pretty woman. And pretty woman, I am not.

He leans against the front of his desk, picking up a file that was left next to his laptop.

"There's a bank manager trying to steal from us," he tells me. He flips though the file, then tosses it to me.

I catch it and scan the first page. It's a typical compilation of information from one of our private investigators. Nothing too exciting: fat white guy thinks he can get away with... well, not quite murder.

"Right. How do you want him to pay for his crimes?" I ask.

Something moves under my father's desk, just a quick shadow.

I force my gaze up.

Dad glares at me. "Am I boring you?"

"No." I clear my throat. "No, I just remembered I had something in my office I need you to sign."

Please follow me.

Dad laughs. "I want the banker strung up by his ankles for the whole city to see. But I don't suppose you'd do that, would you? We could go the old-fashioned route. Take a finger. Maybe the whole hand." He shoves off the desk and whips his door open, striding to my office.

I stare at the shadow under his desk, knowing how close

she just came to being caught. I open my mouth, but I don't have anything worth saying. Not when my throat suddenly closes in anger.

It's the same feeling I felt after I dragged her out of her aunt's pool. How infuriated I was that she would risk her life...

Yep, I'm pissed.

So I don't say anything, instead leaving the door ajar and hurrying into my office. Jameson has made himself at home in my chair, his feet up.

"Comfortable?"

He chuckles. "Your office is too neat. How do you function?"

I shake my head and point to the drawer he's blocking. He shifts out of the way, and I take my time to unlock it. He makes an impatient noise in the back of his throat.

Honestly?

I've got absolutely nothing. A few permits for the construction going on near Central Park, but I can be the signer as easily as him.

"Son."

I meet his cool gaze.

"How about you sit and tell me what the real issue is."

I roll my eyes. "I don't have an issue."

He nudges me aside and puts his legs back up, crossing his arms. "Sit. Talk."

Gemma is going to pay for this—because she might need more time to do whatever the hell she's doing, and I don't want her to face my father's wrath. Just mine.

"If I were to die, who would you choose to inherit our businesses?" I ask.

He blinks at me.

Then bursts out laughing.

He roars so loud, he scoots back in the chair and drops his feet to the floor, slapping his thighs. I hate him for this—for telling me to spill what's on my mind and then laughing in my face.

"Aiden," he finally says. "You're not going to die. And if you do, then I guess I'll just... not."

I scoff.

"I've got it handled. I can see why you'd be worried, because it's a lot of responsibility. But you don't have to, because we're protected." He stands suddenly. "Good chat. Now get to work on that banker—preferably before your nuptials tomorrow."

I nod and see him out. His office door is now firmly closed, and I let out the smallest exhale. I give him a minute—to go inside and shut his door again—then lock my office and stride toward the stairs.

By the time I reach my apartment, I wonder if I'll be able to contain myself—and then I ask myself why the hell I should. She knows what happens when she breaks the rules.

I unlock the door, slamming it behind me. She sits on the dining table, legs swinging. She grins at me, but it fades when she registers my expression.

"What were you thinking?"

Her legs stop swinging.

"Or did you think your little stunt went undetected?"

She swallows.

I approach slowly, still unsure what I'm going to do with her. I guess it depends on what she says next. I part her knees and step between them. Her head automatically tips back, her eyes glued to mine.

"Well?" I prod.

"I, ah..." She looks away. "I didn't mean to get caught."

I stare at her. "Indeed."

Fuck. I thought, at the very least, she might apologize. Or offer up an explanation. Instead, we descend into stony silence.

Her chest rises and falls rapidly, and that's the only sign of her distress. But now there's this, and I'm hard as a rock.

Not good.

I shake my head once and grab her hips, pulling her flush against me. Her ass slides to the edge of the table, and she can feel my cock slide along her panties. She lets out a little sigh, eyes wide. She still doesn't know what I'm going to do, and that's only fair.

Because I don't know what I'm going to do, either.

She's a seductress—but only to me. She pushes my limits. She's headstrong.

I love all of it.

But she'll get herself killed if she continues along this path.

I lean forward and haul her over my shoulder. She squeaks and grabs at the back of my shirt. It rides up, revealing my weapon. Her cold fingers press into my skin.

"You touch my gun, I'll shoot you myself," I warn.

She huffs. "I'm not a complete idiot."

I carry her in the opposite direction of my bedroom—out the door of our apartment and into the elevator.

"What are you doing?" There's fear in her voice now.

Better. Better to terrify her now than have something happen to her. Something almost did happen to her, and it was luck that I found her alive instead of at the bottom of the pool.

Or with my father's bullets in her.

Or burned alive.

I tighten my hold on her thighs.

"Aiden." She kicks at me, but I deflect her blow.

I lock down her legs and finally drop her.

"Where are we going?"

I swipe my card and hit the button for one of the lower floors. We drop, and my stomach swoops. I'll make it up to her. I'll ease the fear later, when she realizes what could've happened.

I take her arm and lead her down a long, narrow hallway. We go through an empty lobby, then a side door. We're in a public-access space now, although things are still very much controlled. She shivers in my grip.

"Aiden—"

"Be silent," I snap.

This is a darker part of the DeSantis legacy.

We enter a room that's thick with steam. There is a shallow pool in the center of the room, and girls lounge in it. I hate this floor—I've always hated it. The women are draped over the edges, and they perk up when we enter. Scantily clad, happy to do whatever you ask for a buck.

They create fantasies for men—and sometimes, women—who don't want to exist in the real world.

But they sell their souls at the same time. It's a trade-off.

Farther back, there are women who don't know anything else. The ones hooked on coke or heroin, who are here because we supply them with enough drugs that they don't care their bodies are the payment.

Gemma's attention latches on to one of the large cushions off to the side. They're separated by nearly translucent curtains. Not enough to hide the fact that there are men here, too, taking what they can buy.

The one she's focused on, there are just shadows moving —a man's back. And if you listen over the gurgle of water and murmur of low conversation, grunting.

Put her with the whores. This is where my father wanted to send her after I captured the princess. Here, with the filth.

"Strip," I say.

She shivers and doesn't move.

"Take off your clothes or I'll cut them off." I let her feel the sharp prick of the blade—her blade, again in my possession—against her hip.

And slowly, she does as I say. She kicks off her sandals and inches her dress over her head, standing before me in just her lace bralette and matching panties. Her injuries are dark red, blue-black bruises surrounding them and other spots.

I ignore them.

"Get in the pool."

Her gaze flies to mine. "You can't be serious."

I don't let my expression soften. I just lift my chin, and my cock twitches when she shudders. There are more threats on the tip of my tongue, but I'm most curious to see what she'll do. How much persuasion she'll need—and how far she'll go.

She takes a step back, eyes narrowing.

The girls have gone silent, watching us, and now the only sound is the slap of skin from behind the curtains. I stride toward their partition and rip it open.

The man isn't one of ours, but the girl immediately stills. He glances over his shoulder, and fury contorts his expression. Until he realizes who stands at his back, anyway. Then it flickers quickly into fear.

"Out."

The girl pushes backward on the cushions, making the decision for him. His dick slips out of her, but the idiot seems stuck. Dumbfounded.

"Get the fuck *out*," I yell.

He bolts for his pants, forgoing his shoes and shirt, and races past me for the door. Only when it's swung shut behind him do I turn back to Gemma.

"Get in the pool," I repeat.

I don't like to repeat myself, and I've pushed my patience to the limit today. I *want* to go upstairs and fuck her into submission, but she would enjoy that too much.

I lift my chin and wait her out.

It doesn't take long.

She steps delicately into the pool. The water sloshes around her calves, then thighs as she wades deeper. It won't go past her hips unless she falls, but she holds her hands out to the sides nonetheless.

Her skin is like porcelain that's been broken and glued back together. Smooth and perfect until your eyes catch on her cracks. Still beautiful, but not the untouchable object she might once have been.

I jerk my head at one of the girls behind her. They're all waiting for my command. Father comes down here when he needs to blow off steam, but he doesn't care.

I first ventured onto this floor to conquer.

"Hold her."

They're quick to follow my order. Their expressions are hungry. One comes up and takes Gemma's wrists, pinning them behind her. These girls are overlooked by almost anyone —but not me. Not when I realized who they saw on a regular basis, with their guards down.

Who would use a prostitute as an informant?

"She's got pretty hair," the first coos in Gemma's ear.

"Pretty skin," another says. She licks Gemma's face.

My girl doesn't flinch. Her gaze doesn't even leave mine as she fights their hands.

Someone grabs her hair and forces her head back, exposing the long column of her throat. Fingers run down her neck, her shoulders. They shove her bralette down, exposing her breasts, and I bite the inside of my cheek.

This is nothing.

This is just a flicker of a snapshot of what her life would be like if she was brought here. They wouldn't be gentle with her. Gentleness, hope, kindness—they all kill in a place like this.

I keep waiting for her to break, but she just shivers as they manipulate her flesh. They don't go lower than her waist, but they pinch her skin, pull her hair. The water splashes up over the lip of the pool, responding to her struggle.

"Down," I order.

They submerge her.

She comes up fighting like a wildcat, doing her best to get free. As soon as she gets an arm free, someone else captures it.

"This is where you would've come if Jameson had his way."

Some of the women flinch—those on the periphery, not participating. The newer arrivals.

The brunette, the first to move, runs her hand between Gemma's breasts, dipping lower. Gemma's chest heaves, and she doesn't take her eyes off me. Even as water streams down her face. The brunette's fingers span wide over Gemma's stomach, then dip into her panties.

I grit my teeth. "Shall she make you come?"

Gemma's head shake *no* borders on violent, even as her head tips back. There are too many hands on her, slipping up and down her arms and legs. Dragging water droplets over her body.

"Hold," I say quietly.

They all stop.

I kick off my shoes and hop into the pool, going straight for Gemma. Some of the girls scatter, but a few remain to keep her still.

I trace my finger down her wet face. "*This* is where you would be if I didn't step in. Men would pick you from the crowd. In fact, you'd probably be good for business. Gemma West, the fallen virgin princess. What would someone have paid for that first time with you?" I lean in until my lips are on her ear. "You'd be used for your holes and nothing more."

I cut her panties off and tuck them into my pocket.

"You're a fucking psychopath," she spits.

I slap her pussy. The sting is amplified by the water, and she hisses through her teeth.

I glance around her, at the two remaining women who hold her against the edge of the pool. One's hand moves higher, brushing Gemma's wet hair off her shoulder. She kisses her throat, then nips her earlobe. I bite back my growl—this isn't about me and Gemma. This is punishment, and it might just serve to torture both of us.

Her cheeks are red.

She's embarrassed by what's happening. The violation of another woman touching her against her will.

"When will you learn that I'm just trying to keep you safe?" I thrust two fingers inside her. I need her to understand, but her terror just fuels my anger. Her cunt clenches. She's slick with wet heat.

Turned on by this situation?

I finger-fuck her, and it's our only point of contact. I ignore the press of my cock against my zipper, begging to be freed, and instead lean forward again.

"Does this do it for you? Would you let a stranger touch you like this? He'd call you a whore and grunt in your ear until he comes inside your tight cunt, only for the next one to be waiting in the wings. You want that life?"

My thumb brushes her clit, and she writhes. She rips her arm free. Her slap comes fast and furious across my face.

The sound echoes. But most of all, it *stings*.

When the fuck was the last time someone hit me?

I touch my lip with my tongue, shocked when blood blooms across my tastebuds.

When's the last time someone drew blood?

"Fuck you, Aiden." She shoves at the women, at me. Her gaze sticks on my lips, but her fight is only beginning.

Maybe I underestimated that.

She wouldn't make it here—she'd bite someone's dick off if they brought it anywhere near her sharp mouth.

The women scatter when she pushes me, but Gemma doesn't stick around. She hops out of the pool and pulls her bralette back into place, stooping to collect her dress. She slides it on and walks stiffly to the door.

Out.

Away.

I smack the water.

"Aiden," the brunette says softly. "That was cruel."

I meet her eyes and hold. She's stronger than some of them —all of them here are stronger than the women in the back rooms—but only Gemma has a talent for holding my gaze without flinching. And *there* it is. She flicks her eyes down to her fidgeting hands.

"I'm trying to prevent her from ending up here." I run my fingers through my hair, frustration tugging at me.

I hate coming here because I hate what they have to go through. It's one thing to choose this living. It's another entirely to be forced into it because you owe money, or you are desperate, or maybe you just have a really shitty family. My frustration runs straight into guilt.

"I've told you once, I'll tell you again—this ends when I'm in charge."

She nods once and moves back. The women here, regardless of their harsh interaction with newcomers, actually do care for each other. They swallow her back into their ranks.

I shake my head and leap from the pool, following Gemma's wet footprints.

One day, they'll be free—and so will my conscience.

CHAPTER 25
Gemma

He traces lazy circles around my breast.

My *bare* breast, when I distinctly remember going to bed fully clothed. And alone.

"Get your fucking hand off me." My voice comes out clear, despite how early it is. The sun isn't even fully up—the sky seems to be lightening from midnight-blue to twilight slowly. Painfully slow.

If it were to be light out, it would be later.

I'd have an excuse to slip out of bed and prepare for the day.

Wedding day.

My stomach lurches, and butterflies erupt through my chest. They're not the good kind, either. I want to puke and gut myself at the same time.

And Aiden's fingers still create trails of fire on my skin.

I grab his wrist and throw it off me. If he was doing it in his sleep, he must be awake now. I don't give him the chance to react and hurry into the bathroom. I flip the lock and bury my face in my hands.

I felt his arm fall across my waist in the middle of the

night, thought he was asleep after a few minutes, and went to sleep on the couch. Away from him.

He dragged me back. Lifted me over his shoulder as easily as he had that first night.

"I hate you," I whisper through the door.

Not just for what he did yesterday, but for what I found.

There's an echo of hands on my skin that I can't scrub off. His harsh words. My own arousal, which took too damn long to go away. I refused to relieve the pressure, instead suffering in silence... and a cold shower. *Maybe two.*

When nothing but silence greets me, I turn away. I'm completely naked—not just my shirt missing, but my sleep shorts and underwear, too. My lips purse, and I have to grip the counter to resist going out there and smacking him again.

I'm not the violent type.

I wasn't, anyway.

But now the violence seems to live under my skin, ready to burst through at any moment. My savage prince seems to have altered my thinking... I just wonder if it's permanent.

If I'll ever go back to the girl I used to be.

Get through today, Gemma. Then figure out the rest later.

Teeth brushed and flossed, I step into the hot shower.

The door swings open, banging against the far wall.

I straighten and step out of the stream, glaring at Aiden through the glass. "That was locked."

"They're flimsy." He holds up a set of picks.

He smirks at me, and he doesn't hide the way his gaze crawls down my body.

"It's bad luck to see the bride on her wedding day," I snap.

His smirk widens into a grin. "You don't believe that."

I force myself to relax and smile. "No, you're right. I could use some bad luck. Maybe something will go horribly wrong before we make it to the altar." I step out of the shower and stride toward him. "Maybe you'll get shot before we manage to say *I do.*"

I tap his chest.

He hasn't stopped grinning, but now I'm within range —*mistake.*

He snags my hips and yanks me even closer, until we're flush from knees to chest. His erection rests against my stomach. I automatically bring my hands up and place them on his pecs. He's shirtless, and I have an unobstructed view of his tattoos. The skull, the flowers. Flowers don't seem to go well with *Mafia hitman*, but it works on him.

"You don't believe that." He appraises me. "You're pissed because of yesterday."

I shudder and pull free from his embrace.

"I'm not just pissed, Aiden." I... I hate that betrayal has taken up the forefront of my mind. "Whatever I thought you were going to do, it wasn't..."

He tilts his head and waits.

"That," I finish lamely.

He pushes his sweats down. I swallow at the sight of his erection and clench my thighs together. How does the *sight* of him turn me on? My brain is clearly not on the same wavelength as the rest of me.

"Do you want me to apologize?" He steps forward, eyes glittering.

Do I?

He stalks me back into the shower, one step at a time. I'm not even sure I'm aware of where he's directing me until the warm spray hits my back.

"Stop." My voice is shaking.

His eyes darken. "I'm not sorry for scaring some fucking sense into you. Now turn around."

I stare at him, tempted to screech in his ear or claw at him. He'd probably get off on that. Those scratch marks I gave him are long gone, but his expression when he got them is still burned in my mind. He likes a fight.

He likes a challenge.

Isn't that why he says he likes—*loves*—me?

"Turn the fuck around, baby. I know you didn't come last night. Let me do the honors."

I squeeze my eyes shut. Fuck it. I can vow to be chaste and hold it over his head tomorrow. So I give him my back.

He runs a finger down my spine, down to the crack of my ass. I shiver and barely hold back my whimper. Just the anticipation has me squirming.

"You're mine," he says in my ear. "Those women's hands on you were my hands on you. They didn't violate you—I did."

His fingers still trace back and forth above my ass, teasing my skin. I'm going to combust.

"Put your hands on the wall."

I'm quicker to follow his order this time, and I get a face full of water. He moves the stream, directing it in the opposite direction, and turns up the heat. Steam billows around us. He's in control, and something inside me just... wants that.

For now.

For a moment.

"You're mine," he repeats, "in every sense of the word."

He pulls me back into him by my hips. He kicks out my legs wider, and suddenly his cock is right at my entrance.

"Hot for me," he murmurs. He bends over me, kissing my shoulder blade. His fingers go back to tracing the skin above my ass. He inches inside me and stops.

I groan at this new form of torture, trying to get more friction. My body is on fire, and all I can do is helplessly grip the tiles.

"Please," I let out.

"Please what?"

"Fuck me," I beg. "Aiden. Fuck me, punish me, just fucking do it."

I imagine he's smirking at me.

I wriggle, trying to take matters into my own hands, and he slaps my ass.

"If you move again..." His threat hangs in the air. "Well, Gemma, maybe this is our lesson. Maybe this will nail down the importance of not *risking your fucking life.*"

His anger roars out of nowhere, and he slams into me.

I scream. The force, the unexpected fullness, brings me higher than I expect. I need relief—*now.*

He thrusts into me hard, my whole body jolting with the motion. I drop my hand from the wall and flick my clit. He grabs my wrist and tears my hand away, and I whimper.

"Aiden, you said—"

"I was going to help you," he says on a growl. "But this is a better lesson. You won't come until you've realized how stupid you were."

The pleasure in my body will destroy me.

I choke on another scream when his finger pushes into my asshole. It's not bad—it's like electricity flowing through my body. Sparks fill me, ricocheting around my brain. I groan and grind down on him.

"Aiden, please." Shame swirls through me. "I'm sorry—"

He stills, buried inside me.

"I'm sorry, please let me come."

"First you ask to be fucked. Now the princess wants to come."

He pulls out of me suddenly and wheels me around. He pushes me to my knees before I can react, and I automatically open my mouth. He slides his wet dick into my mouth, and his fingers wind into my wet hair. I taste myself on him, and I suck hard, cupping his balls. He lets out a low groan.

I love that noise.

He lets me blow him the way I want, my tongue swirling. I suck his dick like my life depends on it.

It doesn't.

The loss of him inside me has my cunt throbbing. I've never been so on edge in my life.

He picks up his pace, his head forcing its way deeper in my mouth. I try to relax, although tears stream down my face at the intrusion. All I can do is hold on to his thighs and try to keep up.

Aiden pulls out abruptly, and his cum spills across my face. I close my eyes as it covers me, and then his hand is there, cupping my cheek. His thumb swipes through it, and he presses the digit to my lips.

I lick him clean, opening my eyes to watch his dark eyes locked on mine.

"Good girl," he murmurs.

My pussy clenches.

He helps me up and steps back. "Ride that edge for me. It'll make our wedding night that much sweeter."

He leaves, grabbing a towel and disappearing into the bedroom.

I sag against the wall and swear at him in my head. Still, there's a thrill in holding off. The sweet lingering pain that reminds me I'm totally his.

I'm a goner.

By the time I step out of the shower, Aiden is gone and Cat has replaced him. She takes one look at me and tuts, holding out a silky robe.

"Nervous?" she asks.

I shift. "No," I lie.

Although, the last DeSantis wedding in New York ended with a death... and contrary to what I told Aiden an hour ago, I really don't want anyone to shoot him.

She helps me into the robe and doesn't call me out on my

bullshit.

I glance at the made bed and start to find two small white boxes on it, a square envelope tucked under the edge of one. I tilt my head, unsure if I even want to look inside them.

"Hair and makeup are downstairs. Aiden told me you should open those before you put your dress on," she tells me. "Um, Aiden said I should be your bridesmaid? Is that okay?"

Tears well in my eyes.

Fuck, I'm getting married today. I'm not sure why it's just hitting me now—I knew it as soon as I woke up. But it's hitting me that I'm getting *married*, and three days ago, my father was killed in front of me.

He was supposed to be the one to walk me down the aisle.

"Oh, no, don't cry," Cat says, awkwardly patting my arm. "I'm sure they'll yell at me for that. Please stop."

I dash away the wetness under my eyes and laugh. "You're brilliant at comforting people."

She lets out a relieved sigh. "It worked, yeah?"

I nod and follow her downstairs. The makeup artist has taken over the dining room table, *stuff* covering every inch of it. She wears a black apron, her hair tied back in a long fishtail braid. She's busy fiddling with brushes, but she rights when I approach and smiles widely.

She introduces herself as Magenta. Cat shows her a photo of the dress I chose, then a few more—I suspect Cat was surfing the internet for bridal hairstyles. They nod, heads together, while I pour myself a cup of coffee.

The hairstylist comes up and leans her hip on the counter next to me.

I glance at her, then have to do a double take. "Jess?"

The dealer from the card game, and Cat's friend. Of course both of these women are probably inside the family. I hold back my shiver when I think of the ones in the pool room. Are they from there? Plucked out of obscurity for talents that have gone to waste on that floor?

"You okay?" She pours her own cup from the pot and blows on the liquid.

"Totally fine."

I must be getting better at lying, because she smiles and nods.

"Pre-wedding jitters are totally understandable. We're going to make sure you look your best, though. Although even in what you were wearing at the game, he still seemed like he wanted to ravish you."

My face heats, and I clear my throat. "Uh-huh."

"Mags," Jess calls. "I've got to dry her hair."

Magenta waves her hand. "Fine, fine. Hurry."

Jess grins. "She's excited to work on you."

I swallow.

"She's got mad skills. Don't worry. I don't think Cat would let anyone near you today if they didn't."

"Okay." I blow out a breath. "Let's, um, do this thing."

For the next hour and a half, Jess and Magenta work their magic. I'm not allowed a mirror. Apparently, the surprise will be *worth it*. Cat's words, not mine. As they fix me up, my mind wanders back to yesterday.

To what I found.

My heart jackhammers with me just thinking about what I stole. It's just another mess of puzzle pieces, but this time... I think I'm starting to get the idea. It happened too fast. I was only in Jameson's office for ten or fifteen minutes before I heard their voices outside the door.

I'd never been so lucky to duck under the desk and *not* have him sit in his chair. Otherwise, my ruse would've been well and truly up.

Aiden saved me from that.

Then forced me to see what would've happened if I had

been caught. Or if he hadn't advocated for me when I first arrived.

I shift on my seat, earning a quick tap to the shell of my ear from Magenta's brush.

I grip the arms of the chair.

Why can I see his point now? Why can I look past his anger and see how afraid he was?

He's as helpless as me when it comes to his father.

"Damn it," I mutter.

"Hmm?" Cat narrows her eyes.

"I, uh, don't have anyone to walk me down the aisle."

Shit, shit, I didn't want to think about that. But it just came out of my mouth, and now there's a pregnant pause. My father is dead—and now I have to get married as an orphan.

My brother would've done it if I wasn't marrying into this family.

If they wouldn't kill him on sight.

"If you cry, I'll have to start over," Magenta laments. "Hold yourself together, girl."

"You didn't use waterproof mascara?"

I choke on my laugh. Magenta's expression is pure outrage.

"Of course I did." She huffs. "One can never be too sure, especially with brides."

I straighten. "Did you do Amelie's makeup for her wedding?"

Cat eyes me.

"I did," she says. "Well, as much as she would let me. Her mother hovered quite a bit to dictate the look. Amelie had little patience for it. But it was right in this room."

Too bad I didn't have a time machine—I'd ask her to stash something here for me. Not that the weapon I brought in did me many favors, but maybe a phone.

"Stop scowling," Magenta demands.

I relax my face. "Sorry."

"It's okay. I'm done. Jess?"

"Yep, close your eyes and let me get the hair spray." A blast of spray later, and Jess pats my shoulders. "Okay, done."

"Dress time!" Cat yells.

The dress designer, who had been lingering near the coffee pot, steps up. She unzips the garment bag hanging by the window, and my smile stalls.

"What is that?" I ask.

It's my runner-up option. The dress stuck to my curves like it had been painted on. It was too scandalous to even consider wearing in front of other people.

Her own smile slides off her face. "Aiden—"

"Fuck Aiden," I say as calmly as possible. "I told you what dress I wanted. Are you saying he interfered?" My mind races with how he could pull that off. Did he switch it with Cat once she got down to her apartment? Did the designer give Cat the wrong one to hold on to when they were packing up?

She shifts. "There might've been a slight miscommunication."

Cat comes up beside me and stares at the dress. I mean, come on. It's more like floor-length lingerie.

"Motherfucker," she says. "Where did you get that?"

"Aiden told me Gemma wanted this—"

Cat waves off her words, then pauses. "Wait, you brought this?"

"Yes, he— He asked, and I didn't know it wasn't what you wanted. I'm so sorry. I've ruined your wedding, haven't I? I haven't made a mistake this bad..." She's flustered. She fans herself, looking like she's about to hurl.

And then I turn to Cat, my eyebrows raised. If Cat wasn't in on this switch, then maybe...

My friend points across the apartment, to the stairs going

up to the bedroom. She had hooked the garment bag of the correct dress around one of the rails to keep it off the floor.

"Holy shit." I laugh, bending over. "I thought I was going to have to walk down the aisle in *that*." I can't catch my breath.

Everything I've been holding back bursts through me as laughter. I laugh until tears fill my eyes, but if Magenta is upset, I don't notice. I only stop when my stomach cramps, and the apartment fades into silence.

"You feel better?"

I straighten and lift my shoulder. "Marginally."

"Great, because we need to leave in less than an hour. Time to get dressed, then I need to figure out what to do with myself."

The designer is pale. "Gemma, I am so—"

"Don't worry about it," I say, touching her arm. "I don't know what he said, but he probably has his reasons."

Dark and lustful reasons, maybe.

Nothing good.

I shove away any thoughts along those lines and move swiftly to the dress. The women follow me upstairs, into the bedroom—it's still not really *mine*. They help me into it, smoothing the skirt and adjusting my hair. Magenta touches up my makeup and lipstick.

"Okay," she says. "You're ready."

"Wait," Cat blurts out. She retrieves the envelope and two boxes, putting all three items in my hands. "Look at yourself and open those, and then come down when you're ready."

I still haven't seen myself.

Cat pulls the sheet off the floor-length mirror in the closet, then they all file out.

I close the door behind them and let out a long breath.

It's hard to breathe through all my emotions, and sifting through them is even more difficult. Like I'm excited, nervous, and horribly anxious. It's ridiculous, really. I tried on the dress and stared at myself in it. I know what it looks like on my body.

But with the hair and makeup...

A lump forms in my throat.

The bodice is fitted with a sweetheart neckline, held up by two thin straps. It flares out into a full skirt at my waist, and it swishes when I move. The starched white satin is covered in a delicate layer of lace. I rotate slightly, revealing the lace that opens up in a large keyhole that leaves most of my upper back bare.

The road rash from our motorcycle crash stands out, but no one said anything about it. Maybe Aiden forewarned them. Still, I touch the healing skin and wince. It's only just starting to scab over.

My sandals are heelless, but I can't help but feel off-balance. Like my center of gravity has shifted away from me.

I set down the two boxes and slide my finger under the envelope's seal. It only says my name on the front. For a moment, my breath catches. I always dreamed that my mother would write me a letter for my wedding day. That somehow she could've predicted her death and prepared for this eventuality.

Me continuing to live without her.

But then I fully slide the folded paper out, and I realize it wasn't her—it's from Aiden. My gaze skips down to his signature at the bottom of the page, and I press my finger into the ink.

Gemma,

I thought you might be needing your something old, new, borrowed, and blue. The wedding dress is new, of course. My wedding gift to you is the remaining three. I hope they're satisfactory.

Now is the time to come clean, and I hate that I'm writing this down instead of saying it to your face. Part of me hopes you won't read this, that you'll go straight for the boxes and ignore this... but you're too smart for that.

Your father and I had an agreement.

My heart stops working.

We were hunting your family, and you weren't retaliating on the same scale—nothing was provoking them into the war our family craved. It was skirmishes like the men who hit our bike: quick, guerilla warfare attacks. Bloodshed. West blood was filling the streets, and it was only a matter of time before something truly awful happened.

Before your family decided to meet ours with matched fury.

Your father saw this coming.

Say what you will about Lawrence West, but he was calm and calculating even in the midst of chaos. Something my father will never understand—but I think you do.

He asked me what it would take to keep you safe. You weren't going to flee town with the rest of the women. Apparently, you made that clear, and he respected it.

But that still left you in danger, with a massive target on your back.

I told him I would marry you. Make you mine. Make you a DeSantis, protect you from those who would wish you harm. Save you.

I SNIFFLE. Dad… Dad never conspired with *me* to save the family—he conspired with Aiden freaking DeSantis to save *me*. I can't keep my emotions in check, and my mind wanders to the last few conversations I had with him before I settled in at Aunt Mary's house to wait.

Please don't be upset with him, princess. He was out of his mind with worry. I confess: I was, too. I was worried you'd do something reckless.

I was worried you'd be killed.

Today isn't going against your father's wishes. Today you're honoring the path he wanted you to walk. Today, you'll make me the happiest man alive.

I won't apologize for my decisions. I won't apologize for the way your father guided you into thinking you were a sacrifice. You were never the lamb being led to slaughter, like I fear you once thought.

Chin up, my love. Today might feel like the end of the world, but I promise you it isn't. It's a beginning.

Aiden

I SET down the note and take stock of myself.

Emotions?

Numb.

Makeup?

Normal.

Dress?

Perfect.

I turn my attention to the first box, the bigger of the two, and lift the lid.

My knife sits nestled in the box. I pull it out and flip it in my palm. It's been cleaned and sharpened from the look of it. No trace of blood. That's neither borrowed nor blue, although I suppose it could be old. The *blue*, though, is the sheath that rests below it. It's soft, dark-brown leather inlaid with turquoise. It has four slits for straps to slide through.

I gather my skirt and quickly attach the holster to my upper thigh, then slide the knife in. It lays perfectly on my skin and is invisible when I drop the tulle back over it.

The second box is smaller, and I crack it open slower. My stomach immediately knots, and I cover my mouth.

"What the fuck?" I whisper.

It's the old. The true, intended *something old*.

My mother's engagement ring.

I sink to my knees and cradle the box in my palms, unable to even pick up the ring. I almost don't want to touch it, because memories of my mother letting me try it on as a little girl burns bright behind my eyes. I used to dance around the house with it on my thumb, pretending Prince Charming was going to swoop down and carry me off.

Into my Happily Ever After.

I close the box with a snap and shudder.

Mom's not here.

Dad's not here.

How the *fuck* did Aiden get this?

Unless... Unless Dad gave it to him when they agreed Aiden would marry me. And Aiden's been holding on to Mom's ring for weeks, probably keeping it in his gun safe—the one place I failed to gain access to in this miserable apartment.

I carefully open it again and stare at the glistening diamond.

There's a tiny, folded piece of paper pressed to the lid of the box. Pain and apprehension sweep through me. If that *is* a note from my mother, I'm not ready to read it. Not after

Aiden's confession. I remove the ring and slide it onto my left hand. Fourth finger.

It fits perfectly.

Like it was meant to be.

But... that's it. Nothing borrowed, unless Aiden meant the knife was borrowed... and is now being returned.

I roll my shoulders and shake out my arms. The diamond catches the light, and I have to pause and stare at it again.

Dad had it. I specifically asked for it after she died, desperate for some piece of her to keep me tethered to my memories, but he refused.

"Okay," I tell myself. I rise and lift my chin. "You can do this."

It's just a day. A moment. A kiss.

CHAPTER 26

Gemma

"Ready," I call to Cat. "That was more emotional than I was expecting..."

Amelie waits for me at the foot of the stairs.

I blink a few times, not entirely convinced I'm not hallucinating, and her grin only widens. She seems *so* much better than the last time I saw her—no more haunted look in her gaze, tan. Happy.

"What the hell?" I shriek, coming to my senses and rushing down the stairs.

We've spoken a handful of times, but I feel like this girl is basically my sister. I throw my arms around her, and she hugs me back tightly. We rock side to side for a moment, and I let myself relax in her embrace.

"I could not miss this," she says. "Not for the world. You look stunning."

I snort and step back, then glance around before I say something I shouldn't. But I don't have to worry—Cat and the others are gone.

"I sent them to wait in the hall. Nosy bitches." She gestures for me to follow her over to the couch. "Aiden told me you needed something borrowed. And luckily for *us*, I splurged on accessories on my official wedding."

"Really," I say. "So that's how it turned out? You run away to Italy and then end up remarrying him?"

She rubs her temple. "Yep. He won me back over, although technically I just married him—we weren't married in the first place. He saw the error of his ways, spent weeks apologizing... Speaking of."

She motions with her finger for me to twirl, and I oblige her.

"Aha, see? No buttons. You must like Aiden at least a little bit."

My cheeks flame, and I avert my gaze. The evidence is stacking against him, and now I'm even more unsure of my feelings toward him. But that's not what a bride is supposed to say. If I voiced any of my concerns, I'd be going off script.

"A bit," I hedge.

She snickers. "Okay, okay, I'll let you live in delusion—for now. You helped me out when I desperately needed it, and I'm going to repay that favor as long as I can."

I raise my eyebrows. "There's only one favor I asked—"

"I know," she says. She fiddles with the ribbon of yet another box on the coffee table, and she sits heavily. "But it doesn't feel like enough. So, I'm at your disposal."

I'm collecting favors, it seems.

"Can you show me what's in the box?" I ask instead. "I'm dying of curiosity."

She hands it over, and I take my time loosening the ribbon. There's something about unwrapping an unexpected surprise... well, sometimes it's good and sometimes it makes you cry. But I trust Amelie not to put anything too emotional in this.

"Something borrowed," she says.

She takes the ribbon and the lid, leaving me staring down

at a tiara nestled in a bed of satin. The silver is cut like lace, with diamonds and pearls imbedded in it. It's delicate, but also seems like it would be a good weapon.

"It's..."

"Fitting for you," she says. "Every girl wants to feel like a princess, but you? I mean, maybe not *technically*, but Mafia princess and real princess are almost the same thing."

The hair stylist left my hair down and curled, although some was pulled back in an intricate knot. Amelie stands, gesturing for me to sit, then carefully places the tiara on my head. She retrieves some pins to keep it in place.

"I thought I might share a moment like this with my sister," she murmurs. "But I'm happy this is helping you. I'm glad I can be here for you."

I clutch her hands. "Me, too."

The door opens, and Cat sticks her head in. She's transformed herself in the time I was upstairs, her face now made up with a smoky eye and glossy lips. "If we don't leave in the next two minutes, Aiden will probably throw you over his shoulder. Or Jameson will throw a hissy fit... I don't want to see either one, to be honest."

"Ooh, I knew Aiden had a bit of caveman in him," Amelie says on a sigh. "How's the sex? Delicious? Kinky?"

Cat shrieks. "I don't want to hear about my cousin's sex life."

I smirk and loop my arm through Amelie's. She came dressed and ready in a pale-blue, flowing dress, a chunky necklace, and sapphires in her ears. Her blonde hair is pin-straight and falls to the tops of her breasts.

I nudge aside a few strands of hair and examine the scar on her forehead.

It was a vicious, angry thing the last time I saw it. Now the scar seems to have settled into a dark-pink line, slightly raised. It very well may disappear with time.

"This healed well," I murmur.

She nods and swallows. "It's still a reminder of what I won't allow. And what I owe you."

I lead her toward the door. I don't really want Aiden to carry me out of here over his shoulder, because he definitely would.

We step into the elevator, Cat in front of us and my three stylists behind us. I wink at Amelie and say, "Yeah, the sex is pretty good. He does this thing—"

"Shut up," Cat groans.

Amelie and I burst into giggles.

Gratitude fills me. I didn't know how much I needed a familiar, non-DeSantis face today.

Sam waits for us at the parking garage, and his eyes widen when his gaze lands on me. Cat smirks and elbows her brother, hurrying past him to open the door to the limo.

Amelie climbs in, then Sam, Cat, and me last. Our driver comes around and closes us in, and I look up at the familiar face.

Breaker—one of Aiden's guys.

He winks through the glass, then slides back in the driver's seat.

"I'd ask if you have cold feet, but I'm pretty sure you're not allowed to back down any more than I was," Amelie whispers. "And just remember, if you hear a loud bang—"

I grip her hand tightly.

"Everything will be fine," Sam reassures us. "We've been keeping watch on the church, the surrounding buildings are empty, and we have more guards than ever."

Amelie gives him a haughty look. "You can't tell me my wedding wasn't crawling with security. It was more high-profile than this, surely."

He tips his head.

Great. I swallow and run my finger up the outside of my

leg, just checking that the blade is still there. It's a small comfort.

The last time the DeSantises tried to celebrate a wedding, a man died.

"It was so last-minute—surely that helps?" Cat asks her brother.

He nods. "Leaves little time for someone to prepare an attack."

I narrow my eyes. "Someone—you're insinuating my family would try something?"

He meets my gaze unflinchingly. "You don't agree?"

I keep my opinions to myself.

"Things are a bit tenser here than I thought," Amelie says. Her hand lands on my knee, and we stay like that on the short ride to the church. "Are you really okay? You seem... off."

I force a smile—not the last one of the day, I'm sure. "I'm grappling with a lot. I'll be fine."

We stop out front, where a few men wait for us. Cat and Sam climb out first, and he takes her arm.

"Ready, Gemma?" Breaker asks. He leans in the open door closest to Amelie and offers me a gentle smile.

"One more thing," Amelie says. She tugs the door mostly shut and pivots toward me. "Can I walk you down the aisle?"

My mouth falls open.

"And here I thought I'd have to walk alone," I manage.

"Is that a yes?"

"I'd be honored."

She hugs me quickly, then shoves the door back open. It nearly catches Breaker's face.

"Ready," I answer him.

He holds out his hand, and I let him help me rise.

"Oh!" Cat rushes toward me with a bouquet in her hand. "I can't believe we almost forgot this."

White roses and baby's breath. A few pops of light-pink

roses, and a few black ones. The stems are wrapped in silk and lace.

I swallow over the lump in my throat. *I'm doing this.* Dad was on board. Mom... she'd approve of Aiden, too. Maybe. After her initial hesitation.

How many people can say they've killed for me? That's got to win him some brownie points.

Amelie squeezes my hand, and we walk up the steps into the church.

Here goes nothing.

We pause in the foyer, and Amelie lets out a big breath. Cat and Sam nod and slip through the door, continuing down. I try to peek, then stop myself. I don't want to know how many DeSantises will be staring at me.

The whole family, maybe.

"Deep breath," she whispers. "And no matter what happens, I'll see you on the other side."

I meet her gaze and tilt my head. There's a lot I could ask, but this is one of the few times where knowing will be to my detriment.

"Ready?" an usher asks.

We nod, and he waves his hand through the opening in the door. Suddenly both doors are drawn open, and the traditional procession music begins to play.

Amelie smooths my skirt and offers her arm. I clutch my bouquet in one hand, held low in front of my waist, and her arm in the other. I don't even look at the people standing around us. My gaze is glued to the man I'm walking toward.

Aiden wears a sleek tuxedo. Black collared shirt under his jacket. No tie. The top button is undone, exposing the tanned column of his throat. And his attention is fastened to me, sweeping me from head to toe.

Heat curls low in my belly.

"You both might start panting," Amelie whispers.

I elbow her.

Her chuckle is so quiet, I almost miss it.

And then we're at the altar, and Aiden descends the steps to retrieve me. Amelie passes him my hand, winking at him. He shakes his head, then meets my eyes again. He glances down at the ring on my hand, and his tiny smirk fades.

"Did you read—?"

"I did," I whisper.

We step back up to the priest, whose Adam's apple bobs as he takes us in.

"You look stunning, by the way," Aiden says.

I glance away and make the mistake of eyeing the crowd.

Oh God. The DeSantis clan fills almost all of the rows. It's a small church, not meant to hold more than a hundred parishioners, but *still*.

"Are we ready to begin?" the priest asks us.

"Yes," Aiden answers.

"Face each other."

Cat steps up and takes my bouquet, retreating back to her spot in the first row. Amelie sits between her and Luca. Sam is on Cat's other side. Jameson is across the aisle with his brother Mac, my card-playing buddy, and the man I can only assume is Cat's father.

I take both of Aiden's hands and look up into his eyes.

The priest begins, but most of it fades away... until the vows.

Then Aiden drawls, "You first, baby."

I cringe. I wasn't sure if we were doing regular vows, but it seems I'm free to say whatever I want. That's how it should be, right? I'm basically vowing to stay by his side forever, or at least support his endeavors forever. And he'll do the same for me.

The least I can do is sprinkle in some honesty.

"I'm still pissed at you," I begin.

That gets a chuckle from the crowd, and a smirk from Aiden.

"But that's not the reigning emotion. In fact, I'm not quite sure how I feel at all. But that's just to say, Aiden DeSantis, that we—"

I'm cut off by a shrieking whine, like a firework.

My first thought is, *guns don't make that noise.*

Something explodes over the choir section, a bright pop of light and an awful sound. It's almost deafening in the confined space, and Aiden and I automatically hit the floor. My ears ring, and I glance around frantically.

In fact, everyone does as they try to find the intruder at the back of the church.

And that's when someone grabs me.

I'm dragged backward by strong arms, and cold metal touches my temple. At the same time, the side and back doors burst open. Two men come in the side and three down the back aisles, their assault rifles raised.

The men move with smooth efficiency, and they're dressed in all black. Kevlar vests, belts loaded with more weapons, helmets—and masks that completely obscure their faces.

"EVERYONE DOWN," the one holding me yells in a booming voice.

I grab his forearm and let him pull me backward, but my gaze goes to Aiden. He's crouched, his weapon already drawn. I shouldn't be surprised that he's carrying at his own damn wedding, but I am.

One of the men strides toward him and kicks the gun from his hand, raising his rifle. He stares down at Aiden, and unbidden terror seizes me.

"No!" I scream. I'd been going with the flow, but Aiden's death will *not* be on my hands. I kick at my captor and struggle to rip free.

The one who might've shot Aiden yanks his head back by his hair. "You come after us and she's dead."

Aiden growls. "Try me."

The man eyes him. I stare holes in the side of Aiden's face, willing him not to risk his life—not for me. Not like this.

But telepathy isn't working, because Aiden slowly rises to his feet.

"Don't." My voice isn't working—I'm not loud enough.

The man takes a canister from his belt and pulls the ring out, tossing it into the center aisle. The four others had been watching the guests, all of which seem frozen. By choice, I'm not sure. It must be a blow to see the heir of the family at the wrong end of a semi-automatic weapon. And his bride, too.

Well, they probably don't give a shit about you, Gem.

I kick at the man behind me.

The canister *pops*, and white smoke erupts from it. In a matter of seconds, the back half of the church is impossible to see.

Someone fires a shot toward the back of the room, and I flinch.

"Take her," the one behind me orders.

Aiden lunges forward at that, his expression furious. The man holding me raises his gun. He fires twice, hitting Aiden in the chest.

My world stops.

Aiden falls backward, and my mind transposes Kai over him. Then my father. But I blink and I've snapped back to the real world.

He hits the altar floor and doesn't move.

My scream rings in my ears. I don't stop screaming, but my fight doubles. I break free for a moment and get to Aiden's side, managing to grasp his arm before someone rips me away. I'm hysterical.

More than I should be. More than I ever would've expected.

"Christ, she's strong," one of them grunts.

He spins me around and shoves between my shoulder blades. I fall toward another assailant. That one grasps my shoulders, letting his rifle swing by its strap for a moment. His piercing blue eyes meet mine, then he drags a black sack over my head. It tightens around my neck—not enough to strangle me, but I hesitate at the contact.

At the threat of being strangled.

That subdues me long enough for them to bind my wrists together with zip ties. Hands grip my waist and hoist me up, flopping me over a shoulder.

We go maybe four feet before something hisses and pops —another canister, I'd guess. This one much closer.

I choke on the smell of smoke through the black cloth, twisting to try to alleviate the burning in my lungs.

"Hold," someone says quietly.

A gunshot echoes from seemingly far away, then the *snick* of it impacting stone.

"Sniper."

"More smoke."

"Move. Right now."

I'm jostled as my abductor carries me, then I'm forced back to my feet. A hand on the top of my head guides me into a vehicle, and I manage to inch away from the door. A body lands next to mine, and multiple doors slam.

We peel the fuck out of there.

I go over the scene in my head, trying to wrangle my emotions. Now isn't the time to lose it—not if this was a rescue mission.

I lean back and silently count to fifty.

There was no blood on Aiden's shirt. How, I don't know.

A mystery for another day. But the close range might've been enough to knock the wind from his lungs.

He's probably alive.

That thought releases the tightness in my lungs.

Aiden thought hope was the worst thing—but now it's the only thing keeping me calm. Whether he deserves my hope is another thing entirely.

I finish counting, then reach up and tug the hood off my head. I swipe at my nose with my bound hands and glance around.

Two men sit up front, one beside me. I watch them all for a beat, but we ride silently. They haven't removed their masks, either. The one beside me reaches over and cuts the zip ties off with a small knife, then resumes his position.

"My brother hired you," I guess. I twist around and spot a dark SUV with the three other men riding behind us, then face forward.

He nods an affirmation.

"Did he tell you to kill Aiden?"

He removes the mask. Those same blue eyes bore into mine, and I do my best not to flinch. I don't recognize him—Colin wouldn't be so stupid as to hire people we know. Cold and impersonal was the only way any of us would've made it out of that church alive.

His dark hair is cut short, slightly longer on top in a way that reminds me of the military. Square jaw, tanned skin. He's got a scar on his cheek that was hidden by the mask.

"We weren't paid for that," he says.

Not a no.

"Do I know you?" I ask, just in case.

He shakes his head. "We haven't had the pleasure."

I grimace. "I wouldn't call this a pleasure."

"No," the driver agrees. "Just necessary."

I fold my arms over my chest. "Go on, then. Why was it necessary to kidnap me from my own wedding?"

They fall silent.

"Let me guess—not your job to tell me?"

The one beside me winks.

Another thing occurs to me. "How'd you get them all to leave me?"

If Aiden is dead, they'll be coming for them.

If he's not dead... he'll be coming for me.

Part of me is hurt by that injustice. He had to know they wouldn't kill me—I knew that, even with a gun to my head, and he's got more experience with this sort of thing. Yet he was still an idiot and tried to save me.

If the bastard died trying to save me from a non-threat, I'm going to bring him back to life to shoot him myself. Honestly, men and their egos.

"We rigged a bomb on all the doors," the driver says. "Bought us an hour unless they can disarm it before then."

My jaw drops. "You can't—"

"When the timer gets to zero, the power cuts out," the third assures me. "It's just a minor explosion, anyway. It looks scary to deter them."

"Well, shit. Fuck." I hit my thigh with my fist. They're trapped in a church.

This couldn't be better.

"We need to make a stop," I say.

"Are you serious?"

I nod. "I don't mind bailing out of a moving car. Would be a shame to ruin the dress, though. So if you could just turn around and go back to the DeSantis tower, that would be great."

"Are you mental?"

I find myself nodding even as the driver makes a quick U-turn and steps on the gas.

"Probably," I say.

We make it back to the tower in record time, and I extract the lucky keycard from my bra. Blue Eyes follows me out of the car and into the elevator. It zips up to the twenty-fourth floor, and I unlock Aiden's apartment.

I stop him with an arm across the door. "No snooping. No reporting any of this back to Colin. Clear?"

He grins. "Yes, ma'am."

Cocky son of a bitch.

I hurry upstairs and yank my bag out of the closet. I stuff clothes into it, my toothbrush, underwear, then carefully extract my stolen items from Jameson's office.

Papers he might notice are missing... so it's best that I'm leaving with no planned return trip. Just holding them in my hands hurts. A painful reminder I was able to shove out of my mind this morning. There's a feeling growing in my stomach that I'm not ready to face yet.

I shove everything in the black canvas bag and zip it closed, at the last second grabbing my boots. The guy waits for me at the bottom of the stairs, his firearm drawn and at his side.

"Chill out," I mutter. "They're all locked in a church, remember?"

"Did you get what was so important to you? *Shoes?*"

I roll my eyes and lead the way out—well, until we get back to the parking garage. Then Blue Eyes takes his time clearing the way and hustles me back into the car.

"Where are we going?" I ask. "Rather, where did my brother tell you to drop me?"

They don't answer, and I cross my arms again. Fuck them. And Colin, for that matter. I had things *handled*.

Dad was going to urge Colin to get out of the city, maybe to have his own life outside the Mafia, and I was going to be protected. In danger constantly, surrounded by people who hate my last name, but...

Aiden had managed to keep me alive so far—or so I thought.

My chest tightens.

Fuck Aiden, too. Staying mad at him is the only way I'll be able to handle living in limbo—whether he's okay or not. He was fucking shot, so he can't be great.

Doubt creeps in. Do I want him to be okay? Or do I want to be free of him?

I touch the ring and try to ignore the lump in my throat.

He's going to be okay—and I will be, too. The question is, where will these men take me?

I don't have to wait long to find out. We pull up to my family's Brooklyn house only a few minutes later. It looks exactly the same as before. I'm not sure why I expect it to be different.

Maybe because I'm different.

"Holy shit," I whisper. I lean forward.

There are way too many cars on the street. Yes, it's Brooklyn, but this is abnormal. Most people go to work and leave spots open. It's a quiet neighborhood.

Blue Eyes opens the door and holds out his hand. I take it grudgingly, moving my skirts out of the way, and swing my bag over my shoulder. No way am I giving him all my possessions, plus the boots. It doesn't matter that we're on the doorstep of my family home. He doesn't seem inclined to take anything except my hand, anyway, and immediately releases me when I'm on my feet.

I push through the front gate. The last time I was here, Kai and Colin were with me. We had just run into Amelie Page for the first time a few streets over, and she... *damn it*, even then she knew I had a sort of fascination-slash-longing for Aiden.

She saw right through me.

My throat blocks.

I consider knocking on the front door for half a second, then think better. I shove the door open and stride inside.

I stop dead.

There are so many people. Family and friends I was raised around. They all turn toward me, perhaps startled. The three assailants/kidnappers/saviors come in behind me. A quick glance back reveals another dark SUV with the three remaining men. They hop out and circle around the sides of the house.

Job's not done, apparently.

I feel ridiculous standing before them in a dress. With a fucking tiara on my head. Actually... I raise my hand and touch the cool metal. I'm surprised it didn't fall out when I was upside down over my kidnapper's shoulder. Amelie's way with pins must be magic.

"Where is my brother?" I ask into the silence. I push aside my apprehension that they're all judging me.

I was about to marry Aiden, after all. From their standpoint, I didn't put up much of a fight. So, they *might* hate me, but then their gazes avert. The following silence isn't awkward or filled with tension—both things I anticipated.

No. I stride farther into the house, and the people part for me.

Another thing that has never happened before.

Turner steps out from the crowd, his eyes wide. "We were informed of Lawrence's will earlier today."

I nod slowly. That, at least, makes sense. "Okay... Colin is in charge? Is that why he suddenly decided I needed to be home?"

"No."

I rotate to find my brother in the doorway, looking like absolute shit. His white collared shirt, a poor attempt at dressing nicely, is wrinkled and buttoned improperly. He runs his hands through his hair, and it stays spiked up in his fingers' wake.

"What do you mean, *no*?"

Colin shrugs helplessly. "It means I'm not the fucking one in charge, Gem. *You* are."

The world screeches to a halt. All I can do is watch my brother in disbelief.

No, no, no.

"I...?"

None of the older women are here, I realize suddenly. They're still *away*. It's mainly men and fighting women. No one who married into the family, no one with children. Definitely no children.

I stare around at the familiar faces, and that off-balance feeling that's been plaguing me all morning suddenly disappears.

I tighten my fingers on the strap of my bag.

"Okay. Right. Did you all show up because..."

"We knew Colin would try to bring you home," Marius offers. "And we all wanted to be here to support you."

"Because you're okay with me running the businesses." I narrow my eyes and glare around the room. "All of them." *Even the illegal ones.* "Even though I was literally moments away from marrying Aiden DeSantis."

"Yes," one says.

It's echoed around the room, a chorus of *yes*es. Some say my name. Some lift their fists into the air. And then I'm left facing my brother, who seems to be relieved at my reaction.

"Yes," he says. "God, yes."

I nod and take a deep breath. The possibilities stretch out in front of me in a maze of opportunity—but I learned something being with Aiden. And it's that there is only one thing I can control: our reaction to the war that Jameson is bringing.

And there is a way to bring it to its knees.

"First order of business..." I glance around. If I can't trust everyone in this room, I'm doomed. Suddenly, my snooping seems okay. Validated. It was as if I had a sixth sense about returning home—and now I have the key to solving our problem.

"I have a plan to end the war," I tell them.

Murmurs break out.

"Silence," I order.

They obey.

Chills break out across my back. Except, now's not the time for revelry—that can come later. After.

When I have a chance to breathe. And process. And stop my heart from aching.

"What I'm about to tell you doesn't leave this room." I stride toward Colin and clasp the back of his neck. He mimics the movement, his fingers sliding under my hair. We used to do this when we were kids and had something important to say. It was like we were locked in on each other, and I get that same rush of energy now.

We stare at each other, and he inclines his chin.

He really isn't mad.

I keep my gaze on him. It's easier to tell just him, instead of a roomful of people.

"I'm sorry I accused you of murdering Wilder," I say softly. "I didn't even ask because I just assumed it had been you. But I was wrong."

Colin's eyes widen, and his fingers tremble on my neck. That admission... that would be enough for him. His forgiveness is quick and easy, like I didn't admit to thinking him capable of murder. Well, he *is*, but he wouldn't be so dumb as to kill the DeSantis heir.

I think of all the lies I've been chewing on.

"The DeSantises have been deceiving us," I say, loud enough for the room to hear. "Wilder's death was an excuse for war. They needed a reason to make it our fault. To justify the hits we've been suffering. But Wilder is alive and well, and I have proof."

The room breaks out into shouts, everyone trying to talk over each other. Everything fades for me, though, and I squeeze my eyes shut.

The awful truth is out in the open now.

Aiden was marrying me to protect me. *Lie.*

He cared about me. *Lie.*

The emotions I've been shoving down since yesterday afternoon thunder over me. The transgressions stack up against him, and bile churns in my stomach.

He *lied to my face* about Wilder's death. Refused to stop hunting my brother.

He killed my cousin in the name of this terrible DeSantis revenge.

And he tricked me into developing feelings for him. But all I've ever been to him is something to possess. The doll to sit on his shelf and look pretty. A collector's item to reveal at parties. *Look what I tamed: the last of the Wests.* He would've made me watch the extinction of my entire family... for nothing.

And I might've been blind enough to forgive him for it.

I guess his love was just another deception, too.

TO BE CONTINUED

In *Stolen Crown*, available now!

Acknowledgments

Woof. That ending, right? You doing okay? Sorry about the little cliffhanger.

I can trace back this duet's origin to one scene: Gemma standing in the window of her aunt's house, and Aiden coming for her. And in my mind, this initial version, she was both terrified and exhilarated by what was about to happen.

It seemed poetic that their story would begin with a sacrifice—and that theme ended up being carried throughout their story. It's such an interesting motivator. I hope you found them as intriguing as I did.

There are a few people I couldn't have done this without: Rebecca, Ari, my lovely author friends Jolie Vines and AD McCammon, and my editors Emmy Ellis and Paige Sayer. Thank you all for putting up with my shenanigans and helping polish this story.

A big, huge thank you to my father. He'll never read this, so I'll tell you: he put up with my random questions, like: "What would you do if you wanted to crash a wedding to kidnap the bride?" Or, "What the *hell* would a Mafia be shipping to smuggle weapons in?" (He wanted to be listed as the co-writer for that one.)

And lastly, YOU are so important to me. Thank you for sharing my joy in dark stories.

Also by S. Massery

Dark Bully Romance

College Hockey

Brutal Obsession

Devious Obsession

Fallen Royals

#1 Wicked Dreams

#2 Wicked Games

#3 Wicked Promises

#4 Vicious Desire

#5 Cruel Abandon

#6 Wild Fury

Reverse Harem Romance

Sterling Falls

#1 Thief

#2 Fighter

#3 Rebel

#4 Queen

About the Author

S. Massery is a dark romance author who loves injecting a good dose of suspense into her stories. She lives in Western Massachusetts with her dog, Alice.

Before adventuring into the world of writing, she went to college in Boston and held a wide variety of jobs—including working on a dude ranch in Wyoming (a personal highlight). She has a love affair with coffee and chocolate. When S. Massery isn't writing, she can be found devouring books, playing outside with her dog, or trying to make people smile.

Join her newsletter to stay up to date on new releases: http://smassery.com/newsletter